RED SERGE

Lorne Oliver

Also by Lorne Oliver

RED ISLAND (Sgt. Reid Series)

THE CISTERN (The Alcrest Mysteries)

PLEASANT DREAMS

(YA Horror Anthology)

RED SERGE
Copyright © 2013 by Lorne Oliver

ISBN 978-0-9738132-4-1

Mum

Thanks for recognizing I was sick and twisted and not putting me in therapy

Mom

Thanks for funding and supporting my sick and twistedness

Acknowledgments

Books are not just the authors, but also belong to those who support the author. Brandi, Jordann, and Wylie are my biggest support. Without them there isn't much reason for all of this.

Mom and Dad were there my whole life encouraging me to do great things. I know they are proud of me.

Karen and Barry, my second mom and dad, are some of my biggest fans and support me in ways you can't imagine. We miss you Barry. Save a seat in the bleachers for me.

I have many friends and family who push me along. I hope to never disappoint them.

And then, of course, there are my technical advisers. Sgt. Kevin Baillie, NCO i/c Professional Standards Unit is always there for me to email countless questions and Sgt. Shawna McPherson who helped me out with questions about facial recognition. As always, any mistakes are my own.

I also need to thank Diane, Desire and Donna for their editing and Cara for the cover art.

Prologue

Bright red blood collected on the giant white rabbit's fangs. It growled deeply with every hot breath. It stared down at the girl. Eyes of a dark red surrounded by pale pink gazed at her.

Kayla stared back.

She had to run. She knew she had to run, but something inside her didn't want to let her body take flight. Fear tensed every muscle. Her feet kicked at the ground pushing her away from the beast. The earth slid under her shirt and scratched her back. Grey eyes watched the pregnant bubble of red engorge itself on the end of the fangs. It was as though she couldn't move until something happened. She stared at the blood and held her breath.

The blood dropped.

It absorbed into the fur of the rabbit's belly, staining it pink.

Kayla ran.

Leigh was dreaming. She rolled onto her front.

The family dog opened one eye to check what she was doing. Its paws stretched out from where they had been scratching Leigh's back. It closed its eye again and went back to snoring.

The girl ran as fast as she could. Arms pumped at her sides. With every step Kayla felt twenty pounds heavier. Her chest hurt. Her heart pounded in her ears. She looked back over her shoulder at the white rabbit following her.

She was only ten.

There was tall grass and overgrown walkways. Trees were taking it back. There were waves. Light in the distance behind trees and blackness.

Leigh knew this area, she had been there before. She had been there in real life. Now she was watching it from somewhere else.

But Kayla never had. Where was it?

Her legs couldn't run much longer. No matter how hard she ran the rabbit was getting closer. It was like in a scary movie. No matter how fast she ran, the walking bad guy - boogie man - was getting closer.

More blood dripped from his fangs. The pink of its chest was brightening to a brilliant red.

Leigh completely twisted around as she tried to get comfortable in her sleep. Her face moved next to the dog's, getting the animal's hot breath against her nose and eyes. The blankets bound up under her thigh.

Kayla tripped.

Her body flew through the air, hands stretched out like a super-hero reject. Her thigh hit something hard. Pain shot through her leg. Her body was instantly chilled from the wet ground. Auburn hair matted to her forehead. There was no other emotion inside her except fear. It was overtaking her. She heard something behind her.

It was the rabbit.

It was there. She didn't want to roll over but she had to. She had to.

Kayla rolled onto her back. The giant rabbit was there. The blood had run and marked a red bib beneath its chin.

Where did the blood come from? Who's blood was it? Was it her blood?

The rabbit bent at the waist and breathed its hot breath into the girl's face. She closed her eyes from the snorting air. It smelled like a mixture of earth and meat. She wanted to scream, but nothing would come out. She had to scream.

She had to scream.

The rabbit opened its mouth. The moonlight made the bloody fangs glisten.

Leigh's brown eyes opened wide.

For one second she laid in bed staring straight up at the splash of light sprayed across the ceiling from somewhere outside.

She sprang up, and caught her breath.

She looked first at the window then at the picture on her wall beside the window. The light of the street lamp glinted off the glass covering the picture of a red-coated Mountie on a large black horse, her father and Handcuf.

She tried to get her breathing under control.

Frix laid beside her. The old Springer Spaniel's sleep was barely interrupted by her sudden rise. Her nightlight lit up the space in the room between her bed and the door. She was eleven, too old for a nightlight, but two years ago a man, a killer, had been in her room. He had been in the entire house. He was the reason for the state-of-the-art security system and the bars on their windows.

Her hand pushed her long brown hair from her face.

Why was she suddenly awake? A dream? She couldn't remember what it had been about. Someone had been running. Something had been chasing. There was screaming.

Kayla?

Chapter 1

My head turns. I could have sworn something was there. A cold chill soars up my spine making my entire body shiver. I put my hands in my coat pockets to pull it in on me a little closer as I look around to see if anyone noticed my twitch.

Cemeteries creep me out – they always have. Exhuming a body is *double* creepy.

My Blackberry beeps. I take a quick look to see it is a text from my wife, then push it back in my pocket without reading it; I pull my coat even closer.

The constant drizzle is soaking right into me. Drips fall from the bill of my ball cap with the Royal Canadian Mounted Police seal on the front.

There are two other men standing on either side of me. Neither motion that they saw my possessed twitch. Three other men stand by a freshly-dug grave, and a newspaper photographer is further over by the entry to the People's Cemetery. He might have taken a photo of my spasm if only he wasn't waiting for the money shot, the casket. What we are doing isn't big news, but it is unusual news and for Charlottetown, Prince Edward Island, that is good enough for The Guardian.

Drip.

My body shivers again, this time from a bead of cold rain running down my back between my skin and shirt. It works itself into the waistband of my dark blue cargo pants and dissipates.

The cold makes the scars over my body ache and reminds me of the stupid things I did and the killers who tried to do me in. My *nightmares*.

Yes, I have nightmares: unseen red eyes staring at me from across a field like the evil creature in a scary movie; women's naked bodies hanging by ropes from trees, blood traveling in rivulets down their skin from knife slices and open wounds that fall to the ground and run under dead leaves into a hidden pool. Then there's the sound of dripping. Large raindrops of crimson splash the growing puddle, sending a splattering of blood up at me. There are the other nightmares of little girls, dead and unwanted, their eyes begging me for help.

Yes, I have nightmares, nightmares that wake me in the middle of the night with bile burning my throat. It's enough for Hillary to put her hand on my body and sleepily ask if I am okay.

"I'm fine. Go back to sleep."

The nightmares are bad enough to send me to the bathroom in case anything is going to come all the way up.

In the shower I lock the bathroom door and keep my eyes open letting the soap burn them so I can keep staring through the steam.

I used to like scary movies. Now I can't sit through them because the eyes in the dark remind me of my fear.

Lately I see the images while I'm awake and going through my daily routine. I see them on the walls across the room. I see them in other people's faces. I see the dead girls and women walking down the street. Am I going crazy?

"Big plans for the weekend, Sgt. Reid?" Dr. Walter Norton looks out from under a baseball cap beneath the hood of his green rain slicker. All I can see is the tip of his greying beard. He stomps at a puddle with his oversized rubber boots. He is retired from practicing medicine and now teaches at the university.

"I do, I do." I'm thankful the old man didn't ask if I have plans tonight. Wonderful Friday night couples therapy to get me feeling guilty for the weekend. "Tomorrow I know Hillary wants to go to the Farmers' Market. After that probably some yard work. Sunday evening Leigh and I are riding with the Musical Ride." I nod to announce I'm done. It's strange telling the doctor, whom I've only ever seen over dead bodies, about my plans. It feels like the principal of a school asking you about your weekend.

"I didn't know you rode horses."

"Yeah, I was in the musical ride early in my career, but I don't ride much now. Too many injuries."

"Jessica got us tickets to the musical ride, so I guess I'll see how you do. It all goes to a good cause, right?"

I nod, "Back into our community."

We both watch as a man climbs down into a grave which, until twenty minutes ago, had lain undisturbed for thirteen years.

Body exhumation is not something that happens often in PEI. In fact, I don't know if it has ever happened. In 2006 changes to the Coroner's Act made it possible for a body to be exhumed in the event that new evidence or advances in science might possibly solve a cold case. DNA has changed everything.

Thirteen years ago a body was found near a fisherman along the northern coastline by Savage Harbour. Back in the 90's you needed a lot of DNA to proceed with identification, you now need much less. In the past thirteen years members of Major Crimes tried to reopen the case, but until now it was not possible to exhume the body. The fact that it was buried at all is strange. Normally it would have been cremated. The hope at the time was that someone would come forward or new evidence would be found. Nobody knew it would take so long.

We don't have any hope of matching his medical make-up with any crime database, but maybe there is a parent or family member still looking for him and perhaps we can match him to them. I hate to think that he went missing without anyone looking for him.

"I still remember when Gary was found."

I look at the doctor whose eyes stare through fogged glasses at the freshly dug hole. The air is thick with the smell of morning and fresh dirt. I can hear cars starting to move about the city.

My watch says it's just after seven in the morning. Charlottetown is coming alive. "Isn't this body listed as John Doe?" I ask.

Dr. Norton looks at me. His lips form into a half smile under the well-trimmed beard. "I named him Gary after the initials written in black marker on the waistband of his underwear, G.L. He was the second floater I had examined since becoming coroner for King's County. He was nasty too. Our best estimation was that he had been in the ocean a couple of months. The elements and sea life had damaged all chances of physical identification and there was no wallet or identification on what was left of his clothes. So Gary it was."

Things happen to a body in the ocean that I hate to imagine. The only thing the investigators had at the time were estimates and educated guesses.

From the amount of body decomposition, they thought he had been in the water somewhere between two weeks to two months. All they knew about where he came from was based on currents and tides.

It was possible that he was from Canada's smallest province, where he now resides, but he also could have come from northern New Brunswick or parts of Quebec including the Gaspe Peninsula along the southern shore of the Gulf of St. Lawrence, or even the Magdalen Islands between PEI and Newfoundland. The Magdalens, although closer to PEI and Nova Scotia but part of the province of Quebec, are a group of islands in the Gulf that are partially inhabited, but have a large tourist trade. I can't imagine a local going missing and not being missed. Sea creatures had feasted from him; eating his eyes, nose, fingers, and much of his rotting flesh. His shirt, if he had worn one at the time he hit the water, was completely missing probably torn off by the violent gulf tides. He still wore blue jeans, held on by a fastened leather belt, size ten black leather boots and white sports socks.

Then there was the underwear with his initials.

They ran a list of what they had found in all of the newspapers where they thought he may have lived. Nobody ever came forward and there had been no matches to missing persons cases from months before or since the recovery.

"They're bringing him out."

I glance quickly at the dirt road leading through the cemetery. The Guardian reporter hoists his camera with a long lens up to his eye. *Newspaper asshole*. He starts snapping pictures as the Cat back-hoe carefully raises the casket cradled comfortably in fabric straps. The smell of death rapidly fills the air and pushes the fresh morning away. John Doe, aka Gary, was buried in a cheap box paid for by your friendly taxpayers. He

16

was prepared as cheaply as possible so who knows what we will find inside. Two men steady the casket on either side as the machine moves the death box to a waiting plastic base on the wet grass.

Dr. Norton moves forward and crouches down next to the box to carefully inspect the seams.

The smell of decomposition still leaks out. What could be left to smell after thirteen years?

Like a sportsman inspecting his speedboat's hull, he runs his fingers along the edges and around the corners looking for any holes or leaks. He looks up at me from under his hood. "It looks good. The bones should be intact. When is your facial reconstructionist coming?" He signals the others to place the hard plastic cover on top of the casket and fasten the two plastic pieces together.

"Monday morning on the ferry. The forensic anthropologist will be driving in then from Fredericton as well."

"I'll inspect everything today and have the skull ready for him."

"Her. They're both women actually."

A beep from my Blackberry; I pull it from my pocket to see who is texting me. It was my wife asking how the dig is going. Her earlier text was to tell me all the milk had been used for Leigh's cereal. Our daughter is eleven and eats more food than I do.

I type one word, "Fine," and press send.

The moment it is back in my pocket my phone starts to chirp indicating a call. I look at the number on the screen then push a button. "Reid." I close my eyes at what I hear. My nightmares are back. These are the older ones about mistakes made. Young blue eyes stare at me from the red lights behind my own eyes. As I end the call and look at the doctor, "I have to go."

He opens his mouth to protest, but stops as his cellphone calls out from inside his jacket. He's getting the same call I just received. I wait patiently for him to answer and growl out a response. He looks in my eyes and gives me a nod. "Let's get this in the van. David can take it to the hospital and then I'll catch a ride with you Sergeant, if that's okay."

~ * ~

The Major Crimes Unit, in basic terms, deals with violent crimes where another person is involved. The crimes that fall under our umbrella are rapes, break and enters that involve someone getting hurt, violent assaults, and homicides or suspicious deaths. Lucky for the good people of PEI we are not that busy with homegrown crimes and spend a lot of time looking into cases for other police officers across the country. There are four members, including myself, and our commanding officer. We are responsible to investigate all of the major crimes across the island and assist the Charlottetown City Police within city limits.

PEI has had only two murders in over twenty years. By the time my wife insisted we leave British Columbia I had hunted and shot down a man who enjoyed killing little girls. It wasn't until the *Red Island Killer* that homicides were something Major Crimes had to investigate in the tiny province. Now here I am heading out to Prince Edward Island National Park to look into another possible murder. It seems there's nowhere you can hide from the ultimate violation.

"This is a nice car. New?"

It takes me a few seconds to realize the doctor is still right beside me. Part of me wishes I had stopped at headquarters and switched to an unmarked police car.

"What? Yeah, well a couple months."

"It's nice. What is it?"

"Ford Focus." I drive a Ford, Hillary drives a Ford. Her father is a devout Ford hater. For him, it's Chevy all the way, or walk. It really pisses him off that we have Fords, which of course makes me want to keep buying them.

"Cars sure have changed. I drive a BMW myself." Dr. Norton goes on about his car and all the cars he has ever owned. I let his voice drift away and just watch what is passing by.

I drive past the Charlottetown airport then the Coke building and head out on Brackley Point Road. Every summer thousands of vehicles travel this highway toward campgrounds, restaurants, and the beach that sits inside PEI National Park.

As we drive past the entrance to the drive-in theatre I take a quick glance at what movies are playing. Maybe this weekend Hillary and Leigh would like to take in a double feature. It's been a while since we've gone to the drive-in. It opened in the 50's and then restored in the early 90's to resemble the 50's era. What's old is new right? The screen itself, hidden from the highway by a row of pines, is over five stories high and seventy feet wide. The mosquitoes are usually as bad as hell, but it is a different way to see a movie. Besides, where else do you pay the price for one film and get to see two?

Further along the road is my wife's favorite place to eat down this strip of Highway 6. Shirley's, across the road from Millstream Restaurant and Trail Rides, is nothing more than a small burger-and-fries shack, but the food is good and cheap. Here you get what you pay for, not like at the Dune's Gallery and Café or Shaw's Hotel further up the road. If you keep going out into the park and get to Dalvay-by-the-Sea Mansion, turned restaurant and inn, you are in for some fancy and expensive food. Granted Dune's, Shaw's, and Dalvay have all been featured in magazine articles on where to eat and are noted in all the brochures for Prince Edward Island, but I am still glad I married a burger-and-fries kind of girl.

After some winding turns in swamp country we come to the entry of the national park.

Between 6:00pm and 8:00am one can drive through the park with no problem, but from May to October everyone has to pay to get into the park during daytime hours. The trick to getting in free is to tell the Park Rangers that you are going to the fish market up the highway. So what if you never make it past the parking lot at the beach just around the corner. This time two RCMP squad cars sit next to the pay booth. Instead of a park worker greeting us it is one of our officers.

As we drive into the park we cannot see the ocean because of the sand dunes covered in patches of green grass that run along the north shore. It is said that this is the most endangered of national parks because every year storm surges erode the sands and humans add to that natural erosion. No matter how many signs are posted asking people to avoid climbing or walking on the dunes, they still have to scramble to the top. Their feet and hands disrupt the grasses which keep the dunes together. They just have to get that special holiday picture that inevitably ends up being an unrecognizable shape on a hill.

In the park is Green Gables, which was the childhood inspiration for Lucy Maud Montgomery to write her Anne of Green Gables novels - unintentionally inspiring generations of Japanese tourists (who use the books to learn English) to travel to the tiny Canadian province.

Today I am not going that far. I turn into Brackley Beach parking lot and line up with the other vehicles.

I recognize some of the cars and look across to the wood snack shop and change rooms to see my commanding officer and fellow Major Crimes members. The white Mobile Command Post trailer and the black 4x4 that pulls it are parked in the far corner of the lot closest to the boardwalk.

On hot summer days the entire parking area is filled with cars, the beach overflowing with bathers. The rain is stopping and the clouds are beginning to part. The day is promising to be very hot. I wonder how long it will take for beach-goers to get over the idea of a dead body found where they change their clothes.

I step out of my car and can instantly hear the waves of the Gulf of St. Lawrence pounding against the sandy shore. The smell of salt is thick in the air.

Given the reason for our presence here, it may be a while before some people return to this beach area. Tourism dropped the summer after the *Red Island Killer* and his "reign of terror." There was plenty of talk and internet chatter about cults, plots, and evil outsiders coming to the island. Some of that chatter drove people away.

People wanted to know what was happening to the island. How did the province go from having only two homicides in twenty years to having a serial killer use the women of the island as his play things? They went as far as blaming the Confederation Bridge which connects the island to the mainland for allowing too many outsiders to come to the island. When it is pointed out that all the people who have killed anyone lately were born and raised in PEI, they quickly drop the entire conversation.

How was it that cities like Abbotsford, BC or Thunder Bay, ON (with approximately the same population as the whole province) had homicides every year and PEI consistently had none? My theory is that you can keep your finger in the hole in the dam for only so long before more cracks appear along the wall. Sooner or later the entire thing is going to blow.

People are returning though and it will soon be forgotten. Robert Pickton's farm in BC (where the remains of some thirty-six of his supposed forty-nine victims were discovered) is now townhouses with happy families skipping along amongst fast-food restaurants and discount stores. This island will be the same.

"Morning, Reid. How did the exhumation go?" Sgt. Wayne McIntyre gives me a nod. He does the same to Dr. Norton as he walks past him. A hand smooth's his goatee.

"It was good. No problems anyway." I slip on aviator sunglasses. The sun is getting stronger, but I don't want anyone to see my eyes. I think about asking what is going on here. I want to delay that, however, as long as I can. My stomach twists like it is in a vice.

It is not often a man feels this awkward standing face-to-face with another man, unless perhaps if one announces he is gay and has a crush on the other. I don't want to look at McIntyre and force him to talk, but I am trying not to look at the buildings either.

My boss doesn't want to look at me because he will have to start talking about why we are here. He knows I am not going to be happy and he doesn't want to be the one to set me off.

Looking around at everyone's faces it seems that no one wants to be here or deal with the why.

I finally try to say something. My mouth tastes sour, I swallow and try again. "What's going on? The call said something about a dead kid."

McIntyre turns toward the buildings. "Marilyn's going to be lead. I'm not even sure if I want you on this considering your past. I don't want to be screwing you up."

"It's a dead kid, Wayne." I walk past him expecting him to keep in step. "I'm fine with this." No I'm not. I clear my throat and shove my hands in my pockets. The smell of wet dirt and grass and the salty seaweed fills my nostrils along with the smell of exhaust. My feet crunch on loose rocks over the pavement.

At the MCP I stop and change into my full-body white suit (nicknamed a bunny suit) complete with plastic slippers over my shoes and a hood that I pull over the slight regrowth of my shaved head. I look more like an exterminator spraying for bugs than a police sergeant. The point is to prevent anyone going through the crime scene from leaving shoe prints, dirt particles, hairs, or skin cells that would compromise the investigation.

Dr. Norton is already in his bunny suit and walking toward the scene on a path designated by the forensic identification officer.

"The body was found around 7:30am by a couple camping on the beach." McIntyre starts.

"Did anyone tell them that's illegal?" For some reason I feel nervous and when I'm nervous I tend to make stupid jokes at stupid times.

"You can mention it to them later."

"Identify the victim yet?" Dr. Norton asks.

"Not yet. The campers found her in the women's change room. Since we don't have a media relations officer anymore…" McIntyre pauses to take a breath. I'm certain in that one second he wants to say something like, "fucking budget cuts," but doesn't. "I'm going to stay out here and handle any media that shows up."

I give him a nod that in a man's world can mean so much. This one means I have enough information, I understand completely, and I'm good to go.

My feet make a swish as the boot covers rub on the ground. The boardwalk of Brackley Beach is built in such a feng shui-esque way that it and the buildings almost blend into the tall marram grass and towering white spruce a short distance away. Sanded boards are sealed with light stain to spare the barefoot bathers, who cross over the path from the beach, from getting splinters and slivers.

As I step onto the raised boardwalk from the parking lot there is a building with toilets then on the right, a large change-room building with showers, one for men and one for women.

I know from experience that they have a chlorine smell inside and instead of good lighting the ceilings are open with only mosquito mesh covering the large openings.

On the left is a snack shop that sells soft drinks, water, unhealthy snacks and fast foods like hamburgers and hotdogs. Next to a few picnic tables are three historic displays standing like triangular pillars for locals to ignore and tourists to stand among to have their photos taken. They talk about the history of the area, history of the park and about the wild and plant life within the park. The final one is an attempt to keep people from damaging the dunes, but (as I said before) people barely ever read them.

I remember reading all three displays the first time we came to this beach to experience the shore. The boardwalk extends in a walking path stopping at the paved Gulf Shore Parkway before picking up again on the far side and disappearing over the dunes toward the beach. As it goes up and over the dunes in a series of steps, the boards are lost beneath the golden sand. In the spring the walkway is usually covered in blown sand and has to be dug out like a snow-covered path.

I have walked through murder scenes before without any hesitation. On this one I want to take my time getting there. I know what's waiting for me and I know how it's going to affect me.

When I was in British Columbia I chased a man the media dubbed *The Playground Killer*. Young girls from 10-13 years old were treated like his play-things and then left lying in the trash or the river - always near a playground close to where the girl had been taken.

Their faces haunted me then and haunt me still, but now they are joined by the adult victims from the *Red Island Killer*. I can feel my heart pounding against my temples and can taste the acrid foulness from my night time vomit as though bits were left behind and are only now breaking free. *Wonderful fucking Friday*.

"Reid? Reid, you with me?"

All I can see of the real Sgt. Marilyn Moore, other than the white bunny suit over her clothes, is her face. Thin sculpted eyebrows with a gentle curve the same red-wine color as her mid-length hair hidden inside the suit, light green eyes, and strong high cheekbones make her face pretty and genuine. She has the kind of face you want to look at. She has the kind of face I want to look at more than I should. Just not in a bunny suit. "Reid?"

"Yeah, I hear we have a dead girl."

Marilyn gives me a nod. She knows me well enough to just go ahead with the details. "White female, pre-adolescent, found here in the change room early this morning by campers wanting an early rendezvous in the shower," She leads the way into the change room building.

Marilyn is a couple inches taller than my 5 foot10 inches and has curves that I can visualize beneath her clothes and covering.

"If they had chosen the men's shower we may not have found her for a couple hours yet," Marilyn says.

I'm hit with stale air that suggests dampness and wood. The outside walls are tinted red which fades as you walk inside.

Beach sand on PEI has a tendency to cling to everything and because of the red clay mixed with it, it tends to stain everything a rusty red. It stains enough that there is a whole company selling PEI Dirt Shirts stained with the sand. It is so bad that the white fur of our dog Frix is tinted red.

There are benches around the room, plastic curtains in front of shower stalls in the back, and empty hooks on the walls. Toward the back, lying on the floor is the body of the girl we are all here to see.

It seems as though she came in here and laid down to stare through the mosquito mesh at the stars in the sky. Auburn hair, almost the same red-wine as Marilyn's, is spread out beneath her head as though she is posing for a photo. Milky eyes stare straight up through the mesh to the clearing sky. Freckles on her cheeks reflect the constellations she may have seen when she first got here. Her legs are straight out, arms at her sides. The girl wears a knee-length white summer dress with crazy swirls of gold and silver and spaghetti straps. The tiny bumps of newly-forming breasts push up from underneath. She is a girl just laying around waiting for mom to call her for supper, except for the dark brown stain through the dress where her legs meet her torso.

Dr. Norton crouches down beside her on the side opposite the Ident officer. Groans escape his lips as he bends down. He checks for a pulse and listens for a heartbeat. It is all just a technicality. This girl is dead.

"She was pretty." She looks to be the same age as my daughter - eleven. This could be my daughter.

My Blackberry beeps from inside my bunny suit with a text message. Thankfully I can't get to it until I leave the scene and change. It is probably from Hillary reminding me to get milk or something.

"She has bruises on her face and neck, signs of trauma in the vaginal area. There's some blood coming from her nose, but nothing else visible."

"Sexual assault?" I ask.

"Can't tell here. Have to wait until she's on the table."

Corporal Greg Eckhart looks up from where he crouches beside the girl. He pushes his glasses into place with the back of his hand. He is the head of Ident, the forensic identification unit. "Hey, Pumpernickel, there's tape residue on her wrists and ankles."

"Pumpernickel? Have you really run out of names?" Eckhart has been trying to guess my first name since the moment I stepped on the island. I have never liked my first name so I never use it and nobody knows it. Even my wife calls me by our last name. I made Eckhart the promise that I would tell him if he actually guesses what it is. I'm not sure if I ever will, but it is fun to see him get so frustrated. I give him a smile, but blink and it goes away.

"There's evidence of manual strangulation." Dr. Norton says. "I'll know more once I do the autopsy."

Eckhart adjusts his glasses again. "I don't think she was killed here. There's no sign of a struggle, no blood, no scuff marks."

"The female witness says she refuses to squat to, you know, pee. That's why she and her boyfriend camped close to these buildings. She says she went to the bathroom around one and there was no body or anyone around."

"Time of Death?" I have the urge to ask straight-forward questions. I don't want to be in here longer than necessary. I can feel the breath of ghosts on my skin. My stomach suddenly swirls into a dozen knots all trying to force out my breakfast of eggs and toast. Yes, this little girl needs the best help we can give her to get justice, but to me she's like a warning - and a memory.

"Who would do this to a child?" Marilyn whispers.

Who indeed? A sick person. A sick man with sick fetishes and sicker fantasies. I know exactly the type of man who would do this. I've seen him face to face. I fought the devil and I killed him.

"Was your other case this bad, Reid?" Marilyn asks.

I look right at her. My body wants me to get away from here. It wants me to run, get to my car, and drive until the memories and nightmares can't catch me anymore.

Run.

All I can handle is a swallow.

"Time of death," Dr. Norton continues – thank god. "Rigor has begun to set in the small muscles of the neck and face, eyes are milky, livor mortis has begun to set. If I were a betting man I'd say she's been dead three to five hours. I'll take the liver temperature and see if I can make a closer estimate." He opens his bag and takes out what he needs.

I spin on my heel heading for the door and fresh air. I can't watch this girl be man-handled again. The killer violated her; is what we're doing any different?

Marilyn hesitates a moment then follows me toward the door. "The witnesses say they saw a man drive away just before they came down here and found the body. That was at 7:15am, an hour-and-a-half ago."

I move from the change room into the warming air. The sun breaking the clouds forces me to blink and let my eyes adjust. I look over at the patch of grass on the sandy dunes. The waves crash on the beach behind them. "So where was she before that?"

Chapter 2

I pull off one latex glove, ball it up in the still-gloved hand then pull that down from the wrist turning it inside out and creating a bag for the other. I place them in a brown paper bag along with my bunny suit. All the suits will be collected and checked for particulates before being disposed of.

From the back of the MCP I stare across the parking lot. My shoulders slouch forward.

When the first call went out everyone came here. The call had been about a child. Everyone comes when a child may be hurt.

Volunteer firemen stand by their cars in one corner of the lot talking to each other and trying to get a glimpse of what is happening. EMTs are waiting by their ambulance ready to take the body to the Queen Elizabeth Hospital in Charlottetown.

Through the bushes I can see a collection of vehicles growing outside the park entrance. The press, tourists who want to enjoy the beach, and by now gawkers wanting to see what is going on. Some of the people here decided it was up to them to call someone else and tell them what was found.

I'm sure the news has passed around the island like rumors in a high school. It is like that game where a phrase is said on one end and passed whisper to ear, whisper to ear until it gets to the end. *Jim likes Bobbi-Jo* ends up becoming *Billy hates balloon goo* by the end of the game. It happens in Prince Edward Island. The entire province has barely more people than many cities. Someone you know or someone who knows who you know lives at one end of the island or the other and is more than willing to tell you all about what they have heard. The lovely island rumor chain.

"So what's it like?" McIntyre walks from the MCP with a Styrofoam cup in his hand. The bitter smell of coffee comes with him.

"Familiar," I say. I manoeuver around my boss, head into the kitchen area of the trailer and pour myself a cup of coffee. I put in three spoons of sugar and some creamer powder. I hate that shit. It never tastes anything like cream. I stare into the ripples in the white cup. Nicole, Sara, Tracy, Allison, the names flash through my head one after the other. Right now all I see are the names. It is not like in the nightmares when I see their faces.

At the back of the trailer radio equipment sits on a small desk against the wall. A table for evidence collection is located behind it, as is a ramp that leads down to the asphalt.

"I changed my mind, Wayne. I'm not getting involved in this. It's going to bring up a whole mass of bad feelings. My wife won't be able to handle me if I get involved with this one." I stare off, but all I see in my mind are the names and faces of those girls I couldn't save in British Columbia.

McIntyre emits a long sigh and raises his cup to his lips. He looks out in the same direction as me but he sees a parking lot filled with people waiting to be told what to do. He takes a quick drink of his coffee. His face cringes at the bitter taste. "Concentrate on the cold case, if you want, but you're also going to help on this one. Talk to witnesses, help with canvassing, and report to Marilyn. I'll get Dispirito to partner with her. Help her until he gets here." He raises his cup as a way of indicating that we are done here.

"I'll talk to the people who called this in. Send Marilyn over when she's done." I drive out of the parking lot and around to where the boardwalk crosses the paved road and heads over the dune. I could have walked through the tall grass to the perimeter road instead of driving, but why get soaked up to my knees if I don't have to? I park behind a white car with the RCMP red and yellow stripes down the sides. On the back quarter panel is a silhouette of a musical rider.

The road stretches on disappearing into the woods that makes up the very west corner of the park.

Half-way up the hill the wood slats of the pathway to the beach appear to dissolve into the fine beach sand that has been blown over the dunes. The winds of the Gulf of St. Lawrence eat away at the island every year. It's hard to tell whether it's the boardwalk going into the sand or the sand going over the path. I have to hang onto the wood railings and pull myself through as my shoes slip in the sand. After three steps I can feel the grains of sand inside my shoes.

A day at the beach means weeks of fishing tiny grains of sand out of every nook and cranny of your body. Leigh would have a shower right away to get rid of the sand and still could find it stuck in her hair afterward.

As I crest the dune Brackley Beach folds out in both directions with rolling green waves topped by white toupees of cresting foam pushing onto the sand. There are batches of black seaweed and debris strewn about.

A white lifeguard tower sits close to the wood stairs leading to the beach. The sand stretches thirty feet or so from the dunes to the water then far off on either side, the size changing of course with the tides. Two people stand next to a small two-tone blue dome tent.

I stop for a moment, closing my eyes, to smell the salt and feel the damp air against my face.

"I'm surprised to see you here, Reid." Deborah English stands at the bottom of the stairs.

"It's my job, Deb."

"Hillary told me about your nightmares so I didn't think you'd come."

"Why is everyone so concerned for me?"

"You should be happy. I'm sure Hillary will ask me how you were when I tell her I saw you."

"Don't tell her."

She flashed me a bright smile. Sgt. Deborah English is a close friend of my wife. Her short yellow-blond pixie cut hides under the flat-top police hat. She was the Media Relations Liaison Officer. When there was a case that hit the press she was the face of the Royal Canadian Mounted Police in PEI.

"What are you doing here anyway? Shouldn't you be back at headquarters getting ready for a press conference or something?" I know damn well what happened with her position. It is just more fun to drill it in. During any fight with my wife, Deb always takes Hillary's side so I will take any hits I can.

"Hillary didn't tell you? Do you want the long version or short?" Her lips are pouty, eyebrows tamed into a gull's wing arch above blue eyes. She looks good in her dark-blue uniform. She is the type of cop teenage boys want to have pull them over. She is a classic Audrey Hepburn beauty which makes her the perfect face for media. Her hands go to her hips and her eyes stare into mine. "Because the division is a million dollars over budget the powers-that-be decided to cut some provincial jobs to hold the province hostage until they give us more money. My job was one of those, so this summer I'm assigned to the Cavendish division."

I look at the young couple packing up their camping gear. "Somebody sounds bitter."

She crosses her arms in front of her. "Instead of admitting their mistakes they're playing with our lives, with my life. Be glad Major Crimes is an essential service and they won't make any cuts there." She looks out at the water for a few moments.

Many of our jobs have time limits then we move on to another position somewhere else whether that be as a regular officer or part of a specialized unit. Sometimes that means changing areas or provinces. When I was in BC I worked five years in Major Crimes then moved here to stay in a MC unit instead of going back to a car.

Deborah says, "I'll take you to the witnesses. They've been packing up their camping gear. I think they just want to get out of here."

"You were first on scene?" I feel more sand in my shoe.

"Yes, Noah Hudson and I were closest when the call came." From June to October there is a Cavendish division which patrols around the tourist area of Cavendish up through the PEI National Park. Through the winter months Cavendish is a ghost town so they close their detachment, but during the tourist season the area booms with a water park, world class golf courses, RV parks, beaches, and a vast array of amusement areas and restaurants so they need the local police. During the Cavendish Beach Music Festival the island population will expand from just over a hundred thousand to three hundred thousand or more, with most of it in the small area.

"Did either of you go near the body?" I ask.

Her teeth bare down on her bottom lip. "I did. I checked for vitals, then backed out the same way I went in. Did you see her?"

I nod but don't say a word. Do I need to?

"Who the hell would do that to a child?"

"A bad guy." I look out over the water at a fishing boat close to the horizon. I can't hear any note of its engine over the sound of the waves hitting the shore.

"She looked like she was Leigh's age, didn't she?"

I don't let my eyes meet hers as I turn to the couple.

"This is Grant Seaver and Ali Shue, both from Saskatoon, Saskatchewan." Deborah turns to me, "This is Sgt. Reid. He's going to ask you some questions."

I give them both a nod. Both of them appear to be in their twenties and both skinny enough that I have the urge to buy them burgers. The guy is wearing only grey sweat pants that sit low, showing his pelvic bone pushing against his skin. His hair is a messy dirty-blond birds' nest that seems to extend to the scruff on his face. The girl looks just as pretty, but a lot cleaner than he does. She sits with her legs sticking out of the tent. Her hands busily move things around inside a fabric backpack. "Morning. How long have you been on the island?"

"Like a week." Grant scratches his arm and neck. There are fine grains of sand stuck to his skin. He remains standing and turns his head to look behind him at the girl. "We, ah, wanted to see the east coast. We've been camping in camp sites and beaches and places. We pitched our tent here last night."

"Do you have a car? I didn't see one down in the parking lot." The truth is I didn't even look.

"No. We took a bus from Saskatchewan and then we walk or get rides, you know, to get where we have to." He rubs his red eyes with a knuckle. I don't think they are red from sleep.

"That's not always safe."

"I can keep us safe. And we don't hitch unless we have to."

"And we're always together." Ali's voice is barely a whisper on the waves.

I know these two had nothing to do with the body. They camped last night on the other side of a hill from where the body was found. Sure there were the winds and the early morning rain, but they must have heard something. Then again, they are young and probably had other things to do besides look at what evil things were happening in the world. I don't even remember a time when I could do that.

"You two found the body?"

"Ali did." He turns back to her. His eyes blink wildly.

Ali doesn't look up. Her hands just can't seem to get things straight in her bag.

"She found it. She needed the bathroom, you know. Like, a guy can pee anywhere but a girl needs to sit, right. That's why we camped here. I went over there afterward, but I didn't go near her or nothing. Then we called the cops, you know."

I lean to the side to look around Grant. "So you went over there to do your business and found the body? Did you see anyone? Did you hear anything before going over there? Hear a car maybe?"

Ali looks up at me. Her skin is white and her eyes moist. They have a tinge of red but nothing like Grant's. She brushes a loose hair away from her face. "I didn't see anyone. I saw her and then I ran back here and I told Grant."

"She screamed all the way, shit." Grant doesn't seem to know whether he should laugh or run. "Look can we just pack and get out of here?

I turn to see Marilyn making her way down the wood stairs. I ask, "Did you see anything else?"

Grant looks to the girl. "I went for a pee before Ali did and I saw a guy get in a minivan and drive away."

"You went down to the showers?"

"Ah, no. I climbed up the dunes and did my thing. I know I'm not supposed to but, yeah. This guy was down there on the road getting in his van and he looked up at me. He sort of waved, then got in and drove to the main road. I didn't see him though, not really. He was a white guy with like dark hair, but that's all I saw." The young man began to perspire across his face even though the wind coming in was cool. "You don't think … was that the guy? Shit."

"What kind of minivan was it?" Marilyn asks.

"It was silver I think. It was still dark out so I'm not sure. Could have been white or grey maybe."

She says, "Any idea what direction the van came from or which direction it was headed?"

"Yeah, it went that way." Grant points straight over the dune. "It went out of the park, I guess. I don't know where it came from, but it was like, just down on the road pointing that way so I'm guessing it came from that way." He points down the beach toward Robinson Island and Rustico Bay.

"That way?" Marilyn points herself and gets a nod. "And what time was this?"

"I don't know, like, 6:30."

"And what time did you find the body?"

Ali the mouse says, "7:30."

"And you're sure you didn't get a good look at the minivan driver?"

Grant rubs his eyes as he shakes his head. "You think he put the body there, eh? Who would do that and then, like, wave?"

"No idea," I say as I think someone who's done it before and doesn't think he will ever get caught.

"Why don't you two pack your things and Sgt. English will get you a ride into Charlottetown. She'll make sure you get a good breakfast." On the last word I look to Deborah and flash her a smile. My hand caresses her arm as I turn and follow Marilyn back to the stairs. Now with the bunny suit gone I see she wears dark slacks and a maroon blouse with a loose collar and topped with a black blazer. Her red-wine hair is tied up so it won't touch her collar.

The moment we are at the top of the stares she stops and turns to me. "What the hell was that?"

"What?"

"The way you touched Deb. What was that about?"

"What? What did I do?"

She shakes her head and continues down the other side of the dune. Her unmarked car sits at a strange angle in front of the patrol car. Over her shoulder she says, "You were touching her in a loving manner."

I don't like how she emphasises loving manner.

The moment she's on the driver's side Marilyn gives me a cocky smile then slips in behind the steering wheel.

I open the passenger side door and lean inside. "What is that supposed to mean? She's Hillary's best friend for Christ's sake. I'm not that stupid."

Marilyn raises a hand. "I never said you were." Not long ago Marilyn and I almost took things too far. My marriage was strained, Marilyn's fiancé hit her, things almost happened. A serial killer had photos of Marilyn and me delivered to my wife. Now things are different. Different for her anyway.

"Are you getting in or not? I'd like to go down the road and see what we can find." Marilyn shouts through the open window.

"Where's Dispirito?"

"Not here yet. Get in." Marilyn moves her notebook from the seat.

"How are things on the relationship side? Are you still seeing that cook?"

Even though I know she drives with reckless abandonment I don't bother fastening my seatbelt.

"Executive Chef Wylie Renier, yes. He owns half the restaurant, you know."

"Which half?" I let out a laugh and pull out my phone. Another text. I don't read it.

"What's that?"

"Hillary. She just texted to say she loves me." I can taste the bitterness of my own words.

"That's sweet," Marilyn says either not noticing or deciding not to mention my tone. "You and Hillary should come to dinner with me sometime at Wylie's restaurant. His food is amazing."

"I think Char is a little too high end for us." To Islanders it is said like Shar as in the first sound of Charlottetown lovingly called Char'town. "We're a burger and fries couple." I look out at the trees that border both sides of the paved road. We are still only a few dozen feet from the shore, but I cannot see it. The car lurches to one side. Another pothole makes it bounce the other way. "Plus we have Leigh. She's eleven. That's too young to leave her alone and she's probably too young for Char."

"Have her stay at a friend's then. It's summer. She has to have some friend's places she can spend a night." Marilyn brakes the car and turns the wheel to

44

get around a spot where a mini-volcano seemed to push through the asphalt. "This road fucking sucks. They obviously don't care about keeping it in good shape."

Robinson's Island is at the far western end of the national park. It is still called an island even though the small waterway cutting it off from the rest of the park had been filled in with sand. A campsite opened there in the sixties with almost 150 spots for people to park a motorhome or set up a tent, but it closed in 2005 because the number of people using it dwindled and the infrastructure was poorly maintained. I'm willing to bet it was more because of the latter. This road, for instance, was once good enough to be used for drag racing. Now it has been all but abandoned due to potholes, cracks in the pavement that stretch the entire width, and the occasional fallen tree that can sit for months before someone clears it.

Today the road and island are used by windsurfers trying to surf the inland bay, hikers, birdwatchers, and nudists looking for a private beach. The small piece of land has been left alone for Mother Nature to reclaim. If you ask the national park people they will tell you that they have plans for it including taking out the paved areas and helping the natural fauna to completely take over, but by the look of this road it is not too high on their list of priorities.

"I remember a few years ago they had a mock emergency on Robinson's Island. It was for Incident Command System training. We had the search and rescue, Coast Guard, parks services, EMT's, Emergency Management Systems, and us all working together." Marilyn brakes hard for a crack in the road. The moment the front tires clear it she slams on the gas. "I think it was a mock plane crash into a campsite. Should I make a reservation for next Friday?"

"I'll ask Hill."

"No you won't."

"I said I will." Marilyn has become a touchy subject in the Reid household. I try my best not to talk about her at home.

Ahead we see a rusted yellow bar blocking the way onto the island. Most of the paint has fallen off, the metal beneath is rusting. The bushes on either side are overgrown making it appear that the bar is suspended in air. Grass has been pushed down on one side as people have walked around heading for their own hidden paradise.

"Rain would have washed out evidence of a car. Maybe we'll get a footprint." Marilyn stops the car in the centre of the road facing the bar.

"If the guy was even up here. Maybe the silver van guy was nobody. If he went for a piss in the men's he wouldn't have seen the body."

The trees and bushes block the wind and drop a blanket of shade over the road creating a cool spooky feel.

As we step from the car I quickly check my watch. Two hours ago I was witnessing a body being exhumed from the ground. "There's a gatehouse there."

A small wooden building sits on the side of the road half hidden behind bushes and bright green leaves. Marilyn wouldn't have been able to see it.

"The grass is pushed down here on the side of the road. This would be a good place to bring someone in the middle of the night, no one around for miles, sounds of the ocean to muffle screams." Marilyn follows the marks where a vehicle's tires have pushed down the grass but never steps off the paved area. Her shoes crunch on loose stones. "It's sad that we look at a place like this and think it would be a good place to rape and kill a little girl."

"We don't know that she was raped." I hope not. My blue eyes catch Marilyn's green ones. We both know what happened to that girl.

I duck under the yellow bar. A few feet beyond the bar the ground is still paved and even further I can see where the grasses have tried their best to grow over the man-made intrusion. Large tufts of grass grow through cracks and expand out. There are spots ahead where the red sand has been blown in. Ahead of us, where the main campsite was, is a half-circle of grass and trees with dunes on the right side. We can hear the waves crashing against the shore. The faint sound of a boat leaving Rustico Harbour comes from further up the point. Every step we take has to be calculated and thought out in case there is anything we need to preserve. I look before taking a step.

In our reports I'll have to write down all of my actions. If the killer did come here the last thing we want to do is mess up anything he may have left.

The windows of the guard shack are boarded. The paint is peeling and the tin roof is rusty with leaves filling the gullies. Green and silver moss has started to grow on the decomposed leaves.

I step carefully around rocks and grass to get closer to the door that is only open a crack. It has a latch half-way up. The padlock is still attached to it, the connecting piece that would have held it from the frame is attached to that. Long screws dangle from it. Paint and wood particles are held inside the threads of the screws.

"It was broken into recently."

"Doesn't make it last night, does it? You think this is the crime scene?"

"I don't." At arm's length I reach out and hook my finger around the edge of the door.

When I was a kid I would have imagined a bear or wolf waiting inside ready to pounce. Yesterday, thanks to my favorite TV program, I would have imagined a zombie with rotting flesh, but today I'm picturing little girls huddled in a corner begging for help.

The door creaks loudly as it slowly opens. My eyes fall onto the faded plywood floor inside the small shack. My body is hit with sudden chill as if the essence of Kayla Schofield, what made her the loving child she was, seems to walk out of the tiny shack and

pass through me. There is the distinct red shadow of
virgin blood painted across the boards. Blackflies
dance up and down trying to get a precious taste. "We
should call Eckhart and get him down here. I'm pretty
sure that's blood on the floor."

Before Marilyn has the chance to dial, her
cellphone rings. She says a few words but mostly
listens. Before hanging up she asks for Ident to come
down here.

"McIntyre?"

She nods. Her dark hair bounces. "Missing girl
over at Bonaventure Campgrounds and Cottages on
the far side of Cavendish fits our girls description."
She stares at me as if waiting for something.

"At least you know he knows the island. He'd have
to know it if he came from Cavendish to here. I don't
think he'd just find this place."

"Want to come for a ride?"

I really don't want to get involved in this case. I
know I will think about all of the girls I had to find
answers for in BC. My own daughter will sit inside
my mind just behind my eyes. I'll have tunnel vision
and soon my wife will complain that I'm getting
obsessed. That is if I let it overtake me. I should tell
her to drop me off at my car and have Dispirito meet
her there. I know that's what I should do. I should do
a lot of things.

Chapter 3

There were rules to every game.

He watched the series of taillights ahead of him go from red to white to red, one vehicle after another, as people slid their transmissions from park to drive. He did the same and followed the snaking line of cars and trucks down a slope and up the ramp into the gaping mouth of the beast. He almost missed the morning ferry.

A man in a bright yellow vest pointed with one hand while the other gestured the vehicles to keep moving. The silver van tipped forward and rolled down to the underbelly of the ferry. At the bottom another yellow-vested worker pointed toward the left side. The driver followed the cars in front of him into the cattle lines painted on the floor. At least he was close to the elevator.

He took his computer tablet and strolled to the elevator. As a last thought he pushed the lock button on his car key. The horn announced it was locked. The sound echoed through the floating parking lot, cut short by the sliding doors.

The Northumberland Ferries ran from May to early December transporting automobiles, trucks, and people back and forth between Wood Islands, PEI and Caribou, and Nova Scotia. Before the Confederation Bridge connecting the tiny island to New Brunswick was built the ferry had been the only way to drive to the island. Although traffic had slowed it was still used by many people and businesses every day. Just a forty-five minute float across the Northumberland Strait and you could be on the mainland. An hour drive after that and you can be in Halifax. Three hours after that you could enter the United States. He wasn't going that far, just home to Halifax.

Never have your fun too close to home.

He joined the line in the cafeteria. His body craved sustenance. It had been a long night with plenty of physical activity that left him satisfied in a manner different than food. His playmate was a screamer, this satisfied him differently than sex. He liked it when they screamed. He ordered scrambled eggs, bacon, and toast with a black coffee.

When in the game always pay cash.

The ferry's engines hummed continuously through the entire body of the boat. They were loud enough that even inside you had to raise your voice to be heard. He selected a small table in the corner and sat with his back to the wall. There was a slight change in the noise from the engines and a jolt as the journey started. The ferry vibrated from the machinery working to propel them against the current in the Strait. He couldn't really tell that they were pushing away from the island specifically, just that they were moving.

The cafeteria soon filled with bodies and the sounds of conversation. His eyes rapidly scanned the crowd.

Some passengers looked as though they could have used a few more hours sleep instead of catching the first ferry. He wouldn't have allowed himself the luxury.

His eyes followed a little girl as she crossed the cafeteria.

His mind suddenly flashed to an Abbott and Costello skit he saw on one of his father's old video tapes. Costello, the fat one, was trying to sing a song with his back to Abbott who was directing someone hanging a painting. He kept instructing the other person to sing higher and lower. Costello thought Abbott was talking to him so he adjusted his pitch higher and lower until he got so frustrated he stomped his feet and yelled. The part of the song he always repeated was, "a pretty girl is like a melody." This little girl was like a melody.

Her mother stayed in line waiting for food, but called the girls' name. *Tabitha.* That was a pretty name. *A melody.* Dark hair fell over her shoulders from under a red hat and onto a matching coat. She was younger than what he liked. She was closer to his daughter's age, but she was growing. Every time her mother called her to come back she twisted as though her entire body was answering "no."

He lowered his head, his eyes on his plate. She was too young. There was no way off the ferry for at least three-quarters of an hour, no place to go or to get away. There were witnesses. He didn't do any pre-game scouting. So many rules would be broken. And he wasn't playing that game anymore.

Everything was changing. It wasn't the taste or the touch he craved any more. He still wanted the innocence, but now he wanted the fear. He enjoyed the thrill. He desired the copper smell of blood. He wanted to see their eyes switch as the last breath was gone. He wanted the kill.

His fingers tore open a paper packet of salt that he sprinkled over his eggs. With a plastic fork he stirred the eggs and mixed the salt inside. Damn liquid eggs. His wife would have bitched about the salt. She would have denied him the bacon and probably the coffee too. Toast, orange juice, maybe eggs. Breakfast was always better away from her. Everything was better away from her. And he always had to have a good meal after playing the game. He had to refill what had been drained. It was his reward. It was her fault he played, his wife's. She wore him down. She made him feel useless and out-of-control. He had to fight back. He had to show that he had power. He was the dominator. Maybe if he killed her he would be satisfied. Probably not.

His eyes darted around the room. He had to control his breathing. Last night he had been a giant, but now he was shrinking. The closer he got to home the smaller he was becoming.

Never stay near where you pick them up.

He checked the time. How long would it be before anyone noticed she was missing? She told him her parents didn't really care. Kayla (she said she didn't like her name) said her mother and father barely noticed when she was around or when she would sleep over at a friend's. They'd notice now, but when? There were no police at the ferry so maybe all was still safe and sound.

Everything was going to come to an end soon though. It had to be that way. His daughter was gaining his attention. He watched her, not as the protective father, but as the predator waiting for the young to drift away from the pack. He couldn't stop. He had to change things.

They had to stop him.

But he couldn't just give himself to them.

One last game.

He picked up a slice of bacon as his eyes gazed at the girl in red. He bet she had a lovely scream. He bet she bled red. A pretty girl is like a melody.

You followed the rules until it was time to change them.

Chapter Four

"So how are things with Hillary?"

I stare out the window as we cross the bridge in the area called Oysterbed Bridge. On my side is a large pottery studio, on the other a red-roofed building that used to be Dayboat Restaurant but now sits vacant. Out in the bay are the floating balls that signify the mussel beds.

"Things are fine. But I can't work on this case with you. She's going to freak out when she hears I'm involved in a case like this."

"Homicide or a kid?"

"Both."

Marilyn runs her hand back through her hair hooking it behind her ear. While driving she lets it hang loose. "What's her problem? She knows what your job is."

"She had to deal with me when I worked on the *Playground Killer* case. We almost split because I got too, *involved.* The girls were the same age as this one, pretty much looked the same, similar anyway. I know I'll get too involved." I end in a whisper that is left hanging for a while.

Marilyn says, "So that means it's best not to get involved all together?"

"Yes, and you see how well that's working out. When Dispirito shows up I'm backing away. I have to or ..." I don't want to finish the sentence. I have to back away or prepare myself for divorce. As we enter the town of Rustico I look at the different license plates on the cars outside Fisherman's Wharf Lobster Supper Restaurant at 10:00am waiting for a spot of lunch.

I can't help but think of Hillary and Leigh. Hill threatened to leave me after that case in BC. It was leave the area or be alone. We moved here and murder seems to have followed me like a foul stink. She often tells me I'm not the same man she married. Maybe she's right. We have been married twelve years, together for seventeen, so having her threaten to leave me puts things into perspective. Of course I have been a Mountie for one year more than we have been together so where does it all come in? This is who I am and what I do.

My Blackberry beeps and I whip it out. The text is Hillary asking how my day is going. Maybe Deborah has called her and told her what's happening. I'll get home later to some silent treatment before getting pulled in to an argument about how I promised not to get involved in kid cases. I can actually feel myself getting angry about the whole thing, but I have no reason for that. I can picture the fight in my head. Hillary doesn't know about this case and I'm not involved in it. I'm doing my job and then I will be done and back onto my cold case file.

Shit, even I don't believe it. I text that I am busy with a case and will call her later.

"Was that Hillary again?"

"Yeah."

"Jesus, she's got you on a short leash. You two still in therapy?" Marilyn probably knows more about me and my life after just a couple of years than my wife does.

I let out a "Yup."

"How's that working out?"

I let my head roll so that I am looking right at her. If my wife finds out that I'm riding with her I will get a lot more silent treatment. Chances are good that Deborah has called and talked to her about what is happening on. My wife has every reason not to trust me with this woman. I said no once, but given the chance again I'm not sure I'll be that strong. I have to get the conversation and my mind away from me. "Didn't your chef win an award recently?"

"My chef? Yes, he won the chef's competition at the restaurant and food show." She seems happy. Her hands don't grip the steering wheel with white knuckles as they did before and her shoulders seem to have relaxed. It wasn't long ago that her shoulders were slumped and she came to work with make-up covering bruises. The man she was supposed to marry hit her and ran her down. At work she has always been strong and in charge, but anyone can put on another face for the public.

I look at her face as she tells me about the dish her chef made and I can see the change. Her make-up has toned down completely. She's smiling as she speaks. Her light green eyes shine more, if that is possible. Every time she moves and her hair dances I get the strange craving for chocolate chip cookies.

Cavendish has one traffic light at the corner of a small cemetery where Lucy Maude Montgomery was buried. A family of Japanese tourists are there taking photos in front of the gravestone.

During the winter the area is so quiet you half expect to see tumbleweeds rolling through. Many residents relocate to hotels and motels in Charlottetown or Summerside to avoid the half-hour drive over icy roads and the harsh northern winds. There are times in the winter when roads are completely impassible. The one traffic light gets turned off in October and is not turned on again until mid-May, with enough fanfare that it is announced in the local media. About May long-weekend, earlier if the weather is good, all the restaurants, B&B's, resorts, little tourist stores, golf courses, and attractions open up and stay open until sometime in autumn whenever the traffic flow slows to the point that they can't justify staying open. As soon as things open in May the population booms overnight. The Cavendish Beach Country Music Festival will engorge the island with double its population for just one weekend and all in one small area.

We drive past the tourist money traps. My family has visited all of them. There is Ripley's Believe it or Not, the wax museum, Avonlea Village that takes people into the Anne of Green Gables novels, Shining Waters waterpark, Sandspit Amusement Park, and some other places that are either there to show you something or get you involved. They are on the edge of being expensive but give your family distractions for the kiddies when all the parents want to do is hit the golf courses and beaches. Leigh loves the mini-putt courses. The Cavendish Boardwalk is a collection of gift shops and food places. There are a few restaurants serving everything from fast food to coffee and doughnuts to fancier meals.

We move from the main area of Cavendish and pass a closed-down amusement park on the left that was there before I moved to PEI. Still in one person's yard is a huge replica of a space shuttle and Epcot Centre from Disney World. Just down the road we turn at a sign reading Bonaventure Campgrounds and Cabins.

From what I know the RV camp is one of the largest on the island. All kinds of people visit Prince Edward Island. Some rent a hotel room as their base of operations. A larger number drive across the

Confederation Bridge in recreational vehicles towing their economic cars behind or they take the ferry across to the island. They park the RV, hook up to electricity, sewage, and water, pop out whatever hidden compartments there are to turn their home-away-from-home into something better than home, then use their car to go wherever they please. They are similar to the hotel people but they can bring more, take more, and have the comforts of knowing who slept in their beds before them.

As we climb a hill through sporadic trees with wide canopies of bright green leaves giving diamond flashes of the sun, we pass a half-dozen log cabins. Each has a small deck out back with a barbecue chained to the foundation. A sign with a blue arrow and the word Office printed in yellow points up the hill. After approximately one hundred yards of trees, the property opens to a large grassy area with just the winding paved road cutting across it. Above it is a large parking lot with another lane that circles around for the larger RVs to turn around. Marilyn parks in front of the only building.

The top floor has small square windows across its entire length and the main floor has large windows with closed blinds. Across the side of the building a mural has been painted depicting the flight deck of an aircraft carrier. A sign in front of the building reads, Flight Deck Restaurant and Bar, fully licensed. Another sign on an arrow points toward a flight of stairs on the side of the building. It reads, Community Center.

Beside an RCMP squad car there are three other cars in the area. A sign post out front (that reminds me of the one in M.A.S.H. with towns from all over the world listed) has arrows that point in all directions: Cavendish, Charlottetown, Summerside, Laundry, Swimming Pools/Showers, General Store, Office. Both the store and office are located around the side of the building.

As she steps from the car. Marilyn straightens her jacket. "You ever been out here before?"

"No. I've heard about it."

"I was here for a wedding once. Pretty complex operation. It's like a self-contained village."

Beyond the building is a giant fenced area where the spots are for the RVs. It is a wooden fence like an old school western corral of logs that have been painted white. Attached to the parking lot is a small shack with an entrance and exit for the fenced area. A four-wheeled all-terrain vehicle is parked facing the shack.

"Who's Moore?" A man walks toward us dressed in a dark-blue RCMP uniform. Sweat glistens on his face. Today is turning out to be hot as hell. I nod to Marilyn and the other RCMP member moves his attention toward her.

His name tag says Corporal Nicholas Freeman. "Missing girl is Kayla Schofield, age eleven. We have the parents in the office. The mother is pretty upset,

63

father's angry. We have two members and a guard looking around the campsite now."

Marilyn doesn't stop walking, forcing Freeman to spin and move quickly catch up to her. She often feels the need to show that she is in charge.

"They say the last time they saw her was around 10pm last night when she said she might stay at a friend's. Friend says she left her camp and was going to the Schofield's camper."

I ask, "Do you believe them?"

"No reason not to." Freeman says.

Marilyn nods. We are not like police detectives on television, we don't see other members as beneath us, but female members often feel like they have to show assertiveness in order to be taken seriously. It's often to their detriment, giving them the "bitch" label. Next year Marilyn's time in Major Crimes will be up and she will either move to another specialty or go back to regular patrol. Members currently out there looking for people speeding or checking out general complaints have likely been in Major Crimes or one of the other specialty units at some point during their careers.

"Did you find her?" A woman rushes out of the office to meet us in front. A baggy red sweatshirt with a picture of the Vancouver skyline hangs from her thin frame. Tan capris pants below the sweatshirt give the impression that she dressed quickly in the dark. The skin around her eyes is puffy and the whites are red. Her brown hair appears wild, like she just stepped from a wind tunnel. It falls in long brown waves with tints of red and lines of grey. I compare her to the younger form of herself laying in the showers over at Brackley. Two men follow. One is dressed smartly and the other wears faded jeans and a golf shirt.

Freeman says, "Sergeants Moore and Reid, Emily and Wayne Schofield. And this is Greg Montgomery, owner of the campground."

"Did you find Kayla?" Emily Schofield's voice rises to a high pitch.

I turn to see a family of four entering the restaurant. They all watch us like they were driving past a car accident. If you look to your right, on the unofficial tour of PEI, you will see two parents about to be devastated. Tip your driver.

"Did you find her? She's only eleven. How far could she get? Is she okay?"

"Maybe we should go inside." Marilyn's voice is as soothing as a mother being patient with an upset child.

Greg Montgomery turns to walk back to the office. Wayne Schofield looks to his wife waiting for direction; she stands her ground.

Marilyn knows there will be no making this woman do anything until she gets what she wants. "We found a body this morning."

Emily Schofield covers her mouth with a hand. "A body …" A wailing sound starts and builds from inside her. It builds and builds as if it were a train whistle coming from down the tracks getting closer quickly. Eyes that had already shed tears erupt as she sobs. She grabs her husband's arm for support as her knees give way.

I jump forward and take her other arm. As his arm moves around his wife's waist, Wayne Schofield looks at me with a mixed expression of thanks and scorn.

"Are you okay, Dear?"

"Bring her back to the office." Montgomery quickly leads the way.

We nearly have to push the woman to get her to start walking forward.

I can hear Marilyn breathing sighs of frustration behind me. She wants to get on with things. We are wasting time right now. This could be our girl, but maybe not. Right now we are at a crossroads not knowing which way to go, whoever we are chasing is getting further away.

The office is just a simple room, barely larger than a closet, with a rolling chair in front of a pre-fab desk topped with organized piles of papers. As we ease the woman into the chair I notice pictures rotating on the computer monitor. Many of the pictures show dogs. Others show Montgomery and another man smiling. Emily Schofield keeps her eyes down on the floor. The moment she is secure I move back toward the doorway allowing the others squeeze into the space.

Wayne Schofield waits a few moments before asking the inevitable question. "What do you mean you found a body?"

"Would you have a picture of your daughter that we could see?"

Emily raises her head and looks at Marilyn with wide eyes, her lips slightly apart. "Wayne, you have a picture on your phone. *Your phone.*" This last is a screeching demand.

We all jump at her voice. I've been here before. This is the part where the parent is certain that once we see the photo of the missing child we will be able to say we were mistaken. It was someone else's child. I know our girl is Kayla Schofield. As the girl's father goes through the pictures on his phone we all know.

Marilyn passes the phone to me, but I don't even have to look at the picture of the girl next to the world's tallest man to know she is the one in the sundress on her way to the morgue in Charlottetown. I have the same picture of Leigh, only my daughter was younger at the time. I can picture her reluctance at having the photo taker and her parents insistence to stand next to the towering mannequin.

"When was the last time you saw Kayla?" Marilyn asks.

"What? You tell us there's a body and now you ask about when we were with her." Wayne Schofield has his chest pushed out and fists so tight that his knuckles are white.

"Mr. Schofield,"

He snatches back his iPhone. "We had a couple of other campers over for drinks around the fire. We're on vacation. This is supposed to be a safe place, isn't it? Safest province in the country? What the hell worries do we have, right?" His hands move as he talks. He makes quick sharp gestures that in any other place would seem threatening.

I take another step into the room a bit closer to Marilyn. She hates it when I try to protect her and takes her own step forward to cut me off.

Emily's hand grabs her husband's forearm. "Wayne, stop." She stares at him long enough to hold his eyes and, without a word, calm him down. She takes a deep swallow and somehow finds a degree of calm in her despair, much like walking into the eye of a hurricane where all is still. Her chin raises a little. She says, "We had our neighbors over for drinks. Kayla came back from the pool with her friends and asked if she could stay at Jane's. Jane didn't know if her parents would approve. Kayla didn't come back so we thought, we thought …" Her voice slips away like a warm breeze.

"Did anyone new come to talk to you lately or ask about Kayla?" Marilyn inquires.

"You think she was taken, don't you? What kind of people do you have here, Greg?

Marilyn clears her throat. "Mr. and Mrs. Schofield, this morning a …"

I spin on my heel and pull Freeman, who has been standing just outside the office, with me. Marilyn has to say what she must and will completely destroy the parent's lives with what they can feel is coming.

I lean in close to Freeman so that my lips almost touch his ear. "I want the gates closed. Nobody leaves the campground unless we talk to them and give them the okay. Everyone in the restaurant stays there."

His blue eyes hold mine for a moment. "That girl in Brackley?" On cue Kayla Schofield's mother releases a piercing scream. Without another word Freeman marches off to do his job.

We have now become a National Geographic program that must be seen at. Everyone wants to know what's going on. They are all thinking, *"Thank God it's not me."* I said that to myself in BC with the other girls. I looked at my daughter every night and wondered what I would do if she was the one taken and killed. And then I did what I knew I had to do. Looking at the Schofield's I'm not sure if I was right. Leigh is the same age as Kayla. Would I do the same now as I did then?

~ * ~

Within twenty minutes the parking area in front of the Bonaventure gates is overflowing with RCMP vehicles. Any officer who is not at Brackley Point Beach is now here preparing to do what Marilyn tells them to do.

"We have four hundred seventy-three campsites for RVs, the whole front field for tents (we don't have anyone out there now) and twelve cabins with seven occupied at the moment. I'm guessing you don't care

69

about the cabins since they're far out in the front and don't have much to do with what goes on up here." Montgomery looks at me as we walk.

Sweat glistens on his face. He looks like he is glad to be away from the office, away from the hysterical mother. He tried putting up an argument when I insisted he call the night guard, who had already gone home, and tell him to get back here. I made it clear that I didn't care about anyone needing their sleep. He had to come back or someone would go to his place and drag him back here.

I look back over my shoulder wondering if I made the right choice to follow Greg Montgomery to the Schofield's campsite instead of staying at the office. "We'll have to question those people too. Somebody saw this little girl leave." Somebody took her. I can't say it, but we are all thinking it now. Somebody snatched that girl in front of all these people and took her away to kill her.

Montgomery's feet stumble sending a few stones from the dirt road free. The fact that we are going to question everyone seems to startle him. He wears a white button-down shirt with blue and red vertical stripes and two buttons open, tan slacks, and leather sandals. He walks with a sway to his hips that makes him look from behind like a woman. If this was Marilyn or Deborah or Hillary I would let my eyes drop to the ass to look for panty lines or to see how the cheeks bounce or roll around each other with each step. Just the thought of it makes me want to look.

I'm man enough to know when a man has a good ass. Oh hell. I let my eyes look down. His slacks are tight around his buttocks but loose on the leg. He looks like he should be strolling a beach in Miami instead of a campground in Cavendish, Prince Edward Island.

He begins with the spiel I'm certain he pours out to everyone who will listen, "Three hundred thirteen spots have full electrical, water, and sewage hook-ups, one hundred sixty have only water and electric. There's a communal dump spot for sewage. Every spot has a fire pit and small grill box for cooking. We have two full-sized supervised swimming pools and a kids' wading pool, kids' arcade by the pools, playgrounds with swing sets and slides, Laundromat, the Flight-Deck Restaurant with a larger community center room above it, general store, twenty-four hour security, free high-speed internet, and a stage area where we sometimes bring in local bands or entertainment." His hands fly all over as he talks pointing in all directions as if telling me the safety procedures in case of a water landing. "Trevor and I, that's my partner Trevor Attanasio, bought this place eight years ago. Back then there were only two-thirds of the sites we have now and only half the amenities. We expanded, revamped the restaurant, and completely renovated the cabins. It was a lot of money and a lot of work, but it was worth it."

"How many people are here now?"

Montgomery looks toward the lines of campers as if he is counting them. He says, "We have about three hundred ninety-eight sites taken right now, I'm not sure of the exact number. Some have families of four, some couples, so I'd say there's over a thousand people. I can give you the exact numbers from the office."

"You said twenty-four hour security?"

"Two guards are at the gatehouse from 7:00 am until 11:00 pm then one guard is on all night doing regular patrols of the grounds including the cabin area."

"So there's only one guard after 11:00 for a thousand people?"

"Yes, unless something is going on like a party or something. Then we'll have more on duty. We cater mainly to families so generally there isn't any trouble. Plus the RCMP detachment in Cavendish is only a few minutes away."

We walk past a camper with bright yellow Tonka trucks in the grass. "And the guard is at the gatehouse, right? Does he do patrols at night?"

Montgomery fixes his collar. "At 1:00 am, 3:00 am and 5:00 am before the second guard gets in at 7:00 am. Then, during the hour they overlap, one stays at the gatehouse while the other tests the chemical levels in the pools and collects the garbage from around the campground. We've never had problems before."

Nobody ever has problems until they do. If people could predict when young girls were going to be snatched and killed, would they ever? With over a thousand people, the campground was basically a village or a small town. With every campsite full they would have between fifteen hundred and two thousand people staying here.

"What's with the name? Why call this place Bonaventure?"

"The man who started the campground years ago was a crew member on the HMCS Bonaventure, the Canadian Navy's last aircraft carrier. It was the greatest time in his life and when we bought it we agreed to keep the name. We've actually adopted the theme throughout the grounds naming roads after decks or levels on the ship, some after other Canadian naval ships. We had a local artist paint that large mural on the side of the restaurant and inside are paintings and photos of the ship and the planes that were on it. It's different anyway. Aren't you tired of things named after Anne of Green Gables anyway? I did a lot of research on the Bonnie and Canada's navy. For instance, did you know that the crew on the Bonnie was twelve hundred people? During the peak season we can have twice as many people here." He smiles at me with pearly whites. He stops behind a long motor home. A purple Dodge Ram truck sits angled at the front. It has a British Columbia license plate, the same as the camper. "Here's the Schofield site."

"How long have they been here?"

"Four days so far. They aren't scheduled to leave for another six."

The camper is an older model without any pop-outs or pop-ups like the more expensive modern jobs. A picnic table sits off to the side with a couple of beer bottles standing on it; one is upside down with the neck in a hole where some of the wood has been torn off. The small fire pit is between the camper and the table, the fire long extinguished. The black ash looks cold and wet. There is a small pile of wood beneath the camper and a clothesline stretches out to a tree. A bottle lays on the ground; I push it out of my way with the tip of my shoe. It stops with clang against a stone. Four of those fold-up chairs you see people carrying under their arms at their kids' soccer or football games lean against the wall of the motorhome under the canopy so that the morning's rain can drip off. I use the key Wayne Schofield gave me and step inside, it smells of sweat and coffee. The bed Kayla had used is a thin single mattress at the back of the camper. The parents slept in the larger bed above where the truck would be when moving. There is a kitchenette in the middle, the dining table folds down for a third bed.

Around Kayla's bed are piles of clothes scattered like any child's. It doesn't appear that she had a plan to leave. The Schofields are not a neat and tidy family; maybe I am not one to judge. I step back out into the warm air where Montgomery has been waiting. He nervously chews on a fingernail.

"The swimming pools are this way?" I point as I step down.

Montgomery's hair is slicked back and down with some type of product. It was already glistening and now shines even more so with sweat. It's slick enough that I can see his scalp beneath. He plucks his shirt away from his damp chest. "Yes, yes they are. Kids make the trek every morning. We have lifeguards on duty from 9:00 am until 10:00 pm, 11:00 pm on weekends. Did you want to see them?"

I nod. I want to see where Kayla may have walked.

Every second campsite seems to have a tree, birch or pine. The roads are packed gravel and red island clay leaving the odd stone loose here and there to trip you. Some dips are still wet from the rain and a couple still have water in them. I look at licence plates as we walk past different campers and motorhomes: Prince Edward Island, Nova Scotia, New Brunswick, Ontario, Maine, it goes on. People come from all over expecting a peaceful vacation. On the backs and sides of each camper are different words naming either the camper or where it was manufactured: Hornet, Summerland, Copper Canyon, Zinger, Chateau, Kodiak. There are large modern units with pop-outs at every angle, making them larger than my own home. Smaller units have only the basics. A few have their own engines and tow a smaller vehicle to putt around in while others get towed themselves. Camp sites vary just as much. Some have nothing but a table and folding lawn chairs. Other people have created a little bit of home with flowering plants, dog houses, and tents for the kiddies. One I see has a wooden deck right outside the door. I wonder if it is taken down at the end of the season.

"Why do some have these built-on areas?" I ask as we pass a camper with a plywood addition covering the side door in a sort of front porch.

"Those are permanent sites. They sign a five-year contract and buy the rights to build on. Some build rooms. Some build decks. Some have play areas for the kids. They leave their campers here year round." Montgomery casually waves to a family sitting outside their RV. "We have people who come here for a weekend, a couple weeks, all summer. During the Cavendish Beach Festival every site will be taken plus half the front field will have tents covering it. This is a busy place. We're hoping to build a small inn. We may even change the name to Bonaventure Campsite and Convention Center."

As we walk I watch everyone we pass looking for any signs and listening to my gut. By now word has spread through the campsite about the police presence and not about being allowed to leave the areas. Is anyone acting suspiciously? Are they trying to hide something? Who has grey or silver mini-vans? Is there anyone alone? Everyone watches with curiosity.

"So tell me about you and your partner." *Because even you two are suspects.*

I half listen to what Montgomery tells me about his relationship with Trevor Attansio from "meeting at a business thing," his words, over ten years ago to visiting the island and falling in love with the rolling hills and laid-back attitude to how Attanasio does all the handyman work while Montgomery himself is dedicated to the paperwork and business side. The rest of my mind is busy taking in different aspects of people throughout the campground.

There are so many people we have to question before we can even begin to look for whoever did this to Kayla Schofield, assuming he's not here. Assuming he is not a she.

I check my watch. It's almost 11:00 am. The eyes I see looking at us are questioning when they will be able to leave. They have tee times or plans to hit the water park. Either way they don't want to be sitting around their campers on such a nice day swatting mosquitoes and waiting for their turn to be questioned. Some will consider it an interrogation. Among this many people some will have things to hide. How long it will take depends on how much each person is willing to share.

The rows of camping spots sit on either side of the dirt roads. The Schofield's campsite is located along a series of straight roads like planned city streets. The remainder resembles a mismatched town with streets heading off in different directions, cul-de-sacs, and dead-ends. Each corner has a pole with the name of the roads. We pass the corner of Banshee and Captain F.C. Frewer.

"Banshee?" I point up at the blue sign.

Montgomery searches for some sort of kick to his memory. "The F2H-3 Banshee was a Canadian fixed-wing fighter plane that flew off the Bonnie. There's a picture of one in the Flight Deck." He has obviously had that question more than once.

"Reid, wait up." Marilyn jogs her way down the road from the direction of the restaurant and office. I can see the cruisers are still blocking the entry and exit lanes. "Hey, find anything out?"

I glance quickly at Montgomery between us. There is nothing much to say, but talking with a civilian makes me nervous. "Kayla didn't take any clothes, it seems, so if she went willingly she was expecting to come back. There are some bottles around the camper so I'd say the parents are right in their account of drinking."

"I don't know if there's much to get out of them. It doesn't seem like they're hiding anything. Still sucks that the last time they saw their daughter was just a blow off."

I know how that is. How many times has Leigh been around me and I just send her off with a "go fool around on the computer" or telling her I'm too busy right now?

Marilyn continues, "McIntyre's here now, I left him to babysit the Schofields, and Dispirito finally showed. He's bitching about showing up wherever we were instead of where we are. Eckhart's done at the beach and has moved on to Robinson's Island. The night security guard is back too. LeBlanc is watching him in the restaurant. I'm thinking we should canvas everyone to find out if they saw anything; what do you think?"

"Unless she went willingly, somebody had to see or hear something. I want to check out where the swimming pools are, then I'm all yours." On cue we hear the sounds of kids screaming and the sound of splashing as someone jumps in the pool. We go through three more intersections - Banshee and Majestic-class, Majestic-class and HMS Powerful, then HMS Powerful and Club 22 before even seeing the pools.

As we cross each intersection Montgomery gives us a quick lesson on what each means. "The Bonaventure was a Majestic-class aircraft carrier. There were six made from the same template for the Royal Navy in England, but they were never used by the Royal Navy. Two were bought by the Canadian Navy, two by the Australian's, and one by the Indian Navy."

"What was the other Canadian ship called?"

"The HMCS Magnificent," his eyebrows do a little dance, "which served from '48 to '56. It was replaced by the Bonaventure." Montgomery is proud to be telling us this history, almost as though he was part of it.

"The Bonaventure was named the HMS Powerful when it was first commissioned. It was named after Bonaventure Island which is a bird sanctuary in the Gulf of St. Lawrence."

"Club 22 is just a nickname the ship had like calling it the Bonnie. It has a big 22 painted on the flight deck. I always thought the restaurant should have been named Club 22, but the name was here before we were."

On the right is a long rectangular building with the word SHOWERS printed along the outside and a door on either end, marked Men's and Women's. The first swimming pool we see is the wading pool. There's an orange plastic elephant it the middle. As it comes into sight a little girl slides down the extended trunk slide into the shallow water. She waves to her mother sitting on the edge, her feet in the warm water. At the far end a pole stands in the water, like an old fashioned Maypole with a continuous shower of recycled pool water raining down. There are different toys – balls, floating boards, foam noodles – that every evening have to be fished out of all three pools. The other two are regular swimming pools ranging in depths from one to two and a half meters or three to eight feet. Between the two is a high perched lifeguard tower. A woman, probably in her late teens, sits up in the chair. Dark sunglasses look down at us hiding her eyes. Her cellphone sits on the arm at easy reach for texts from friends who aren't working during summer vacation. Five children play together around the furthest pool. Two girls look to be around Kayla's age. The other three are boys all ranging from younger than the girls to one being older looking, but looks can be deceiving. My own daughter is eleven years old but without any help can easily pass for fifteen, sixteen with an early blossomed body and darker features. Hillary has been asked if Leigh was her sister.

I tap Marilyn's arm to let her know to take the lead. Kids talk better with women.

She says, "Hey guys, can we talk for a minute. I'm Sgt. Moore with the RCMP. This is Sgt. Reid." All of the kids look at each other hoping for reassurance that they should stay there. When I was their age police terrified me. There was no reason for it. I just knew police put people in jail. Having them come up to me like this would have made me want to run. "Do any of you know Kayla Schofield?"

Montgomery puts a hand to his chest. He leans in close to my ear, close enough that I feel his warm breath on my neck. "Are you sure you should do this without the parents present? These are my customers, my family, I don't want to piss them off."

I ignore him. A small red Honda drives past us heading toward the exit with a man at the steering wheel. There are golf clubs visible in the back seat. I glance back over my shoulder and watch as Freeman turns the car around. Illinois plates.

The smaller children shake their heads and go back to sword fighting with the foam. The three girls look at each other waiting for someone to take charge and decide whether they are going to talk to us. One girl places her hands on her hips. She's skinny enough for me to think of Ali (a victim of *The Playground Killer*) and wears a yellow bikini too skimpy for a tween. The tiny mounds that will one day develop and wide hips

81

handed down through evolution do little to indicate the woman she will become. Her brown hair with blond streaks is tied back. She has done a good job of keeping her head out of the water. A few wet strands cling to her neck and shoulders.

"I know her," she says in a strong voice denoting she won't back down for anyone.

"What's your name?" Marilyn asks.

"Jane St. Claire."

"Jane, go home." This voice booms from behind us. "Can someone tell me what the hell is going on?"

Jane drops her head. Her arms wrap around her body as she sulks off heading down Club 22 toward the back end of the grounds, all of her bravado gone. The other two girls pause for a moment then jog to catch up with her. A few seconds later the other kids follow. The man who got them to scatter stands with his legs shoulder-width apart, arms crossed over his chest. Dark hair is swept to the right. Thin wire framed glasses are barely noticeable.

Montgomery doesn't know where to look. He says, "Mr. St. Claire, this is Sergeant Moore and ..."

"I don't care." He raises his hand to silence Montgomery. "I really don't care. I'm missing my tee time at Gables. Now I'll be charged for not showing up and not cancelling. Who's going to pay for that?" Spittle erupts from between thin lips. It disappears into the fabric of Montgomery's shirt.

"I'm sorry, Mr. St. Claire, I know this is inconvenient but the police are ..."

"Sorry won't cut it. We're being held prisoner." He takes a step forward.

Marilyn takes a quick side step to put herself between the two men forcing, St. Claire to step back. "Mr. Montgomery has nothing to do with what is going on here, sir. Any complaints can be directed toward me." St. Claire does not move, his muscles don't seem to twitch. As he looks from Marilyn to the owner of the campground, only his eyes show he is uneasy. Marilyn raises her chin - *atta girl*! "Last night a girl the same age as your daughter disappeared from this campground. I can't say what happened to her, but I will tell you it wasn't good. We now have to find whoever did it. This brings us here, to you good people. Please let us do our job and we'll be out of your hair as soon as we can."

Considering the circumstances causing us to be here, I should probably feel badly about being turned on by the way Marilyn stood up and spoke to this guy. The sun seems to shine from her hair making the deep red seem lighter. She is one strong, beautiful woman who demands control of every situation.

His facial expression mirrors someone who just let out a stink bomb of a fart and had all eyes turned on him. His arms slowly sink to his sides. His face seems to get longer. The anger still burns in his eyes. As he asks, "Kayla Schofield?" I recognize the *American* in his voice. "Jane asked if she could stay over last night, but my wife had a bad headache so I said no. I wanted her to be fine by the morning so I could go golfing. The girls just talk all night. I just wanted to get some sleep."

"So you saw her last night? What time was that?"

Shrug of his shoulders. "I don't know, around 10:30 pm."

"And where's your camper?"

"They have a spot down at the far end of the grounds." Montgomery quickly answers. "They're on The Island. It's named after the command center on the main deck of the ship.

St. Claire crosses his arms over his chest again. This time it is not in defiance, but because he doesn't know what else to do with his arms. His voice becomes so soft I have to strain to hear him. "I wouldn't let Jane walk her home or even half-way. Kayla had to walk all the way back by herself. What happened to her?"

Marilyn shakes her head as she says, "Can't say."

"It could have been …" He turns to look in the direction his daughter went as though he could still see her. Right now St. Claire is thinking that if he let his daughter walk her friend back to her camp, Kayla would be safe but Jane wouldn't be. Should he be sad or happy?

Young Kayla Schofield, with her auburn hair, had to cross the entire campground by herself at night. There were no light posts around the campgrounds to mark the way. Most people had fire pits or their own lights. There were plenty of places where she would not be seen. There were plenty of places where a mini-van could have pulled up beside her and forced her inside. A scream may have been noticed or, if there were parties happening, no one may have heard. What the hell happened?

~ * ~

Something in me says this is not going to be your average run-of-the-mill homicide. I know that I can't get involved. In my mind I keep seeing images of Kayla lying on the wooden floor dressed in a summer dress staring up through the sun roof at the pre-dawn sky, the kind of sky that looks like black and blue were mixed together on a painter's palette. When I focus on removing her image others replace it. Everything around them is fuzzy, but one after the other a girl walks in with a blank expression on her face: Nicole Tait, Sara McDonald, Tracy Field, Allison Crenshaw, all victims of the Playground Killer and all constant stars of my nightmares. I wake in the middle of the night with their images burned in my mind. No, I can't get involved in this case.

I stay at Bonaventure for a couple of hours questioning people who saw nothing then get a member to drive me back to my car, back to where the body was found. When we get there the boardwalk area is still taped off. Two RCMP Members keep watch, but the parking lot is half-full of beachgoers who make their own paths through the grass to get around the boardwalk.

Throughout the day I receive only three more texts from Hillary. "Did you eat lunch?" I respond with a yes but leave out that it was a sandwich at the Flight Deck. "How is your day going?" I text back one word – "busy."

Her last text comes as I stand by my car staring at the Brackley Beach showers wondering why people harm children. "I heard the news. Are you working on the case?" I clear the message and put the Blackberry in my pocket.

I know I'm being a prick about the whole thing. Marriage is a major responsibility at which one must work constantly to make things go somewhat smoothly. I'm tired though. I think we are both tired. Both tired of the mistress that always seems to get in the way - *my job, my career*. Just as I believe in two types of security guards, I think there are two types of police officers: those who can let go once the badge is off and those who can't. I can't. My head is constantly sorting through cases no matter what I'm doing or where I am or who I am with. That's why Hillary hates it. She sees it as me putting work before my family. I say I don't. I say that the two of them are always in my head while I am at work just as much, if not more, than the number of times work is on my mind while I'm with them. She doesn't believe me. Hillary says she is too tired. We have known each other for a long time and have been married almost as long. Maybe it's all my fault. Maybe I'm going through a mid-life thing. Maybe we'd be better off apart.

Prince Edward Island is divided into three counties reflecting royal theme, Prince, Queen, and King. The larger towns have their own police forces as well. Queen's County, which is the center third of the island, is under the jurisdiction of the Queen's County Detachment located on Maypoint Road and therefore named the Maypoint Detachment. Twenty-six Regular Members are responsible for policing over 37,000 people. The Major Crimes Unit, at one time, worked out of the detachment until we moved to Headquarters on University Drive inside Char'town. The Provincial Police Dog Unit, Mobile Traffic Unit, and Forensic Identification all still operate from the Queens County Detachment, however.

I stop at the detachment to talk to Corporal Eckhart leaving my Focus, then walk next door to the Maypoint Plaza mini-mall. It's your typical quick stop kind of place with a convenience store, realtor, firearms control office, Chinese food restaurant, and Yogi's Food & Bar. The last being my destination.

Yogi's has been the MCU's Friday-after-work place to unwind long before I came to the island. Since our unit has moved to HQ we continue to make the trek through a couple of the city's busiest intersections and up the hill to grab a quick drink and, maybe, do an informal debriefing before the weekend. Because it is so close to detachment the assholes who don't know their limits tend to stay away. Cops need a place to unwind. Cop shows on television always a bar the officers frequent because it happens in real life. Usually we never have more than a couple of drinks because it is only the place where we either vent so that we can spend the weekend thinking of only our families or where we can spend an extra hour because we are dreading spending the weekend with our families. I'm more one than the other. If we want to get completely sloshed we'll go somewhere else where there aren't any of our fellow officers.

I step through the door and wait a few seconds for my eyes to adjust to the dim lighting. My nostrils instantly fill with the smell of cooking oil and the soya sauce aroma of Chinese food wafting from the kitchen shared by Yogi's and the Magic Wok. Half-way up along the right is a small bar with stools. On the wall behind the bar hang shirts emblazoned with the bar's name and cartoon likeness of Yogi Bear. There are other pictures of the bear on the wall. I've often wondered if some copyright laws are being broken but I've never verbalized the question. One man sits at the bar, his head bent over a glass. He doesn't flinch at the sound of the door. I sit at the MCU's usual table, second on the left, and take one of the two preferred lower seats next to the wall. In the almost-empty room I can hear the music and noises from the video gambling games by the far wall. A glass of beer appears in front of me.

"There you go by. You all alone tonight?" Karen's Newfoundland accent always makes me laugh. Every

Friday she has our drinks to us before we sit down and without us having to say a word. She's in her forties, I would say, short with happy cleavage and a pleasant smile. Her blond hair, darker roots showing, is held on the top her head with chopsticks.

"Big case," I say as I reach for the pepper shaker. Only here do I sprinkle a little pepper into the foam of my Alexander Keith's. The white foam immediately dissipates. Something my grandfather showed me.

"That girl found this morning?"

"Yeah, everyone's in on it."

"But not you, then?"

I take a quick sip of the golden liquid. "No, not me. I have issues."

Karen throws back her head. Nails painted mauve squeeze my shoulder. As she walks away she says, "Don't we all, by, don't we all."

I watch Sports Center on a big screen in the corner without paying much attention to it. The Blue Jays have lost three in a row; Daniel Botting is the youngest person to win a NASCAR race. Half-way through my beer a group of five teachers comes in and sits at an adjacent table. Their drinks arrive shortly afterward, all in tumblers or wine glasses. Their voices quickly rise to louder than a casual conversation. Apparently some student named Nathan is destined to be dead or in prison before he's an adult. I feel a bit like a creep sitting alone at a table for eight, my eyes flipping to check out the teachers in their skirts that look too short for teachers, blouses that seem to have too many buttons open, and dress-down Friday blue jeans, all the while pretending to watch the latest results of competitive beach volleyball. I'm down to the dregs of my Keith's and thinking about leaving when the door opens and Greg Eckhart walks in.

As Eckhart sits down he drops a large brown envelope in front of me. Karen appears next to him with a bottle of Coors Light.

"There're your pictures, Lorne, Kevin, Denis, Scott, Magnus, Phillip," he spews out the half-dozen names in rapid succession. All of which are wrong.

"Give it up, Greg."

All in one movement, he takes a drink and pushes his glasses back up his nose with the back of his hand. "I told you, you can't use my first name until I know yours. So, Moore knows you requested those photos, right?"

I give him a quick nod. The teachers burst out in laughter. Two plates of wings, one of nachos, and two plates holding fried rice and some combo of Chinese food arrive at their table. The odours of grease and soya dance over to us making my stomach growl. How long ago was that sandwich?

"So, I've been thinking -"

"Ident boys can do that?"

"Funny. Your first name has to be something pretty embarrassing. Maybe a girl's name or something like River or Badger or something. Were your parents hippies?"

"No."

"Any Native in you?"

My arms are starting to tan with the natural progression of summer, but I am still your stereotypical white guy. I have blue eyes and I've noticed in the morning mirror that they are starting to look exhausted with lines spidering out from the corners. My dark hair is shaved very short. My jaw line is still hard and defined squaring down at the chin, though I am sure it will not be long until everything is rounded. I lift my shirt and flash him my white stomach. There are muscles there but the stomach is starting to get rounder as I age. I'm still in my thirties. I shouldn't feel this old. And yes, men can be as vain as women. "Do I look Native to you?"

There comes a whistle from the next table.

"Keep your shirt on, Reid. You won't believe this damn security guard," Marilyn says as she sits right beside me. Her knee touches mine. A glass holding vodka and cranberry juice magically appears from Karen's hand.

I signal her, and she bends lower than she really needs to as she takes my empty glass, for another beer. "Which security guard?"

"The night guard at Bonaventure. He lied right to my face. He told me he did everything by the book. Showed up at 11:45 pm, did his patrols at 1:00, 3:00, 5:00, *on the dot* then stayed in the guard house while the guy who came on at 7:00 am was checking the pools and all that. Doesn't he know I'd already talked to the other guards and the morning kitchen crew? The guy's an idiot."

"So what happened?"

"Well for starters he arrived to work late, not early. I don't know about his patrols but the breakfast cook said that when he got to work at 7:10 am the security guard's yellow Sunfire was gone."

"You think he had anything to do with Kayla?"

"Doubt it. He eventually said he took off right after the morning guard started his pool check. I guess he did it all the time and, this is a direct quote, "nothing ever happened before." So basically there was no guard watching the entrance to the RV park from just after 7:00 am to about 7:45 am."

"Meaning if our guy was from the park he could have dumped the body at the beach and made it back in without being seen. Convenient."

"RV camper reports are all over the board. White man, black man, grey van, silver van, gold van, white van, Dodge, Chevy - it's all over the place. The guards of course don't remember anything but then they are more concerned with people going in than going out." Marilyn dips her finger into her drink then puts it in her mouth slowly pulling it out. Her pale green eyes stare off into space. I force myself to look away folding my arms over the brown envelope.

"We have no credible witnesses, no motive."

"He's a sick prick, that's his motive." Eckhart finishes his beer. We all go silent for a few minutes staring down at our drinks. During that time the table of teachers leave.

Marilyn taps the envelope before taking a drink. "What's that?"

A full mug of beer magically appears in front of me. I repeat the pepper trick. Eckhart waves off an offer of another.

"Pictures from a case," I say.

Eckhart gives me a knowing look. I respond with a slight shake of my head then drop my eyes. I'm not involved in the Kayla Schofield case, so nobody needs to know I have the pictures from this morning. He announces he has to go, but not until thanking me for his drinks. I didn't know I was paying, then again he broke some rules for me.

For a few moments Marilyn and I are alone at the long table. She lets her hair down so that the curls fall over her shoulders. It was not long ago that a moment like this would mean my hand under the table rubbing her firm thigh and us whispering inappropriate things. As it is now she has stated her relationship is too involved for that. And I'm married; we're working on the happily part.

"I don't know how I'm going to catch this guy." Marilyn lets out a sigh.

I look up as Dispirito comes through the door. The breeze from outside makes his blond hair do a little dance. He's tall, around six foot four inches, and probably the best looking male member of the MCU.

"You catch him the way you would any bad guy, good police work." I stare at my drink.

Dispirito sits. His drink arrives.

"We talked to everyone at the RV park. And nobody really saw or heard anything. Can't find the mini-van." Marilyn circles her finger around in her drink making the ice tink on the sides.

"Her parents?"

"They were drinking past midnight with some others who concurred that Kayla never came back after asking if she could stay with the St. Claires."

Dispirito says, "Did you know most serial killers are caught by fluke?" The scar on his right temple seems to glow white in the odd lighting.

"This isn't a serial killer, Al." There is a sense of thankfulness in her voice. Marilyn cocks her head to the side. The Bordeaux-coloured hair falls down her arm.

"No, but I'm just saying. Did you know John Wayne Gacy was caught because he had the lead detective over for dinner?" His eyes move back and forth between us. "The detective realized what he smelled in Gacy's home was autopsy smell. Cocky bastard."

Marilyn puts money on the table. "Speaking of autopsies, we have one to attend in the morning. I hate going home when there's something like this going on. I feel like I should be out there doing something more. Well, I'll see you in the morning, Al. See you

Monday, Reid? Hey, didn't you say you and Hillary had something tonight?"

"What?" Damn!

It takes me fifteen minutes to get back down the hill and drive all the way down Queen Street. to the new condos near the waterfront. Dr. Jeff Cheverie has an official office in a building close to the downtown, but for "special" clients he uses the office in his apartment. Hillary's car is parked across the street. I complained about not being able to make it during regular doctor's hours so we became "special." I ring the buzzer for his apartment. A sweet sounding voice asks who I am then invites me in and unlocks the lobby door with the push of a button.

I check my phone. There haven't been any more texts since Hillary asked if I was working on the case. Is she pissed? Was she testing if I would remember?

"Mr. Reid." I'm welcomed at the front door by a lovely young woman with flowing locks of chestnut brown. I know it's Mrs. Cheverie, but still I'm surprised. She is in her mid-twenties. The good doctor is more my age, late thirties. "Jeff and your wife are in the office."

I a nod, then proceed through the nearest door. As I open it I hear voices from inside the room. They stop instantly. Hillary looks at me from her place on the end of a love seat. I smile and her eyes drop. My smile fades.

"Reid, you made it." Cheverie pushes up from his chair and crosses the room in three long strides. He gives my hand a quick squeeze, then releases. "Hillary said you might not make it because of the thing out in Brackley."

I look from him to her. She doesn't look up. I say, "Ah, no, I'm not, that's not my case. I helped question people, but I'm not involved." I slide onto the love seat beside my wife and quickly press my lips to her cheek.

She sniffs. Does she smell the beer on my breath?

"Your wife was just telling me about your dedication to your job." Cheverie settles back in his chair. He has an iPad tablet in his right hand and a stylus pen in the other. The pen sits ready to take notes on whatever I have to say. The Doctor has silver in his hair. Square glasses sit perched on the end of his nose. The strong scent of his cologne fills the room.

I clear my throat.

"She says you often bring your work home."

And you don't? I bite my tongue.

Hillary seems to be concerned with her manicure. I know she is waiting to hear what I have to say.

Cheverie flicks the pen against his chin. "How would you feel if Hillary brought work home?"

I stare across at him. I don't want to be here. He knows it, Hill knows it. I say, "She works at a bank. It's a completely different thing."

"For argument sake, let's say she had to bring work home often." That little black stylus is ready to write down my answer.

"I'd hope I was supportive." I turn to look at my wife. Her black hair is cut in a soft angled bob, her make-up delicate and minimal. Her strong jaw is clenched hard as if she is forcing herself to keep from yelling at me.

Cheverie asks what Hillary is thinking, "Are you saying your wife isn't supportive?"

Bam! One second too late to realize I just stepped in a trap. "She's very supportive."

"Are you too involved in your work then?"

"My job isn't black-and-white, nine-to-five. Criminals don't work on a set schedule. Sometimes my brain gets ideas when I'm at home. If someone gets killed on a, a Friday night I can't call up the victim's family and say, "Oops sorry." I'll look for the killer on Monday after my coffee and doughnut."

"I know that, Reid." For a moment I forgot Hillary was here.

"There's no reason to get defensive, Reid." Cheverie's stylus taps against his tablet. "I'm just trying to understand your relationship a little better. Let's all take a moment to calm ourselves."

A moment to calm ourselves? What I really want to do is tell him to fuck himself.

I can't look at the doctor. Hillary doesn't want to look at me. Instead I let my eyes wander the room. We've been here a few times. Usually we talk about our past our marriage.

This room is more a den than an office. Cheverie has a desk off to the side, the top of which is

97

immaculate. Framed copies of his degrees hang on the walls. Among them is a large wedding photo of him and the woman who let me in. Another is a black-and-white of them walking hand-in-hand on a beach. The happy marriage we all should strive to have. My eyes return to the desk. On one corner is a small photo of a teenage boy standing next to a car. There's a large smile on his face. His blond hair is a curly mess sticking out beneath a baseball cap.

I rise, cross the room, and take the small frame in my hand. "This is your son?"

Cheverie hasn't let his eyes leave me. He puffs his chest a little. "Yes it is."

"Nice car."

"A 2012 Mustang. I bought it for him for his seventeenth birthday." I would swear his chest has puffed even more, the big man showing off his money.

"Seventeen." I put the photo back down. "So your wife was what, seven when she had him? No, wait, you have dark hair and so does she, but your son is blond." I plop down on the love seat. My eyes lock with the doctor's. I can feel Hillary's gaze burning into the side of my face.

Cheverie crosses his hands over his lap. "Trevor is from my first marriage. Very good, Detective."

"It's Sergeant."

"My apologies," he makes a noise that sounds like a snicker.

"Do you know what you get when you break down a therapist?"

98

"No please enlighten me," he pauses a moment, "Sergeant."

I stare into his eyes. I know this is going over the line, but I can't help it. I say, "the rapist."

Nothing is said for a whole two minutes as we size each other up. I feel my wife staring at me, but my eyes never leave Cheverie. I can't win the fight at home so I need this one. Finally he crosses his legs and suggests we go on. I know deep down I can't win this fight. Marriage counseling helps many people. Dr. Cheverie has helped people to have better relationship, but at some point you have to wonder when enough is enough. I know I will be sleeping on the couch tonight. I know when we go to the Farmers' Market tomorrow and the Musical Ride Sunday we will plaster smiles on our faces and act like we are happy. I don't know where this is going.

Worse than that, I don't know where I want this to go.

Chapter 5

Leigh Reid opened her eyes. Sleep clung to her lashes. For a second, one second, she saw everything so clearly. Everything from her nightmare the other night was right there. The giant white rabbit with large white fangs shining with saliva and dripping blood that stained its fur, tall grass, the girl with dark hair and her screams. She thought she was going to hear those screams forever. Then she blinked and most of the dream was gone as though it had never been there. The only thing remaining was the dry taste in her mouth, her heart slowly returning to a normal beat, and the feeling that someone was watching her.

She always felt that way. Ever since she overheard her parents talking long ago that the Red Island Killer had been in her room and saw the picture of her riding Dakota on the beach. Her dad put him in jail. Still she felt like someone was watching. Her dad put a peel-away frosted covering on her window so that nobody could see in from the street and had a security system installed with motion sensors in every room and hallway for when they weren't home and magnetic sensors on the windows and doors for when they were asleep. They had a dog, but Frix would only bark if someone broke in to steal the couch. Her father said there was nothing to be worried about. Their home was a fortress. Yet every night before going to bed, he went through the house locking the doors and windows then looking through the curtains to see if anyone or anything suspicious was out there. No matter how safe the house was, Leigh felt compelled to dig through the boxes in the basement until she found her old Disney Princesses nightlight. Even with the distorted pink and yellow light that shone up the wall beside her bed, she didn't feel safe.

Her bedroom was that of a young teenager even though she was still only eleven. There were pictures of horses along the walls. Some were just pages from magazines, some framed pictures or paintings she got as gifts. The photo of her riding Dakota was poster sized and attached to the wall holding the window. There was another of Titan, the horse her father rode during his years with the Musical Ride. Clothes adorned the floor like patches of cloth islands on a hardwood-floor ocean. Besides a book shelf with Goosebumps books, books on horse care and training, and a mismatched collection of CDs, the only other pieces of furniture were a dresser, a vanity table with a full mirror on the back and a chair in front. Stuffed into the frame of the mirror were pictures of friends, Dakota, and family. She hadn't changed or even thought about the pictures for a long time. On the table top surrounded by cosmetic implements was a laptop computer. Leigh ran a finger across the mouse pad at the base of the keyboard. The screen burst to life with updates from Facebook.

She looked past the computer to the mirror. Her long brown hair flared out on the sides with deep lazy curls. She had her mother's brown eyes and was told she looked like Hillary Reid. She didn't see the body of an eleven year-old girl. Underneath a faded tank-top was a chest a sixteen or seventeen year old would be happy with. She pushed her arms forward and together, making her breasts push together and upward like the women in that Shakespeare movie she watched in school last week, she knew that some grown women would probably appreciate having like a chest like hers. Her hips were wider than she would have liked and she had a roll in her stomach that her Mom called *the last of her baby fat*. She didn't think she was good-looking no matter how much her mother and father told her that she was beautiful. She didn't get why the boys in her class looked at her a little longer or why older boys watched her walk by. Her Dad liked to say that when she started dating he was going to sit in the living room cleaning his handgun and was going to interrogate the boy. Leigh didn't want that to happen. She planned not to tell him whenever she started dating.

As she stared at her image in the mirror her imagination had the giant white rabbit peek out at her from the long flower covered curtain that was her closet door. Only while she was awake she didn't know it was the rabbit. She just felt something.

"Leigh, are you up?"

Leigh's heart jumped. She turned to the door expecting - expecting something. What she saw was her mother leaning into the room. Her black hair, cut in a short bob, hung from the side of her head. Leigh liked the way her mother looked. She was attractive and spent time at the gym toning and tanning her body. Lately she had been spending more time out.

"Are you coming to the Farmers' Market with me?"

She knew some kids who would be at the Market. "Yeah I am."

"I'm leaving in twenty minutes. Be quiet when you come downstairs; your father is asleep on the couch."

"Did you guys fight again?"

"No, honey, we didn't fight. Your dad just had work to do. Twenty minutes." She slapped the doorframe and slipped into the hallway.

Leigh Reid was a contradiction. She went to the bathroom and showered. There she still felt as though she was being watched but she could lock the door. She had the body of a woman, but she was still a kid who didn't know what she could do. She scratched a tiny itch on her boob and suddenly the entire thing was itchy. When she got out of the shower she shaved her armpits and legs with her mom's electric razor, not sure why completely but knowing that it was more acceptable to have smooth legs and, besides the hair under her father's arms looked like it just didn't belong. Once back in her room she put on mascara and a dark eye-shadow. There were a couple of lumps that clung to her lashes and the shadow was not spread evenly. She spread gloss across her lips. It was a light pink so that her father wouldn't notice. Her mother let her use make-up and tried to teach her how to put it on properly instead of making herself look raccoon like, but she was too young to have the patience to do it. Her father still breathed heavily every time her saw her wearing make-up. Her fingernails were painted black.

She hated brushing her hair, but it had to be done. She did a rough job so that it wasn't all wild and sticking out, then tied it in the back. With her curling iron she made a strip of hair on either side of her face hang down in waves.

After dressing in matching underwear and bra, hip-hugger jeans, and a black T-shirt with a U shaped neckline, the phrase "I Wanna Be A Vampire" written in blood red across the chest, she turned to the computer. She clicked a tab and quickly typed in the web address for a different web site. It was a random chat site. You picked a room and talked to random people from all over the world. Last week she talked to a girl from India and then a boy from Paris. The rooms you were sent to usually went by chance so that when you clicked one you didn't know what room you would go to or who you would talk with, but there was a way to find the people you knew. She logged in as *HorseRider*. A few seconds later a name she recognised appeared in the listing of people in the room, *Lapin*.

Lapin. "Morning."

HorseRider. "Hi, how are you?"

Lapin. "Good. What are you doin'?"

HorseRider. "Going to the Market with Mom. Then who knows? Beach maybe."

Lapin. "That the famous Farmers' Market?"

HorseRider. "Yes. It's pretty cool."

Lapin. "If you go to the beach you should take some pictures. lol"

Lapin was thirteen and from Halifax, Nova Scotia. His mother had called him her little rabbit because of his buck teeth and then because of the movie, 8 Mile, his friends called him Rabbit. That was why he used the French word for rabbit as his login name. They talked almost every day about whatever was going on. Mostly they talked about her life. She said she had to go and would talk to him later.

Lapin. "Hey guess what."

HorseRider. "What?"

Lapin. "My family's coming to the Island for the Music Fest."

HorseRider. "Awesome. Me 2. Later."

Downstairs she stopped in the living room to look at her father. He laid there on the couch, half-covered by a knitted blanked, Frix laid between his legs. Dad slept on the couch a lot more often lately. As she stepped closer she saw photographs all spread out across the oval coffee table. They weren't photos from when they'd been at the hot springs in the Rocky Mountains or any of their times to the beach. Instead, were they photos of a girl dressed in a white summer dress with swirls of gold and silver all over it. There were close-ups of bruises around her neck. Her eyes were this unnatural milky white. Leigh bent over to get a closer look at the red-brown hair. She knew this girl. She dreamed of this girl. Giant rabbit. *Grand lapin.*

"Leigh, get away from those." Hillary Reid crossed the room with her purse in one hand and a towel in the other. "I'm not going through this again." She laid the towel down over the photos on the table. "Let's get going."

"Mom, I wasn't …"

"Let's go."

Leigh wanted to see the photographs again. How could that girl in the pictures be the one she had dreamed about? Did she really dream about her or did seeing those pictures make her think she did?

Chapter 6

The front door latches shut. My eyes open. I don't move. I hear Hillary's Flex fire up and back out of the driveway before I push myself to a sitting position.

When we got home last night I grilled steaks on the barbecue beside a tinfoil pouch of vegetables with butter. I didn't have to stay outside the whole time, but I did. Hillary and I then sat in the living room eating. Leigh was still at a friend's. The two of us didn't really speak. We watched the local news, without a word about the headline story of the body of a girl from British Colombia being found in the Prince Edward Island National Park that RCMP are investigating as a suspicious death, without even looking at each other. I didn't want to look at her, maybe catch her eye, and have another blow-out about how I promised I wouldn't get involved in a case like this or about what I said at the therapist's. I asked her about her day. She blew the whole thing off by saying it was just like every day. She waited for an hour after our daughter got home before getting up slowly and saying she was going to bed. I said I would be along shortly. Thirty minutes went by. I went upstairs and saw that she was reading. I asked if she wanted anything. Hillary said no and turned her bedside light off. The next time I checked on her, she was sleeping. I took the pictures out and spread them over the coffee table.

Somewhere in there I fell asleep.

Now someone has placed a towel over the photographs and a blanket over me. Pain is cupping the inside of my right eye. The television is off. What was I watching before I fell asleep? I can smell coffee coming from of the kitchen. Hillary can't start her day without a cup of coffee. I wonder if she made more than one cup. There's enough for one more cup.

With cup in hand I sit back on the couch and remove the towel from the table. Kayla Schofield is still there. Some are close-ups of her angelic face and the bruising around her neck. They are a far contrast from the white summer dress with gold and silver swirls. Her legs and feet are bare as though she went walking the beach in the early morning then went to lay on the shower floor before slipping away and being found. Years from now they will tell ghost stories about the girl in the white dress skipping through the sand at Brackley Beach, or through the grass out on Robinson's Island. People will camp out hoping to see the girl and then swearing a gust of wind was her spirit asking for peace. It'll get spun into some sort of romantic fantasy instead of people seeing the brutal truth here on my coffee table. I quickly stack the photos together and push them back into the envelope.

A shower is what I need.

All the hot water does is bring a flood of images and questions to my brain. Kayla Schofield in her sundress. Why her? What made her so special? Killing this way, strangulation, is so personal. Why does this seem so personal? The entry booth at Robinson's Island. What made him chose that place? Was there a significance or was it seclusion? Is this guy a local? Has he done this before? The last image is of Hillary yelling at me about how involved I got in the case out west. Am I getting involved? Is this going to be as serious as in BC or is it just a single event?

I remember him watching me. I remember his eyes. The Red Island Killer. That was personal. I remember.

I open my eyes. My heart races in my chest. I feel the blood pulse rapidly through my veins. Someone's there. My hand swipes the steam from the shower door. Nothing is there. My clothes are on the toilet. The door is closed and locked. I am alone. My heart begins to calm as I feel the sting of soap in my eye. It was nothing more than one of my shower panic attacks.

111

I dry off quickly and get dressed, my body still damp beneath my jeans and golf shirt from the slack-assed job I did with the towel. I know I'm not going to be a popular guy today no matter what I do.

~ * ~

The Charlottetown Farmers' Market is one of the must-see places for tourists. It started in 1984 and now is a full-blown event on Wednesdays and Saturdays during the summer, only Saturdays in winter. The building with green wood-shingled walls, red trim around the edges, sits on the edge of the experimental farm in view of RCMP Charlottetown headquarters. I pull into the parking lot from the round-a-bout on Belvedere Avenue and search for a parking spot. The market has been open barely an hour and the prime spots by the building are gone. I have to go down the slight hill and find a space between a car with Arkansas plates and a Hummer.

When I step from my car I can already smell the sausages grilling outside the front corner next to Old Goat and Dog knife sharpeners. I stand in line at the grill for a mild Italian with mustard and diced onion. Just outside the main entrance a young woman makes free balloon animals for the kids. A little boy walks away with penguin in hand. Another woman is playing a guitar and singing. Beside her is a small table of CDs she has for sale. The woman, with long blond hair, smiles as I walk past her.

The Farmers' Market is no place for the timid. I have to push my way through the crowd of people going in, going out, and standing in the middle of the hallway having conversations with long-lost friends. The inside of the building is a rectangle with vendors on the outside as well as in the middle. I get swept away in the current of people. There is a wide variety of product here. There are cheeses for sale, meats that include bison, beef and chicken, different varieties of fish caught around the island, baked goods, bread, vegetables, handmade crafts, artisan work, prepared foods, a stand that makes smoothies, one with different flavored oils and vinegars, a mini-donut stand. Everything has a connection with the island, most coming from the red earth itself. I jump out of the moving current and stop at a vegetable/artisan booth. In the front are bags of organic micro-greens. Along the back are knitted slippers, sweaters, and baseball caps with paintings of island landscapes on the fronts. I smile at the woman standing behind the table. She has long black hair linked together in two braids. She smiles at me, sees that I'm not interested in buying, and returns to her conversation with the woman from the next booth.

"Busy place."

I glance to my right at the man who spoke. He investigates a bag of greens.

"Yeah, it can get pretty claustrophobic."

"Do you know if the fish guy is any good? He has some nice looking salmon, but you never know."

I say, "I've never bought from him, but he must be good. I buy my fresh fish from Lobster on the Wharf down on the harbor. That or I go out to Rustico."

"Maybe I'll do that then. I'm heading out that way anyway."

"You just turn right at Fisherman's Wharf and you'll find the place that sells fresh seafood. That or ask a local." I nod then step back into the current of people and get swept along toward the smoothie booth.

I ride the wave of slowly moving people, avoiding those who stop solid in the stream like large boulders in a river forcing the water to crash off of, and flow around always looking for my two ladies.

Leigh stands between L'il Orbits Donuts and Out of Africa, the stand that sells authentic African food, with two others. I recognize both girls. One is from her class at school and the other from the equestrian lessons. All three of them are eleven, but my daughter does not look it. She smiles at a boy who walks by, taking a look at her and her low neckline. He has to be in his late teens. Leigh's lips turn upward in a pink smile.

Her friend Angie has long blond hair with streaks of unnatural red, black make-up circles her eyes and clumps on her lashes, and black lipstick covers her full lips. She and Sasha have the thin curveless bodies that eleven year olds are supposed to have. Sasha has light brown skin. A green bandana holds her black hair back. Once the boy has walked away, their three heads are close together whispering and smiling, hopefully about Barbies or dolls or something. A father can hope.

The moment Leigh sees me her smile disappears. "Hi Dad." She leans her weight onto one hip. Her friends look at me but don't say a word, no smile, nothing.

"Hey Sweets, what are you doing?"

"Nothing."

"Did you know that guy?"

"No." She looks at her friends. Though I can't see it, I can feel the eye roll. I can practically hear it. "Mom said you got us tickets to the Music Festival. What night?"

I look around trying to find one face in a river of faces. "I don't know. I think it's the whole weekend. I volunteered to work it so they gave me the tickets for you guys." The Cavendish Music Festival is probably the safest festival around. It may fill up the island for a weekend, but it fills it up with country-music fans. I've never heard of a riot at a country-music concert. "Where's Mom?"

"Sitting at the café with Deb. Are you like working today?"

I nod.

"She's gonna be pissed, Dad." I can't hide anything from her.

The café is a small side room with wooden picnic tables painted green like the outside walls. They have been serving coffee since the market first opened.

"I know. And watch your mouth." I grew up with profanity and I'm known to swear. When I was a kid the only time my father would not let me use profanity was in the presence of my mother.

"Dad, can I stay at Sasha's tonight? We want to go to the movies."

I shrug my shoulders. "I guess so, just ask your mother."

I walk away, leaving the three of them alone in the stream of people. So many people all crowded into one place it is ideal for pickpockets and kidnappers if there are those things on Prince Edward Island. There is at least one of them.

The café is a small extension on the side of the building. The general island topics of the day are the weather, crops, golf courses or the price of lobster. In the 80s there probably would have been a grey cloud of cigarette smoke hanging in the air here. Today the topic seems to be the body found on the beach. People want to know if others have gone out there to see the spectacle. I hear people talking about whether the girl or her killer are from the island. "Oh no, must be from away." The press has been doing their job, but they don't have everything yet. The radio stations have a news update every half hour, usually with nothing new to report. I hear someone say it must be the father, the sick bastard. I think of turning on the person speaking, but hold back. Everyone has their own opinion. They will hear or read whatever is reported, and whatever their friends or colleagues have to say and, then will make up their own story. Me blasting at one person about how they should wait for us to do our jobs before they talk about it won't help. It might make me feel better, but might also start other rumors.

I see Deborah English lean toward Hillary to say something. *There's Reid? Here comes the prick?*

From looks alone the two of them could be sisters. English the good, blond. Hillary the bad sister, with black hair. My wife is lovely. She is thin and attractive, though the look her brown eyes give me is not the most flattering. Her skin has a light tan from frequent visits to the salon. We have been together seventeen years, married for twelve, and though things have not always been good they have never really been that bad. Not that I would say anyway. We've had our arguments. Hillary threatened to leave a few times when the job took over my life. We fight about the usual finances and stupid things we both tend to buy on impulse. In general we have a good relationship and have had a good marriage. Hopefully the therapy will remind us both.

"Hello ladies."

English waits a moment to see if Hillary is going to say anything then says, "Hi Reid, how are you?"

I shrug my shoulders. "Alright. You?"

"Good."

I lean down and kiss the top of Hillary's head. I smell and taste the cleanliness of her freshly-shampooed hair. She says, "I thought you'd be working today," over her shoulder.

I run a hand back over my short hair. "Actually I'm going to the autopsy. Ah, I know we wanted to come here and ..."

"That's fine, Reid. After yesterday I've been expecting it." To others it seems strange that Hillary calls me by my last name, but since I won't answer to my first it only makes sense. She still doesn't look at me. An overwhelming sense of guilt falls over me like a full-body wave. "I saw those pictures you were looking at."

My eyes go to English. There's a slight angle to her lips like she is enjoying this. "Yeah, I should have put those away."

"You should have," Hillary turns on her seat and looks at me.

I lean down with one hand on the table, one on the back of Hillary's chair. My eyes quickly look around to see if everyone is looking or listening. In my mind they all are. I look past my wife to English. Her blue eyes try to look away but always seem to come back. "What do you want me to do, Hill? A girl got killed."

She turns to face me. "And it's not your job this time." Spit flies from her mouth and lands just above my lips.

"I have more experience at this." I look at English. This time she stares down at her coffee.

"I'm sure they can do it without you, Reid." Hillary turns away. All of her words are cold and sharp, like a knife run under the cold tap for a while. I'm willing to bet everyone in the room is looking and listening.

Word has probably spread to anyone stepping from their parked cars, *go to the café and watch the fight*. Hillary turns back to me. The corners of her lips are up slightly. "Or do you think Marilyn is incompetent?" She asks in a soft voice.

My teeth clamp down on my tongue. Pain shoots through my mouth stopping me from saying anything. Marilyn has been an issue between us and something almost happened once or twice, but I don't think Hillary ever believed us when we told her nothing happened. It didn't help that a psychotic serial killer gave her photographs.

After a few moments I release my tongue. The pain doesn't go away. I can feel my cheeks are burning. I say, "I didn't come here to argue with you. I have to go."

"Sure."

"We'll talk later?" I mean it as a statement, but it comes out sounding like a question.

This time she turns her whole body to face me. There is anger in her eyes along with something else. Something like satisfaction. She says, "Yes we will," and turns back to the table. Her hands wrap around her coffee cup. I look rapidly to English then turn and walk away.

~ * ~

As I enter the morgue at the Queen Elizabeth Hospital I see that the autopsy is almost finished. I'm wearing the full bunny suit with paper booties over my shoes, hood up over my head, and mask covering my mouth and nose. The smell of death and an already decaying body quickly slip through the mask and past the Vicks Vaporub under my nostrils. TV cop shows almost never get this right. The smell of a decomposing body sticks with you. It is a stench like no other. It is that bile smell that erupts the moment the chest cavity is open. All of the gasses and internal organs mix together to create the worst odor; it sticks to your clothes and clings to your hair follicles so that you smell it long after leaving the room. I am glad I was not there for the initial cutting, but still the stench lingers.

It is a very cold room. Stainless steel work tables, sinks, a back table, more steel, with microscopes beneath a light box for X-rays, ventilator hood, computer in the corner, a rolling tray of items used to do the dirty work. All of it cold and impersonal.

Though this is the main morgue for the province it is very small. The work space, cut room as we call it, is tiny and claustrophobic. With the work table in the center over a drain, a doctor, an assistant and a couple of cops, there is little room for manoeuvring. The cooler where the bodies are kept on rolling tables has only enough room for six to eight of them and it isn't like on TV where each body has its own individual little door. They all get pushed into the same room. There's no privacy in death and after that small cooler is full there's no more room at the inn.

All eyes turn to me. I'm a distraction from the distasteful task at hand. The only one not looking is the eleven-year-old girl laying naked on a steel table. I avert my eyes from her and look at the others eyes instead. Even in death staring at this girl's naked body seems wrong. The last eyes that she saw while alive didn't mind it. They probably enjoyed it. As my eyes settle on her I see there is little left resembling the once innocent young girl. The 'Y' incision has been made, her insides taken out and weighed then placed in a silver bowl, much like Marilyn's boyfriend would use in his kitchen. Because of the way she was killed, all of the indignities have to be done.

I have to look away. That could be my daughter there on the cold table with bunny suited men and a woman looking at her naked body then going beyond that to look at her bare insides. I look up at Marilyn's light green eyes watching me. Her face is flat. Her body is formless in the scrubs, showing none of her curves. By now she must know about the photographs in an envelope on my passenger seat. It's not that I wasn't allowed to have them, but that I should have asked her. Eckhart stands back, a Nikon hangs from his neck. Every few seconds the back of his hand touches his glasses due more to a nervous habit than necessity. Dispirito stands next to Marilyn with one hand across his body and the other holding the mask over his mouth. He seems to be the only one who has some form in his bunny suit. Everything seems to fit tight around his muscles. He looks at me and nods.

From his look I sense he is thankful for the distraction. Dr. Norton's assistant barely acknowledges I'm here.

"Reid, I thought we were autopsying Gary on Monday." Dr. Norton looks my way for a split second then back to work. I'm guessing he wants to get this over with.

"What? Gary? Oh, John Doe, right. No I'm here for this. I want to help."

"Well you're late."

"Yeah, wanted to skip the gory stuff."

"I thought you were going to the Farmers' Market."

I look at Marilyn. "I did already. What do we have?"

For a moment I'm not sure if anyone is going to say anything. Eyes bounce around the room. Finally Marilyn gives a slight nod and Dr. Norton clear his throat.

"We have a very healthy young girl. Perfect lungs, perfect heart. Quite a shame." The doctor indicates for his assistant to begin the work of sewing up the patient's chest.

Patient? Is that the right word?

Norton continues, "On the exterior exam there was bruising on both forearms, more so on the left, bruising to the abdomen and neck. Considering their colour, they were made shortly before death."

"He held her down then." I take a step closer and feel a chill push through me. My spine seems to go straight. The fine hairs on my neck stand up and make my skin tingle almost as though Kayla Schofield's ghost is standing beside me.

With a snap, Dr. Norton pulls off his blue surgical gloves, disposes of them in a hazardous waste bin, and pulls on a fresh pair. He says, "That's a safe theory. On her right forearm is some bruising, see here, but on her left is where most of his weight was. I would be willing to bet this large bruise is where his palm pushed down." He reaches across the body and holds his gloved hand over a dark purple bruise on her white skin. "Why he did this, I don't wish to theorize."

Because his right hand was busy undoing his pants.

"The bruising on her abdomen I would say is from the killer kneeling on her. There was some internal hemorrhaging just prior to death. The X-rays show a slightly different story."

Nothing, it seems, can hide from the pathologist. Dr. Norton, though retired from general practice and mostly working as a professor at the University of Prince Edward Island, takes his position seriously. In bigger cities that have hundreds of thousands or millions of people, there are full-time medical examiners. In many cases there is a whole team looking at death and human cruelty on a daily basis. Thankfully PEI is not like that. We have three ME's taking turn on call. It somehow usually ends up that Norton goes to the more gruesome cases.

Dr. Norton takes down the black-and-white film of Kayla's arms and slides two of a skull onto the light box. Suddenly a side and rear view of this child's skull is in front of me. This is what we are reduced to. "There are several hairline fractures at the back of the skull as though she was repeatedly struck, but not hard enough to cause any internal trauma."

I turn to Eckhart. "Were any weapons found?"

"We didn't find any, no."

"What if he, ah, he pushed her head against the floor in the entry booth?" Dispirito talks a lot with his hands. His left one is in a claw shape imitating what the killer might have done if he grabbed Kayla's face and pushed her head into the floor of the entry booth to Robinson's Island. Al Dispirito is in his late twenties and has the tendency to relate to the victims of crimes more than he should.

"Possible," says Dr. Norton. "The hyoid is broken."

"Isn't that normal with strangulation?"

"In an adult, yes. In children and adolescence the hyoid is still developing. God's way of letting kids play dangerously."

"The hyoid bone is a horseshoe shaped bone found here," he points at the x-ray, "just below the mandible between the chin and thyroid ligament. It doesn't actually connect to any other bones, only ligaments. Its function is to control the movement of the tongue, pharynx, and larynx. Basically it helps us make noises and swallow. It's what gives humans the ability to have spoken language. It was believed Neanderthals didn't have hyoids until one was unearthed with a full hyoid proving that Neanderthals may have used spoken word three hundred thousand years ago. As you grow your hyoid ossifies and, by your mid-twenties becomes solid. In children the hyoid is flexible, rubber almost, and would take a great amount of force to fracture. I can only imagine what he did to her to break hers."

"Damn."

We all look at the X-rays on the light box unwilling or unable to turn around and face what was done. What makes a man do this to a little girl?

Marilyn says, "Now tell him about the rape."

I have never felt more like a deer in headlights than I do at this moment. Five sets of eyes drop to the floor as if in silent prayer. I don't want to hear what this girl went through. But I must. I have to understand the pain in order to have the will to stop the animal. Was this a snatch, rape, and kill or was it more? Was there ritual in the act?

Dr. Norton takes a deep breath and lets it out slowly. "You might have seen the vaginal bruising on the victim."

Actually that was the one place I didn't look.

Norton goes on, "Extensive exterior bruising, interior tears. Semen was present. We'll send it to Halifax and see what comes up. But there was more damage than flesh on flesh. Something else was used in her. A pipe maybe."

"Jesus," I am not a big fan of religion but sometimes no other words suffice. Nobody speaks for a few minutes letting the doctor's words sink in. The others have heard these revelations once already and even now their faces appear stunned. Who could do something like this? Who could do it to a child? A grown adult man takes a child, beats her, brutalizes her, then kills her. Why? Why do all that and then kill her? She's already dead emotionally and would probably never recover, so why finish it? Guilt over what he did? The whole act didn't give him any satisfaction? Or was it just so she wouldn't have to live with what had happened to her? Maybe he had a sudden flash of empathy.

Marilyn breaks the silence. "I'm calling Queens' District and having them do a grid search on Robinson's Island and along the entire road back to the beach entrance if they have to." Her voice is quiet while her tone spits anger.

"I'll supervise and be there in case they find something." Eckhart pushes his glasses. "By the way, I found a few hairs on the outside of her dress yesterday. There were visible roots so I sent them to the lab in Halifax."

"Her sun dress wasn't bloody really, and neither was she, so I think he washed her up after he was done, dressed her, then positioned her. We're going back to Bonaventure to talk to anyone we might have missed and also to have our presence there. After I talk to her parents about the old fracture first." At Marilyn's words Dr. Norton takes down the skull X-rays and replaces them with one of Kayla's right arm. The film paper makes the sound of thunder as he clips it in. Marilyn says, "Probably nothing, but the parents are always the first people you check out."

"What about the branding?" Eckhart asks.

"Branding?" I stare at Eckhart. How could this girl have a branding?

Dr. Norton and his assistant gently roll the girl onto her side. A blue-gloved finger points to the back of her right calf muscle. There is one circle with two oval shapes off the top cut into the skin. It is more than cut. I can see the flesh all around the three shapes is red and charred black.

"That was burned into her flesh," I say before anyone else can. My eyes stare at the mark no bigger than a quarter without blinking, or moving away. I remember another mark, no bigger than a quarter, seared into the arm flesh of four little girls and coming from a ring attached to an evil man's keys. That symbol though was in the shape of a heart. I remember finding it in the pocket of the man I killed. It was not only a sign of how sick he was, but also a sign that I had the right man. For him it was the sign saying he had been there, like someone putting their initials on the first page of a novel they just finished. At that moment I was so happy to find it. I had the right man. The Mountie got his man. Then I walked away and threw up at the thought of being happy about it.

"Yeah," Marilyn is staring at me. "A fucking rabbit. Do you believe it?"

I shrug my shoulders.

"Any idea why?"

I shake my head.

"Any guesses?"

"I saw on some show, Law and Order Special Victims Unit I think, that some pedophiles have symbols to recognize each other."

"Like a friggin' fraternity with a rabbit insignia? I gotta get out of here." Dispirito rips the mask from his face as he walks from the room.

Marilyn is still staring at me.

I pull my mask off and follow her partner.

~ * ~

"Reid, wait up." I stop, still on the sidewalk leading around the outside of the hospital, and turn. Marilyn slows her jog to a light trot. The waves of her red-wine hair bounce over her shoulders. I see that under her bunny suit she wore a pair of charcoal slacks and a white shirt. A jacket the same dark grey as her pants is now on, two buttons fastened in the front. This is a much better look for her. The slacks are tight at her hips and flair out slightly as they go down to small heeled shoes. No high heels like the women of television cop shows. The jacket seems to be stretched over her breasts. There's a good reason my wife is jealous of her. She says, "What am I missing?"

"I don't know what you're talking about."

"Yes you do. Don't give me that. I saw your face in there and it wasn't just a, *this is one sicko perve-*

face, like the rest of us had on our minds. You know something. I'm going to put it through ViCLAS, so you better tell me now before I really get angry."

The Violent Crime Linkage Analysis System (ViCLAS) is a national database created by the Royal Canadian Mounted Police along with other police forces to track violent offenders and the crimes they commit across Canada. You sit in front of a computer answering a never ending number of questions on the Crime Analysis Report with all of the known information of your crime. Computers toss it all around, and hopefully you see if something similar occurred somewhere else. Marilyn will be able to find out if somewhere else someone sexually assaulted an eleven-year-old girl with a pipe and branded her with a rabbit head or some variation of such. The disgusting fact is that people who do violent crimes such as this one are people of habit and have a need to do it, particularly when it comes to sexual crimes. ViCLAS could tell her that other girls in Ontario had the same thing happen to them. Maybe they have DNA that can be compared to our sample. Maybe they have a suspect. It provides police services across the country the opportunity to connect crimes that otherwise would go unsolved because before 1991 they would have thought they were on their own.

A man walks quickly past us from the parking lot toward the front entrance. He has a worried look on his face, a Wendy's bag in one hand, and a large drink in the other. The smell of burger grease and fries follows.

There is no sign of yesterday's rain. Any dips where it would have collected in the pavement are already empty and dry. A white, yellow, and green ambulance turns off its siren as it turns from Riverside Drive to Murchinson Lane and then onto the Emergency Entrance road. Its red lights continue to strobe. I start walking to my car near the back of the parking lot. Marilyn keeps up my pace. We pass her Jeep parked in one of the police spots and she continues walking. Dispirito's car is gone. One car length past hers. Two. Three.

I stop. "*The Playground Killer* branded his victims, okay? He used a heart shape though." I stare into her light green eyes. I don't know where else to look. "That guy raped these little girls, beat them to death, then for shits and giggles he sat there heating up the heart ring on his key chain with a Bic lighter and burned it into their arms. Do you know what he said when I asked him why? Why did he brand them?"

"No."

I lean in close. "He said he liked the smell. That's what he said, he liked the smell."

"That when you shot him?" She asks with a blank expression on her face. Marilyn knows the story. I was cleared. Internal affairs said it was a clean shoot. I was trying to bring him in for questioning, he fought back. I pulled my gun and shot him to save my life. I was cleared. Only I have real doubts in my actions.

I say, "Pretty close, yeah."

"You think this has something to do with him or with you?"

"What, like a movie sequel? Jason comes back to get his revenge? The second one is never as good as the first, Marilyn. This is just some sicko with similar tastes."

"Look, Reid," her hand strokes my upper arm, "you need a break from this. I know about the pictures Eckhart gave you. There's no reason for you to have them. We're doing everything we can for now. I know what I'm doing. Dispirito is a good cop. He may not have a good head for autopsies, but he knows how to investigate. Tomorrow we're going to go around the island talking to any and all registered sex offenders. Why don't you take Hillary out tonight?"

I shrug my shoulders and look around the half-empty lot. "She's pissed at me."

"Why this time?"

Shrug. "The job. My dedication. PMS. I don't know." I started a fight with the therapist.

"Fuck you. Every guy wants to blame it on PMS. Maybe you just did something stupid that you don't remember. Or maybe she's right and you should forget about this case entirely. Why don't you buy her flowers or take her to dinner at Char or something?"

Is her boyfriend so hard up for customers that she has to keep pushing me on him?

As she starts walking away she says, "Do it."

I enjoy watching her walk away for a few moments before turning and walking to my car. Hillary would smack me for looking. And I think right now she may be too pissed off for a public venue. There has to be something else I can do.

Rabbit.

I pull out of the hospital behind Marilyn on to Muchinson then right onto Riverside. Around the next bend Riverside becomes the Perimeter Highway. It is supposed to be a quicker way around the city of Charlottetown, however during busy weekday traffic it can sometimes be as slow as going through town.

Heart.

I lose track of Marilyn somewhere along the highway as her lead foot shoots her well ahead. I know the Schofields have moved to a city hotel because they want to be alone. It won't be long before the reporters find them, if they haven't already. I'm glad I am not going to be part of that conversation. Marilyn will have to ask them about any possible abuse, how was Mr. Schofield around Kayla, did anyone have it in for any of them. They will be angry at her, of course. It is a waste of our time to investigate the innocent, but in an investigation like this we are going in blind without any facts. We start with a pile of rubble and have to move each piece before we find the path. If there is one. Marilyn has probably already called the detachment in the Schofield's home area in British Columbia to check into their background, friends, work, relationships.

British Columbia.

I turn onto University Drive and into the parking lot of the Atlantic Superstore. In front of the Empire Studio 8 movie theatre is a large collection of cars, probably there for the matinee. I wonder what movie Leigh is going to. I walk into the grocery store and grab a green basket. An angry wife needs something. A dinner made by me - PEI jacket potatoes, corn on the cob, good-sized lobsters, a French baguette from the bake shop and three grilling steaks. I quickly stop at the flower shop for some apologetic lilies, then get in line at one of the operational check-outs. Whenever I come here there are always just two of the nine check-outs working with a full house of customers. While I wait, I look around at other services the Atlantic Superstore has to offer. Pharmacist, toys, clothes, optometrist, cooking class, hair styling, and in the spring I can get my taxes done. One-stop shopping.

My hand hovers over the garage door button for a second before I remember that last weekend's project is still in my parking spot. Leigh, disgruntled as she was for being told to mow the lawn, decided to trim a couple of decorative rocks inlaid in the ground. Yes, a couple. Now the rocks have nice white chips on top, but the lawn has an uneven look to it and both the riding lawn mower blades are bent out of whack. My own fault for telling an eleven-year-old girl with a sixteen-year-old attitude to mow the lawn, I guess. My argument was that I mowed a much bigger lawn with a push mower when I was younger. I got as far as putting blocks under the front end of the John Deere and taking the blades off.

Part of me wants to open the large door just to see if Hillary's SUV is in there.

We live in a nice housing development, just out of Charlottetown on the west side, called West Royalty. Family orientated housing. Lots of green. Lots of kids. In October the little loop we live on goes all out for Halloween with decorated houses and mood music. At Christmas nearly every house has colourful lighting. At the end of August we will have the annual block party. It is the dream. Nice neighborhood, two-story house with two-car garage, deck out back. So why is it, when I am standing here in the driveway looking at the front of our house, I wonder how the hell I got here? All I want to do is run away.

The first two years of our relationship were up and down. I can't say it was love at first sight, but it was attraction at first sight which then built into love. I had already been a Mountie for a year working in Northern Saskatchewan earning my stripes. It was a friend's wedding in Ontario where we met. After that first meeting we talked on the phone and wrote letters and sometimes we would meet together for rendezvous. Three years after meeting we were married in her home town. Then it was off to Ottawa where I became part of the Musical Ride. A year later Leigh was born. I don't remember ever wanting a full-fledged family, but here I am in my mid-thirties with a wife mad at me every time my job comes first and an eleven-year-old daughter who looks seventeen and thinks she's going on twenty-two. Eighteen years of being a Mountie, twelve years of marriage, and I still don't know how I got here. I know we moved with my posts, living in Ottawa, British Columbia, then Prince Edward Island. I just don't know how I became a *we*.

I walk in. The television is on but a short wall blocks any view of the living room. Someone is home. In spring our home smells of fresh lilacs. Right now it smells of citrus air freshener. I put the plastic shopping bags on the floor next to the wall, paper-wrapped flowers on a small table. One of the lobsters twitches making the bag crinkle.

The first thing I notice is the overnight bag sitting at the base of the stairs. Hillary's purse sits on top. Dread and fear falls over me. I slip my shoes off and creep forward like Indiana Jones in a pit of snakes. One noisy step and venomous fangs will lash out. I peak around the short wall into the living room. My wife sits on the couch facing the television. There's a glass of red wine on the coffee table. Her eyes flick at me. I try to smile.

"Everything all right, Hill?"

"Yes." She takes a sip of her wine and smacks her lips. "I want to talk."

I cross the room and slowly sink into my chair. "This have something to do with the suitcase? Somebody get hurt or something?" No, I'm not really that naïve.

Frix folds herself off her end of the couch leaving behind a few strands of red and white fur.

"Nobody's hurt. Leigh's going to spend tonight at Sasha's. I already told her some of what is going on."

Guess this makes me the last to know. Damn wonderful. Hillary holds her wine in both hands. Her wedding and engagement rings clink against the glass. Her eyes stare downward. I don't know where to put my hands or where to look. Frix waddles her way to where I left the evening's groceries for grilled pepper steak, lobster, baked potato and corn all cooked on the barbeque. She's now more interested in finding out what is moving in the bag than I am in cooking it.

I know my cue here is to ask what is going on. Hillary always says things to get me to ask the question. *"This is so interesting,"* she'll say while reading a magazine or even just making a noise, but then she waits. Usually I stay quiet to piss her off. After a minute or two I break and ask the question. This time I stay quiet.

The plastic bag moves. Frix swats it with a paw. She's an old girl, but playful when she wants to be.

On the television a man eats something that looks like a chocolate covered bug. After five minutes I hear myself say, "I'm not working on the dead girl case, Hill. I went to give another pair of eyes. That's it."

"That's only one of the things, Reid. This isn't even really about you. I have my own life. I'm so tired. And I'm lonely."

"Lonely?" I can see the train bearing down on me. I can feel the heat from its engine and smell the steam. I'm Gordon Lachance yelling, 'TRAIN,' in the movie Stand By Me, but my legs won't work. There's no avoiding this.

Hillary seems to have forgotten the liquid in her glass. It's merely something to fixate on. It is something to help get her mind straight and her thoughts in order. Finally she says, "Your job takes up eighty percent of you. I'm not happy with only twenty percent. Not to mention I share that with Leigh. We need more of you. She needs more, Reid."

"I don't know what to do, Hill. This is who I am. This is who I was before we met."

"And who you are is great."

"Then what's the problem?"

"I want more. When my husband is with me I want him to be thinking about me, not some dead girl or other victim or whatever. When he makes plans I want him to be there. And not just physically, Reid. When you're with us you're never really *with* us." Her phone, sitting face down on the coffee table, pings. She hesitates then snatches it up. She looks quickly at the text message. The phone ends up on the other side of her.

She seems to have lost her place.

"So what do you want from me," I ask.

"I want something you can't give me, or you're not willing to give."

137

"Do you want me to quit my job? I've wanted to be a cop my whole life. I never wanted -" The rest of that is supposed to be, *a wife and kid,* but I don't say it. I should not even be thinking it. Does she know what I was going to say?

Rabbit.

"I don't want you to quit your job."

"Then what?"

"I don't know." Hillary sips from her glass. Her phone pings again. This time she doesn't look at it. Instead she pushes it under her thigh to muffle the sound.

"Who's that?"

"I don't know."

"Is it Deb? Does she want to know how this is all going? I guess this'll be the topic of HQ on Monday."

"It's not Deb." Hillary looks away.

"You just said you didn't know who it was."

"And she wouldn't say anything." She puts her glass down. In one move she gets to her feet and slips the phone in her pocket. Instead of stepping over my legs as she would usually do she walks around the far side of the table. "I can't do this anymore. Not right now."

"Do what?" The high pitch of my voice startles me.

"This, Reid. I'm taking a few days away to clear my head." A tear glistens down her cheek. "You should do the same."

"What about the Musical Ride tomorrow?"

138

She lets out a sigh and I catch her massive eye roll. That's where Leigh gets it from. "I'll be there for Leigh."

For Leigh, not for me.

What I should be doing is getting to my feet. I should cross over to her, take her in my arms and hold her tight. I should start kissing her stopping each tear with my lips. I should tell her I love her and I will do whatever I can to change.

I hear the door to the garage open and close. The rumbling of the bay door comes through the wall. Her SUV starts and I see a flash through the curtains as she pulls onto the street and drives away.

I never say, *don't go*.

Frix barks at the bag of lobsters.

Chapter 7

The Charlottetown weekend experience, enjoyed by many, is a visit to Maid Marian's Diner in Sherwood, a suburb of the capital city. People have been visiting this place for years and have made it a family tradition that continues generation after generation.

Even on the night the original building burned to the ground, people came out from blocks around to watch it go up in orange flame like it was a pyromaniac convention. We sat in our car across the street at the Esso station for a while watching it burn. It didn't strike us as stupid to be sitting at a gas station across from an inferno for at least thirty minutes.

It's Sunday morning. I pick Leigh up at her friend's and head to Maid Marian's. Neither of us speaks a word on the way there. Neither of us speaks as we get in line outside the doors.

This diner has tables squeezed in as tight as possible. Finding a seat is done on the honour system. The servers are too busy running from table to kitchen and back to seat anyone. Everyone lines up starting just inside the doors with eyes skimming the surface for any open tables. You watch the people that were early enough to get a seat. Are they leaving? Nope, they're just sitting down. That table is getting their food. That table of four is almost finished. Everyone gets ready to move. Occasionally a scout will be sent out to look around the middle display and around the corner. They pop back into view with arms waving. On a busy morning, like today, it's very likely to happen that as people are rising others are sliding into the booth. How the servers keep everyone in check is beyond me. It takes us thirty minutes waiting in line, moving one step at a time, before we slide into a table.

A waitress quickly makes the dirty plates disappear and does a quick wipe with a wet cloth before putting menus down on the moist tabletop. I ask for tea, Leigh for chocolate milk.

"Mom's not coming?"

I say, "No, I thought it would just be the two of us," and let my eyes drift to the TV high in the corner. There's a soccer game on. The red and white team is beating the yellow and white, 1-0.

"Oh." Leigh says and drops her eyes. She absently starts rearranging the salt and pepper shakers putting them together in front of the napkin dispenser instead of on the sides. It wasn't long ago that restaurant servers would have brought her crayons and a coloring page without question. Where is my little girl?

After Hillary left last night I spent a lot of time flipping through channels. I watched half a game show then an episode of Hoarders. Most of the night involved shining my high browns, the boots that go along with the red serge uniform, and flipping through the photos of Kayla Schofield. I fell asleep on the couch and woke with a sore neck in the morning.

"Can I get a turtle?"

"What?"

A waitress suddenly appears beside us again with our drinks and her ordering pad. All orders here are still written by hand. I order two sunny-side eggs, sausage, and toast. Leigh gets two over easy eggs, pancakes, and bacon.

As soon as the waitress is gone Leigh continues, "So like, yeah, um, Sasha's dad, her parents got divorced two years ago, so he buys her things to get her mom mad and um he like yeah…" she takes a drink. "He bought her a turtle last week and it's so cute. Can I have one?" She pushes out her bottom lip and bats her eyelashes. "Please?" My head is suddenly full with worries about the state of the English language.

"Ask your mother."

Instantly her lips purse and her eyes do a half-roll in their sockets before she turns her head.

"Don't roll your eyes at me."

"I didn't." She slumps back in her seat. Her hands drop from the table. "I wish I'd brought my computer," she says softly to herself, but I'm sure it's meant to strike a blow at me.

"You did." I bite down on my tongue. As Hillary often reminds me, I need to pick my battles with our daughter. This isn't the place, and certainly not the time. I hold my breath for a moment then exhale slowly. "Are you ready for today?"

Not many non-members get the chance to ride during a Musical Ride performance. On this trip across Canada they are asking to each area to find a young rider to display their talents in front of the crowd. Our Commanding Officer told them about Leigh. I guess I've bragged a few times.

A shrug of her shoulders. "Sure,"

"Are you nervous?"

Her shoulders bounce.

Our food arrives in front of us with very little fanfare. I busy myself with eating instead of trying to think of ways to start a conversation. After five minutes I realize Leigh hasn't been eating much. When I look up she's staring toward the salt and pepper shakers still on guard in front of the napkin dispenser where she put them. Her eyes are rimmed with moisture teetering on the edge of tears.

"You okay?" My fork hesitates as I'm about to stab at another piece of egg.

Leigh shrugs her shoulders again and lets her chin sag. A big fat tear drops from her eye and streaks down her cheek to her chin.

"What's wrong? You don't have to worry about the ride. You've practiced a hundred times."

Her chin wrinkles. Her face squeezes into something that resembles a bulldog. "I'm not worried about that." Her voice quickly rises in tone. "You and Mom are fighting and you're probably going to get divorced and I don't want you to." More tears fall.

"Leigh, calm down."

"But I don't want you to leave." Tears streak down one cheek. With her sweatshirt sleeve over the heel of her hand, she wipes them away.

"I'm not leaving. Who said anything about divorce?" Did her mom say something to her? Did she overhear something? I want to know, but don't want to ask. I've learned that, more often than not, some things are better off not being verbalized. You especially don't ask questions you really don't want an answer to.

Leigh hammers both hands into her lap. She says, "Nobody, but," she snorts back a bubble of snot, "you're fighting all the time now. And Mom slept at Deb's last night and …" Her covered hand comes up again and swipes across her nose.

"Don't use your shirt for that."

At least now I know Hill stayed at Deborah's. Many different scenarios went through my head last night. Were those texts from Deb? Maybe there was a new man in the picture and the texts came from him? Was she staying at his place? Where would she have met this mystery man? It would be a cliché if it was the therapist. A hundred thoughts plowed through my head until I didn't know what was what. I couldn't distinguish in my head who Hillary was any more. It kept my mind off the dead girls for a while. But then sleep came and so did the girls' faces.

I lean forward on my elbows suddenly aware of eyes and ears at the table across from us. "You have to calm down, Leigh. Moms and dads fight sometimes. It doesn't mean we don't still love each other or anything. Nobody is getting divorced. There's just something going on with my work, but I'm not going to get involved with it. I was, but now I'm not." Who am I trying to convince?

"Is it about the pictures of the girls that were on the table?"

I drop my eyes. Hillary had every right to be mad at me for that one. I say, "You shouldn't have seen those."

"What happened to her?"

"Bad stuff." This is the part where I want to treat my daughter like the little girl I wish she still was. I want her to be innocent and free. I'd like to hold off a while on her being touched by the evil of humanity. The one time in your life you shouldn't have to deal with pain and the worst of things is when you are a kid.

"Like what?" She fills her mouth with pancake. A little dribble of maple syrup tries to escape and I watch her tongue track it down.

I could tell her what happened to Kayla. Maybe that would set her up for getting older, make her stronger, make her more diligent in looking for the bad things. She started getting her period a year ago, so would it be wise for her to know what is out there? You try to keep your child safe from all that crap, but then they go out there unprepared and naïve. *Yes, Leigh, she was taken, stripped naked, raped, beaten, had something rammed up her vagina so hard it ruptured her, then she was strangled so viciously that it looks like he stomped on her throat.* No, I can't tell her that. Even I don't want to know that.

I say, "Bad stuff, really bad stuff. Just promise me you'll be cautious and aware. If you get a bad feeling about something, listen to it."

She gives me an mm-hmm.

We meet Ken Oliver at the Charlottetown Civic Centre as he unloads Dakota. Leigh wraps her arms around the horse's neck. She is a black-and-white paint with an abstract pattern over her body. A white patch on her back actually looks like a saddle that fades into the black with elegant lacing. The two of them, girl and horse, are a team. Together they have done well in English riding competitions. Tonight she is going to do a display of her riding abilities just before the main show of the RCMP Musical Ride.

147

To take you back in time the Royal Canadian Mounted Police was originally the North-West Mounted Police formed in 1873 to police and maintain social order in the western territories of Canada so that people would come from Europe and settle there. Almost immediately, the Mountie in his scarlet tunic and dark blue breeches sitting on a horse holding the lance became a symbol of Canada and was used to advertise the vast space.

The first Mounties were mainly from the British Cavalry; they wanted to perform the classic cavalry drills to show their horsemanship abilities. Unofficially the Musical Ride started as early as three years after formation, but the first recorded Ride was in 1887 in Regina. Over the years they traveled around the world performing for kings, queens, presidents, and common folk. They became the symbol of a country. Nowhere else in the world is there such a recognized police force image as the Royal Canadian Mounted Police.

When it first started there were twenty men in the Ride. Now thirty-two riders go on tour every summer to help charities in various locations across the country. Everywhere they go all they ask for is an area to house the horses in separate stalls, bedding, and hay. All money made from the event goes to local charities. After a few years' service members volunteer to be part of the ride and, once they go through their training, they become ambassadors of the ride, the country and the goodwill that the country and the

Mounties represent. I was like many of the riders and wanted to be part of it to show my pride and wear the red serge in situations other than official ceremonies. I still feel the same pride every time I wear the red uniform that features the crossed-lance patch on my sleeve above the patches for pistol and rifle marksmanship.

One of the Musical Ride transports sits just outside the part of the community center where the horses are stabled. Much expense has been made to bring in dirt for the arena where the ride will take place. I can smell the fresh earth and hay donated by local farmers. The truck-trailer has images of the ride painted across the sides. This one is used to house all of the riders' equipment and uniforms.

It doesn't take long for me to get back into the rhythm of things. I had gone to Ottawa a few times over the past few weeks to train with this year's contingent of riders. A couple have been in it longer than the usual three years because there aren't as many volunteers for the ride as there once was. In practice runs, we wear a toned-down version of our Red Serge. This is the uniform that has made the Mountie an icon. You can tell the boots of riders because the oxblood is worn off on the insides from where they rub against the saddle leather. Our breeches of midnight blue have a yellow stripe down the outside of each leg. In practice we wear plain white T shirts with the RCMP buffalo crest over the heart. We also have large brown gauntlet-style gloves. After practice we will put on our scarlet tunics, high in the collar, and the wide flat brimmed Stetson hats completing our Red Serge. You put the uniform on and you represent the police force, the country, and the history of a nation.

I wore the Red Serge at my wedding and I will be buried in it.

I sit atop of Africa, a beautiful black horse with just a touch of white on his forehead.

As we circle around the outer edge Africa throws his head every time we pass the spot where people are standing. These horses are bred and trained for this ride, as well as duty on Parliament Hill in Ottawa and in parades. Through their training they become used to having things a certain way and can be as temperamental as a teenager if anything is different. Africa's usual rider stands by the gate along with Superintendent Kevin Baillie, the Officer-in-Charge of the Musical Ride, with whom I rode with during my time with the troupe. The horse twitches his head toward his usual rider as if to say, get this guy off me. Leigh is also standing there.

Near the end of practice as we circle around, Hillary is standing beside our daughter. That's a good thing, right?

"Reid, I was just telling your lovely wife about the time we went to Germany," Baillie smiles behind his bushy moustache. He wears the tan colored Stetson to top off the red uniform, but I know under that is a head of disappearing hair.

I bring Africa to a stop beside them and re-adjust how I'm sitting. I try to remember anything that happened during my time with the Ride and what stories he could be telling. That was so long ago. "I don't know what you're talking about," I flash a friendly smile and let my eyes move over to my wife.

"We got to the barns in the morning and there was Kellerman asleep in the hay with his pants down around his ankles. Reid poured a bucket of water on him to wake him up."

I give my shoulders a shrug. At least I'm not in trouble.

The moment we are dressed in our Red Serge, everything becomes serious. There's time for a few quick photos with guests before we mount and head for the arena. Leigh rides near the start of the show. I peek out to watch her show her English riding and jumping skills. The moment all thirty-two of us ride out everything is forgotten. I don't think of dead girls or an angry wife. All I think about is the ride.

However, the moment we are finished and marching from the arena, it all floods back as if a switch has been thrown. It's such a sudden flash of faces and blood that I almost slide from the saddle.

The first face I see is Marilyn's.

The second is Hillary's.

Neither look happy.

The moment I am stripped down to T shirt, breeches and high browns I see the two of them walking toward me with Supt. Baillie.

151

"We found another body," is the first thing Marilyn says to me. No, *"how is it going, nice ride,"* just straight to the point.

My head turns to my wife then looks down. She wraps her arms around her body. I too feel a sudden chill. I ask if it was a young girl. I hope not.

"Yeah it is. Pretty much the same as Kayla. Dark hair, thin, young-looking body but with the beginning signs of womanhood. No guarantees that it's the same killer, but I'd be willing to bet on it." We all look over as Leigh leads one of the horses outside. "We were searching for the," she hesitates trying to find a nice way to describe the tool he used, "weapon and found her. Dr. Norton says she's female and probably early adolescent. He thinks she's been buried about a month or so."

Nobody wants to say anything. I study the red mud on Marilyn's shoes. Leigh is over with the riders washing down the horses. These animals are taken care of better than most humans.

Marilyn adds, "She was recently dug up."

"By animals?"

"Not sure. The body was mutilated by animals though. Tomorrow we're going to search the whole island for more graves."

Baillie clears his throat. He is the only rider still in full Red Serge. "We don't have to leave until Tuesday morning so I'm sure I can get some help with searching."

"That would be appreciated."

I can't say anything. The job and my marriage are butting heads. I steal a glance at my wife. Hillary stares over where water from a hose splashes against the horses' backs. I can hear her strong breaths. No matter how much I want to join the search I have to stay back.

Chapter 8

He closed his eyes behind dark sunglasses and leaned his head back. Only three days earlier he'd felt the same vibrations of the Northumberland Ferry radiate through his body. This time he sat on a bench on the deck; a cool breeze curled up his neck and pushed into his face. It eased his body and mind. The wind cooled the sun's rays that heated his skin. It couldn't reach the burning sensation deep inside. That was something unnatural, something wild. This was why he knew the end game he started with lovely Kayla was right.

He wanted to kill again.

"Why do we have to go to Prince Edward Island? I thought we agreed to go somewhere else this year?" His wife angrily washed dishes Friday night. He had come back from his business trip feeling refreshed and ready. His wife didn't understand it. After all that driving when he should have been exhausted and run down he was like a new man. He had a lot of fight in him she had to push down. And he let it happen.

"I told you, I got tickets for the music festival." He sat at the small kitchen table almost afraid to move. In his head he thought, and *we* didn't decide. *You* told me we were going somewhere else. "I thought I would surprise you."

And I want to feel blood between my fingers.

"You don't even like country music."

That was true, he didn't. He said, "Sure I do."

She let out a snort, "Since when?"

He looked down at his hands. He felt the edges of his mouth curl into a little smile as he pulled some dry skin from the edge of his fingernail. A bubble of blood came to the surface. "You don't know everything about me," he whispered, then popped his finger in his mouth and sucked the blood.

There was a splash as his wife dropped the cup she was cleaning back into the water. She spun around, dish-cloth still in hand, dripping water on the new kitchen tile she insisted on getting. "What is there I don't know about you?"

Oh, I don't know my dear. How about that I've raped and killed at least two girls a year for all of the eleven years we've been married, and that happened in four provinces and one state. No wait, Kayla makes five provinces. At first it was for release, but now I just want to kill something. And how about while I've

156

been sitting here I've imagined killing you in six
different ways?

He looked up at her. Something made her eyes
twitch as she looked at him. She almost took a step
backwards before he realized he still had the smile on
his lips. He let it slack and shrugged his shoulders.

She snorted again and went back to the dishes. In
that one instant had she seen who he truly was? Was
she afraid? Could he do it?

He opened his eyes. He was back on the ferry again
and quickly turned looking around the deck. He
wondered if the girl with the red hat was there. Maybe
she was heading back to the Island.

A woman walked out of the door leading to the
game-room and onto the deck. She sat three benches
in front of him. He had noticed her before boarding
the ferry. The woman, dressed in an RCMP uniform,
was dropped off by another officer in one of their
patrol cars. The tall driver got out and leaned against
the door of the car as he cracked a Pepsi. When it was
time to board, she gave the other cop a kiss on the lips,
took a square case and a backpack from the back seat
and walked down toward the boat. The other officer
watched her for a moment before driving away.

Now she was there in front of him. She didn't have
a clue. She didn't even have an inkling of who was
behind her. Or should he say, *what* was behind her.
His smile formed again.

She removed her cap and shook out her hair. It was
short, like a boy's. She turned and looked over her

shoulder. Her blue eyes fell on him through oval glasses.

His breath caught. She looked so young. She looked barely older than the girls he played with. If only she had long hair he could change the game completely.

She smiled in his direction before turning back to the wind.

She was slim and short with tiny breasts and rosy cheeks. She would be the perfect girl to test himself, the perfect woman. Through his eyes he saw red, blood red. He wanted to hear the screams. He wanted to feel the muscles go taut as he touched them. He wanted …

"Daddy,"

He blinked his eyes quickly. His daughter stood in front of him with a curious expression on her face. Her dark red almost brown hair faded into the blood he saw behind her. He had to catch his breath. She was ten. She was getting into the age where she would be lovely, before being jaded by age. What did her screams sound like? What did she taste like?

That was sick. It was *his* own daughter.

"Daddy, can I have ice cream?"

Her younger brother stood behind her almost blending into the background. Their father noticed that the girl said, *can I have ice cream*, instead of, can *we*.

"What? Ah, no." *Just get away from me.* He looked at the cop.

His daughter stomped her foot. Her arms crossed over her tiny chest and her lips formed a pout. She said, "Do you want me to go ask Mom?" in the same commanding tone as his wife. She was the same. She was going to be the same. She was going to grow up, take a husband, and tear him down until there was nothing left but a shell, a zombie going through life without feeling anything. She was like Cinderella's step-sisters taking the cue from their mother to treat Cinderella like nothing more than an insect on the floor. But this was no fictional girl; his daughter had her mother's eyes.

And the boy was going to be just like Daddy.

He felt his body shrink as he searched his pocket for some money. He felt his wife's eyes watching him from somewhere behind. She probably sent the child to him. She had to remind him what gender was in charge. Because he bought tickets to the music festival they were on this ferry. He had to be put in his place.

Oh, how he wanted a scream, almost anyone's would do!

Chapter 9

I back into the flow of the shower and let the hot water cascade from my head to my shoulders and down my naked body. The bathroom door is locked, but I can't turn my back to it. I still see his eyes staring at me from the darkness. I can feel his anger towards me. I know the sick asshole is in prison, but he's also here.

He's in my head.

Everything is in my head. Criminals I hunted down and arrested or killed, my wife, my daughter, bosses that I disagreed with, every girl that ever said no. They all run through my brain in a continuous line, but his eyes are always there behind me. A line of little girls stare at me from behind the parade. Fear begins inside me and flashes out to every nerve ending. Before the panic takes over my body, I quickly wash my shaved head, my hands push the soap out of my eyes, and I step through the curtain into the cool bathroom.

I hate being in headquarters before everyone else. There are at least two people in the building at all hours. They are on the second floor in Informatics answering 911 calls for the RCMP, monitoring who is going in and out of HQ, dealing with passwords and all of that. If there is an investigation underway on involving wire taps or cameras there would be at least two more people locked in a room in the basement listening and recording. I hear noises and my imagination likes to play tricks with my brain. Have I always been this paranoid?

I detect Marilyn's scent before I enter the offices of the Major Crimes Unit. All of us who work here usually enter the building through the door to the back parking lot around the corner from the MCU. She came that way. I inhale her perfume and shampoo as I come from the basement stairs by the doors leading to the parking lot. I scan my identification card and punch my code into the security box outside the door. It beeps and the lock clicks allowing me access. Our offices are not like the homicide units you see on television shows where anyone can walk right in and (as a season finale or for ratings' week) shoot the hell out of all the officers inside. Here you have to pass a guard who's situated behind bullet-proof glass and a locked door before being allowed access to the building. Every other unit is also behind another locked door. This is no TV show.

I smile at Susan Daly, the MCU receptionist, sitting inside the door. She is a dull woman. Her blond hair is in a loose perm, as if styled in the eighties, and she always wears light-coloured, unassuming clothing. Her job here is almost to not be here. She answers the phones, directs calls, and gives messages while trying not to hear a thing. To keep her mind elsewhere she has framed photos of the family dogs, cats, and turtle on her desk. The rest of Major Crimes is a big open space except for McIntyre's office in the corner. His door is closed, blinds shut, but there is a little light coming through. He's always here before the rest of us, especially when there is an important case going on. I wonder what his marriage is like. I'm willing to bet he's already had a call from the CO and it's only 8:00am. Our desks are in an open area where we can bounce ideas off each other. Marilyn is the only one here. She stands by the bulletin and white boards along the wall.

The only messages on my work phone are from the facial reconstructionist telling me she will be on the 11:00am ferry if someone can pick her up. I write the time on a yellow post-it and stick it to my computer monitor.

"How are you doing?" Marilyn steps in front of my desk holding a manila folder against her chest. Today she's wearing black pants and a creamy blouse that hints at the dark bra she's wearing. A black blazer is folded over the back of her chair. Her eyes droop down in sadness and her head tilts to the side.

I don't answer her because I don't know what to say. Instead I ask, "Anything new?"

"Not yet. The body is in the morgue. I'll join Dr. Norton this morning and Dispirito is heading back out to Robinson's Island after the triangle meeting. Are you coming?"

I shake my head to indicate no and say, "Facial reconstructionist is coming. And I, I just can't."

"I'm sorry I didn't call you the other night." I had called her shortly after Hillary said she was sleeping somewhere else. I'm not really sure what was on my mind at the time. Something I don't want to admit.

"It's fine." I nod my head.

"I wasn't sure if calling you was such a good ..."

My hands play with the papers across my desk. "I get it, Marilyn." I don't really. All I wanted was someone to talk to. I'm sure if I say that enough to myself I will even believe it. "I get it."

"Well," she starts playing with her fingers. "When you and Hillary get into, you know issues, you tend to get interested in me."

Dispirito comes through the door. This morning he's suited up. Nothing fancy, but more formal than his usual casual appearance.

"I get interested? You don't get interested?" I look at Dispirito then to Marilyn's green eyes.

Marilyn's voice drops. Her eyes do the same. "I don't think that's what either of us need. I'm good with Wylie. I don't, I can't,"

164

I look back to the papers. I say, "Yeah, I get it." I press the post-it against the monitor again.

"Did Hillary say why?" Marilyn leans her hip against my desk. I suddenly smell chocolate chip cookies.

"The job I guess. Same old stuff." I flip open the folder regarding the John Doe we dug up on Friday.

"You think that's it?"

I look quickly at the file without really seeing anything. It's just a distraction to try and get her to go away. "What do you mean?"

"If it's the same old thing then why did she leave?" She leans down to get close to me. Her hair falls from behind her over her shoulder, caressing her cheek. I feel a rush of heat inside my chest. "She doesn't think there's anything going on with us, does she?"

LeBlanc and Longfellow both come through the door together talking about how good the game was on the weekend. I don't know to which game they are referring. Are they still playing hockey? No, that should be over. Basketball? Baseball? Football maybe, the Canadian Football League has started already, I think. Was there another reason why Hillary left? Who kept texting her? Why is Marilyn staring at me?

"No," Questions start bombarding my brain. The case of the dead girl had only happened two days ago so why the sudden move to pack a bag and hit the road? If she didn't go to Deborah's, where did she go? What did she pack? Maybe I should go through her things when I get home to see if anything is missing. She slept out again last night. I could drop by her work and try talking to her. I shake my head quickly. "How - how's the little girl case?"

"Going nowhere. We went back out to the RV camp before finding the other body. Either nobody saw anything, heard anything or knows anything, or they are all in on it together. The girl left her friends, disappeared, and was found dead miles away. Alien abduction, maybe. And now we have a second body that may or may not be connected."

"ViCLAS?"

She shakes her head and the red-wine waves dance back and forth over her shoulders. Under regulations her hair should not be touching her collar, but when you are in the specialty units you are given some slack. If you saw the officers in the drug units you would never think they were RCMP. "Nothing yet. It takes time to go through the whole database. It takes time for lab results. It all takes time. Then we find a second body. And the killer gets further and further away."

"Did you tell him about visiting the sex offenders?" Dispirito waltzes over with hands in his pants pockets. "That was a treat. Gordon and I drove all over the island. All of them say they were nowhere near Cavendish or Brackley, but we found three violations. I'm surprised how many registered offenders we have here."

"Real friendly bunch too," Longfellow adds.

"You're sure none of them were in the area?"

Dispirito moves his eyes between us. "That's what they say. We're checking into alibis."

"What about New Brunswick and Nova Scotia? Did you give them a call about sex offenders? It's just a short bridge crossing or ferry ride." I check my watch.

"I called, but haven't heard back. I'll call again." Dispirito says, then goes to his desk.

Silence falls like a blanket. There is a lot going on right now between Marilyn and me - the dead girl, the wife who seems to be leaving me, and past "almost" indiscretions that sit between us like a wall or giant boulder. I don't really know what else to say. I chose, "Do you want to get together and talk later? Over coffee?" then realize how wrong that is.

Her mouth opens. She looks to the other people in the room. They are all looking at their own work without a care as to what we are doing. I look down at my papers. Coffee isn't what I have in mind. I don't know what's in my mind. I look over at the white board where Marilyn has all the information on Kayla Schofield and the new Jane Doe. Her mouth closes then opens again. "I don't know, Reid. I'm busy with this. I'll call if I can." Her voice sounds like she is forcing the words out.

"Moore, Dispirito, LeBlanc in my office." McIntyre stands in the doorway to his office. Everything about him is in place except for a tuft of black hair sticking out over one ear. Marilyn drops the folder she is holding on my desk and quickly ties her hair back with an elastic band from her wrist. "Reid, you want to get in on this?"

"Ah, no, they've filled me in. I have my John Doe case to deal with." I don't need to be in on the major case management meeting to know what is going on. Basically it all forms a triangle. McIntyre is on top controlling everything and calling the shots with the other two points being Marilyn as lead investigator and LeBlanc as the file manager. His job is to collect all of the witness interview reports, evidence files, paperwork, video tapes, and photographs so he can transfer them onto DVDs for the crown attorney when it comes time to go to court. Right now they are talking about what they have done, what they have found out, and making a plan for what comes next. They have nothing - no weapon, no witnesses, as far as they know there is no DNA, but they have to wait for that to come back. The only thing they know is that the killer might drive a silver mini-van and he may have a rabbit shaped brand like the one the Playground Killer had. Why?

Why would someone do this to little girls? Why would he leave her like that? What happened to the other girl? Why was she buried?

Why are you thinking about getting involved, Reid? At what point does work and life co-exist? Do people with regular jobs have this much trouble finding the line?

Why did Marilyn leave her file on my desk?

McIntyre's door is closed. Did she mean to leave it? I flip open the top. My stomach churns. A normal person with a normal life would probably turn away from a photograph of a face unrecognizable as human. I lean in closer. There is a fair bit of flesh however there is more exposed bone that has been reddened by the earth. You can tell she was dressed in a thin summer dress and that she had dark hair.

The boss's door opens I close the folder. Marilyn crosses to my desk, smiles in my direction and takes the manila folder. What does that mean?

I open up the John Doe folder and stare at it for a moment before diving in. Thirteen years ago, when the body was fished from the ocean, the investigators had even less to go on than what Marilyn has to work with. I have been over the file before and can easily recall all of the finer details. First page is your basic police report, filled out first in pen then typed by the MCU investigator thirteen years ago. Technology then was not where it is now. I put this report aside. The lead investigator was Sgt. Tom Gallant, now retired. Responding officer was Constable Robertson. The body was found floating in the water by brothers Greg and Kyle Arsenault a kilometer off of Savage Harbor. There is a list of witnesses who were there when the body was brought ashore. Most of whom, I'm willing to bet, saw the body and then regurgitated their breakfast. Seeing a body in a state of decomposition is disgusting enough; seeing a body that's been floating in water for a while is even worse.

The medical examiner's report is next. Because of the long exposure to the water and elements there was not much to report. Height was 172 centimeters. I check my chart and see that he was around five foot seven. Weight was hard to determine since there was extensive bloating, but Dr. Norton estimated it at around 150 pounds. So he was a short heavy guy. Apparently he was muscular, according to what was left. To determine hair colour they had to go to the nether regions which were still secured inside jeans and underwear - dark brown. So he was average, maybe a bit below average.

I take out the stack of 8.5 x 11 glossy photographs. The first few are of the body. It's a disgusting bloated thing barely discernible as a human being. Try leaving hotdogs in a pot of water for a week or two and see what they look like or what they smell like - you're not even close. I turn those photos over and move them off to the side. The next photos are of his clothing. Each item was spread out onto red garbage bags in order to get the best picture possible. The first was his belt. It was made of black leather with carved eagles all along it, except in the back where the words, Jack Daniel's Old Time Whiskey, had been stamped into it. Looking closely at the photos, I can see there are still flecks of white paint on some of the eagles. They had probably all been white when he bought the belt. Was it old and well-worn or was the paint washed away in the sea? The buckle is comprised of eleven small rings connected to each other in a circle and held to the leather belt with a metal bar. It doesn't say anything in the reports if investigators contacted the Jack Daniel's company about when this type of belt was made. I wouldn't mind contacting them about samples. There is a picture of the label on his faded blue jeans, Broadway, with English on top and French underneath, another the inside of his underwear waistband, Fruit-of-the-Loom, and block letters written G. and L. in black marker. The last photos are of his black boots. They were short leather boots that barely went up past his ankles. On the insides were zippers. They were winter boots with a good centimeter or more of insulation. The bottom sole was coming off the right one. That was it. No shirt, no jacket, no jewelry, no wallet. He was just a man in blue jeans and boots - the object of a country song.

I flip back through the pictures, taking a close look at his clothes, and wonder what it all means. The Jack Daniels' belt and boots could mean he was a biker. Montreal, Quebec is well known for its biker feuds. What would it take for them to drive to the Gulf of St. Lawrence and dispose of a comrade? But then again, did bikers write their initials in their underwear? Who did? Army? Sailors on the hundreds and hundreds of cargo ships from all over the world, that used the seaway to get to the big cities further down on the Great Lakes? That would make sense since the investigators reached out to Canadian and American east coast police forces. If he came from overseas, they had no definite way of checking. How long could a crewman go missing on a giant cargo ship heading out to the open ocean? Would they turn back or try to contact the coast guard? But what if he was the recipient of foul play? In police work you have to make educated guesses as to what may or may not have happened. Sometimes you are completely wrong. Other days you are totally lucky.

I turn to look at McIntyre's office. They are in there talking about the little girl and what needs to happen next. Here are two cases that seem to have no suspects. The only difference is that John Doe could have been an accident. Kayla Schofield's death was no accident.

My jaw hurts. The last thing I need is a toothache. My wife wants little to do with me, my daughter blames me, and now my mouth is rotting away. In the back of the folder are reports and lists of what the investigators did. They searched for missing people and put out what they knew about the body, but there was not much to go on. I'm starting from scratch and thirteen years behind.

I look at McIntyre's office again. On my fifteenth glance the door opens and everyone files out. Marilyn is writing notes in her book. Dispirito runs a hand back through his blond hair. The two of them grab coats and head out the door. Their day ahead will have them swatting mosquitoes and staring at the ground. Later they will have to go over everything they have already done for a second or third time. They will probably talk to her parents again, talk to the people at the campgrounds again and feel hopeless.

In the back of my top drawer I find a bottle of Advil. I pop two pills with a swig of cold coffee. Step one on the way to the ferry, coffee.

"Reid," I look up at Susan by the door, "phone call on line two. It's your wife."

I stare at Susan Daly as though she just told me Charlottetown was being overrun by zombies. That I could probably handle. I take a deep breath and pick up the phone. It takes another breath before I push the flashing number. "This is Reid." Why the fuck did I say that?

"Ah, hi, it's me."

My tongue catches in my mouth. I say hi back, but I can't think of what else to say. Is this a good thing? Is this a bad thing?

"How are you feeling?"

"I'm okay. You?"

She hesitates. "I'm doing fine."

Hillary is doing fine. I don't know what this is. An explosion of questions fly through my head. "Where have you been staying?"

"Leigh called me." She ignores my question. "I tried to explain that this wasn't your fault and that it was my idea. She's upset, but I don't think she's mad at you."

"That's a good thing." Sometimes, more often than not, I don't think before speaking. "She shouldn't be mad at me."

"But she should be mad at me?"

I glance down at my desk. "I'm not the one who left, Hill. You didn't talk to me at the ride. I don't even know why-"

"You know enough, Reid." I can hear talking in the background. She is probably at her job at the Royal Bank in the Confederation Court Mall.

"I don't know anything, Hillary." I realize how loud my voice is. My shoulders slouch forward. I can feel eyes on me. "Why, why don't we have dinner or something so we can talk face-to-face. Talking on the phone isn't helping. Not while we're both at work."

The silence is deafening.

"Fine, Reid. I'll come for dinner tonight." The clicks on her end and all I hear dead air.

I look up and catch myself in LeBlanc's eyes.

"You alright? Was that Hillary?"

He heard me say her name so he knows, but wants to make me feel better about it. The trouble with working closely with other members is that everyone gets to know everything about you. There's no privacy in a sea of people whose job it is to find out everything. I have no idea how I've been able to keep my first name hidden from them this long.

"It was. I'm good. We're going to have dinner tonight and talk." I put my keys in my pocket as I get to my feet. "I have to meet the ferry." I won't look in anyone's eyes. If Marilyn was still here I would be lost and feel the need to talk it all out. Hillary's eyes don't do that to me anymore. I really wish they did.

174

I hop into an unmarked police Charger, make a stop at Tim Horton's for a couple of coffees, then head across the Hillsborough Bridge out of Charlottetown. In PEI the Trans-Canada Highway crosses the Confederation Bridge from New Brunswick and runs along the south shore to the Wood Islands where the Northumberland Ferry from Nova Scotia docks. The drive there has spectacular views of the shore and Hillsborough Bay. Today I just can't take the time to enjoy the view.

Wood Islands is not actually a set of islands. The Northumberland ferry takes 75 minutes to travel the 22 kilometres from Caribou Island in Nova Scotia. During the peak times of the summer, two ferries run from 6:00am until 11:00pm. Just like the Confederation Bridge, it costs to leave PEI but is free to enter. Automobiles, including transport trucks, park on the bottom two levels of the ferry. Travelers have to leave their cars and go upstairs to the cafeteria restaurant, a game and lounge room that sometimes has live music, and the open air deck on top. As I park next to the terminal, the larger of the two ferries is already tied up and people are walking off the boat.

Cassandra Michaels is the only person walking off the ferry with the unmistakable yellow stipe down each pant leg of her RCMP uniform. Her blue jacket is zipped over the tan shirt of the uniform. She carries a box-type briefcase with a handle, the top flaps connecting with the handle through the middle. In her left hand is a small duffle bag.

On the island, duffle bags and backpacks are called kit-bags. The explanation is that the bag holds all of your kit.

"Sgt. Michaels, nice to meet you, I'm Sgt. Reid." We shake hands as I take her duffle.

"Call me Cassie." She has a strong French accent.

"Reid."

"No first name?" I shake my head. "Be careful with these. They're full of the tools of my trade." The bags go in the backseat. Cassie takes off her cap and runs her fingers through short brown hair, cut almost in a boy's style. It makes her look younger than she probably is, but the cut emphasises her oval face. She slides oversized sunglasses over her eyes and takes a healthy swig from a water bottle before slipping into the passenger side. "Look at all those cars speeding off the ferry, like cockroaches in the light. It's been awhile since we've made the crossing but I don't remember driving so fast."

"Yeah, some people are crazy." As soon as there is an opening I pull out behind a motorhome with Ohio plates. I wonder if they're going to Bonaventure campgrounds.

"Crazies everywhere. How long have you lived here?" For ten minutes or so we talk about our lives as if we are merely two co-workers. In the greater sense of the RCMP I guess we are. There is nothing at all about death or bodies until she finally says, "I've reviewed the case file you sent. No evidence of foul play?"

"Inconclusive."

"No fractures or signs of trauma?"

I watch a car quickly catching up to us in the rear-view mirror. "There were plenty, but most of it was post-mortem. He was in the water awhile so there's no way of knowing what his body may have gone through. Fish, logs, boats - all could have beat him up." The car signals and whips past us like a race car using the draft. I think for a moment of flipping on the lights and siren. Son of a bitch didn't know who he was speeding past.

"Well, hopefully, I can give him a face and someone will recognize him."

"How exactly do you do that, put a face on a bare skull? I'd like to know the process so I have some clue about it."

"Oh, of course. I will look at John Doe's race and age so that I have the right measurements for skin depth and features. Using cotton balls and tape I will build up the skull in areas such as the nasal aperture and orbital bones so that none of the clay will go into the areas and possibly damage the skull." From the tone of her voice Cassie truly enjoys this work and talking about it. "The next step is to ensure all available teeth are placed or replaced accurately. That is if we intend to reform the face with its mouth open. Everyone notices teeth. You may notice a stain or if one is missing. In what condition were his teeth? Did he have dental work or were they neglected? Or are there signs of old dental work; perhaps his socioeconomic status has changed over time. The teeth are the only part of the skeletal structure visible to the naked eye, so positioning the mouth open can be very important."

"This guy's teeth aren't so great. The front ones are there, stained but otherwise okay, the back ones though are either missing or rotten. That's why they couldn't get an identification from dental records."

"That limits things. I guess we should be lucky the mandible was even there. I heard of a floater that basically had the tendons chewed off by sea life, so the lower jaw was lost. I will mount the skull on a stand in the Frankfort Horizontal Plane and glue tissue depth markers right to it."

"Frankfort Horizontal Plane?"

Michaels swigs her water. "It's the natural alignment of the head on the human body, in basic terms. It passes through the two orbitals and two tragions." She must see my confused expression because she adds, "The bottom of the eye-orbit lines horizontal to the top of the external auditory meatus. The ear holes." She has a lovely smile.

"So the eye hole connects to the ear hole? What about the tissue depth markers what are those?"

She looks out the window for a moment with the expression of someone trying to decide how to explain something to a child. "In the early eighties data was collected and put into tables of different tissue depths. Not everyone is the same, but there are enough similarities in skin-thickness to make educated guesses. You first break it into those of Asian heritage, African heritage, and European heritage. You then keep breaking it down by body size - slender, normal, and obese. And then gender. I will cut a pink eraser to the estimated measurements and glue them directly to the skull. Do we have an anthropology report?"

"A professor is coming in today."

She nods and continues. "The report made thirteen years ago will help with knowing approximate size and race, but an anthropologist may be able to fill in some details. So, once the tissue markers are in, the technical part is done and the art begins."

"I have to put in prosthetic eyes and start with modeling clay to build the face. There are measurements to approximate nose and ear size, but the shape of such items is not always predictable. I have to stay as neutral as possible so I don't put my own influence on the reconstruction and taint the possibilities of getting a good identification. The last step is to add hair and anything such as glasses or earrings that may have been found with the body." Cassie takes another drink then looks at her empty bottle.

"How long does something like that take?"

"A few days of solid work, in ideal conditions."

"Really? That fast? And then we'll have a face for this guy and hopefully find out who he is?"

"That's why you called me in."

As I pull into a parking space outside the morgue doors at the QEH I see a blue Cavalier with an oval sticker on the back bumper with the letters UNB (University of New Brunswick).

"Reid, right on time." Dr. Norton is where I last saw him, in the autopsy room. There is the odor of something rotting in the room that makes me fight back the urge to gag. The doctor leans over a metal table on which is the body of the latest victim. "Your body's over there. I'll be with you in a few minutes."

Marilyn stands beside the doctor. She looks at me quickly with a slight nod.

The body of John Doe is on a metal table off to the side. His foul stench lingers in the air but is overtaken by the new odor of the other. Cassie clears her throat behind me. Standing beside the floater is a woman dressed in blue surgical shirt and pants, mask over the mouth and nose, beanie covering most of the hair. All physical evidence was taken from the body thirteen years ago so there is no need to wear the bunny suites unlike the doctor and Marilyn.

Dr. Norton doesn't look up from his work, but says, "Sgt. Reid, this is Doctor Cheryl Baron, forensic anthropologist from the University of New Brunswick in Fredericton."

She holds up her hands showing the gloves and signalling no handshake, but she does give me a nod. "Pleasure to meet you, Sergeant." Bright blue eyes hide behind oval glasses. They are so bright I wonder if they are contacts. But then why the glasses? Her high cheek bones give the impression she is smiling. I may not be able to see her entire face, but I am sure she is good-looking.

Introductions are made all around with Sgt. Michaels before we get dressed into hospital gear. Dr. Baron goes over the body of John Doe as though looking for that one missing jigsaw piece. The grave wax has already been removed. It is a waxy substance that is formed when a body has been exposed to moisture for a time human body fat mixed with water - delightful. Cassie gets right in there hovering over the skull.

I stand back letting everyone do their work. As Cassie and Dr. Baron move to the light wall to look over John Doe's X-rays, my eyes follow them, but stop at the corpse across the small room.

Her skin is grey. She wasn't treated with as much care as Kayla. This one seems to have been discarded. A child's toy thrown away, forgotten. Someone has to remember her. Parts of her flesh on one arm looks as though it has been gnawed, maybe by one of the many coyotes that lives on the island. The other arm is missing. I have the sudden image in my head of wild dogs pulling at her limbs, their heads shaking back and forth until joint and ligament let go. She has long dark hair like Kayla.

Like my daughter.

"So this guy was in the water for how long? Sgt. Reid?"

"What?" I look at Dr. Baron. Those blue eyes are impatient. "Between two weeks and two months, probably closer to the latter."

"You're lucky to have anything at all."

"I hope we have some more luck and find out who he was." I cross my arms over my chest. "Somebody has to be missing him." He couldn't have died and meant nothing to anyone. Imagine dying and being completely forgotten. Wife leaves you, child angry at you, it could happen. The little girls of the world get all the attention and this guy means nothing. My eyes drift to the other table. I'll bet we find out who she was by tomorrow.

He meant enough to initial his underwear. You only do that to stop yours from being mixed up with others. Somebody knew he existed. Now here he is barely recognizable as a human being on a cold table, bright lights above him, doctors probing at whatever is left. Nobody needs to be like this.

Or like her.

I have to fight the urge to cross over to her and inspect her ankles. Is there a rabbit mark there? Did she meet up with the big bad rabbit?

"I'll have to prepare the skull. All the flesh and hair has to come off before I can start my work." Michaels bends over at the waist and her face is just centimeters away from what is left of the dead man's head. I don't even want to be in the same room, let alone that close.

I look up and catch Dr. Baron staring at me. She locks eyes with me for a moment, then looks back to her work.

A phone begins to ring and vibrate on a side table.

"That's my phone. Reid, can you get it?" Marilyn twitches her head at me.

With a snap I pull off a latex glove. The display says the call is coming from Dispirito. "Hey, Al, it's Reid. Marilyn's up to her elbows in stinky stuff." I give her a little smile. If we can't make jokes things get too serious.

"I need you guys out here." His words rush at me through the phone.

"Us?"

"Yeah, are you with Dr. Norton?" His deep swallow echoes through the line. Behind his voice I can hear others calling out. Every breath he takes thunders at me as if he's in a panic. "What, what are you doing there?"

I look at the people around the little girl's body. I say, "My John Doe thing. I've got an anthropologist and reconstructionist and …"

"That's a bone doctor, right?" Dispirito interrupts me. "Bring him too."

"Her, the Doctor's a woman."

"Whatever, man, bring everyone."

"Where?"

"Robinson's Island. Bring everyone you can. Come now."

I hang up the phone and look at the others. All eyes are on me and I'm sure they can see it in my face. I don't want to go to Robinson's Island. That is the last place on Prince Edward Island that I want to go to, but I know I have to.

Chapter 10

It's like returning to the scene of a crime. There's a scene in the movie Platoon, of the soldiers going back to where they had bombed, that plays in my head; only this time it's taking place along the green-edged road to Robinson's Island. The road is blocked off just past the walkway from the parking lot to the beach. The police tape by the shower has been removed. As I stop to talk to the officer standing there I feel the eyes of tourists and "looky-loos" on me wondering what is going on. Questions blast at me from the reporters, probably the same questions Marilyn got when she passed well ahead of me, standing as close to the squad cars blocking the road as possible.

"Sgt. Reid, what's going on?"

"Does this have anything to do…"

"…With the little girl's death?"

"Can you answer a few questions?"

"Sgt. Reid,"

"Sgt. Reid, why the large police presence?"

I don't even look at them. I tell the other officers that Sgt. Moore called for me and drive through as soon as they move a wooden barrier. I didn't have anything to say to the reporters. I don't know what is going on. I'm not involved.

Dr. Norton and Dr. Baron follow close behind in the coroner's car. Sgt. Michaels stayed behind at the hospital to get started on removing flesh from John Doe.

I park the car at the end of a long line of other cars all pulled as close to the ditch as possible. There are RCMP radio cars and white trucks all along the side of the road practically in the ditch. Ahead the Mobile Command Post sits next to the entry booth where blood was found. A black unmarked SUV sits beside it. Standing beside the truck is Marilyn, Dispirito, McIntyre, and a young-looking member dressed in the dark-blue tactical uniform with a ball cap. Marilyn turns and marches straight toward us.

"We've got bodies," she says before she is too close.

My feet kick some rocks out of the way. My legs stop wanting to work. "What do you mean?" Bodies? As in plural? What the hell was this?

She runs a hand through her thick hair. Behind her I can see Eckhart in his white bunny suit in the tall grass of Robinson's Island. There are officers gathered around the MCP waiting for orders. I

186

recognize a number of them as riders in the Musical Ride. Holding a Styrofoam cup Supt. Baillie walks over to McIntyre.

"I've been on the phone all the way out here. We found a body yesterday over there in a shallow grave, so today they did a grid search. Twenty minutes in they found a patch of dirt in the grass further east. At almost the same time English found another to the west." Marilyn points in the other direction. My eyes do a quick search for the blond woman. "Dispirito halted the search. Police dog went nuts, so its handler thinks there's a body. Two bodies."

"What type of body? Is this connected to the girl? Is it the same MO?" Shit, now I sound like one of the damn reporters.

"No idea. I haven't seen it yet. Dr. Norton, if you can suit up, Dispirito can take us to Eckhart."

He strokes his beard quickly. "Of course. Dr. Baron should too. If there are bones we'd have to wait for her anyway."

"I've worked on numerous crime scenes in Canada and the US. It's safe to say I'm more experienced at retrieval of remains than anyone else in the province." Now that Dr. Baron is out of the autopsy clothes I can see that the parts of her body that were hidden before are lovely. She has a full bottom lip with a piercing below and to one side. I wonder if it is something from her youth she's holding onto or if it's something she decided to get as she got closer to mid-life. Light brown curls circle her face. She stands tall and straight

187

with the air of being confident and in control. Still it is those blue eyes that make me want to look at her and look away all in the same moment.

"Umm." Marilyn looks at all of us for a moment. She nods and says, "I'll talk to McIntyre about it." The two doctors walk off and disappear inside the Mobile Command Post before Marilyn speaks again. "I don't know what this is about, Reid. Two bodies buried here. This whole thing is going to explode and the entire island is going to be different. The Red Island Killer was something they could push back to whispers, but this is going to be too much. I've lived here my entire life. This is a peaceful place to live. What the hell?" Her hand goes back into her hair. Green eyes stare at mine. Hers say she's confused and worried. Mostly she's overwhelmed.

I put my hand on her shoulder and squeeze tightly. "Let's just hope this one isn't homegrown." Islanders have bad feelings toward those *from away*. The general belief is that all of the crime across the island is because of people *from away*. People who were not born in Prince Edward Island are *from away*. Drugs are *from away*, robberies and rapes are committed by people *from away*. It really kicked them in the balls when the Red Island Killer turned out to be Island born and bred. And yet people still think there is some sort of off-island influence there. "What do you want me to do?"

"I don't know. I don't even know what I need to do."

The two doctors head off through knee-high grass, Dispirito leading the way, watching with each step where they put their feet.

"Do you want to walk through it with me? It's what, one now, we've got two bodies to go over." Marilyn's face looks sad, as if she's fighting to keep full control of herself.

I want to take her in my arms and tell her we'll figure this out together. I force myself to look away from her. (She's not the one I should be thinking about.) Yellow police tape has been strung across the entire entry to the island behind the MCP. The whole island is a crime scene. I look back at Marilyn and want to caress her red-wine curls. I look over her shoulder. A dog barks from the black SUV. I have to think about Hillary. I have to think about my marriage.

"Yeah, let's change and go." I check my phone. Hillary hasn't texted me at all today.

"Have you met the new dog handler?" I shake my head. The moment we're up to the MCP she introduces me to Corporal Ty Bauer.

"Hey, you're the man with no first name. Greg told me about you."

"I'm not allowed to use Eckhart's first name."

"He offered me a hundred bucks if I can find out yours."

Up until two months ago RCMP on Prince Edward Island did not have its own dog unit. We had to call in the Charlottetown City Police K9 whenever one was needed. Bauer is young and seems smaller than what I thought a dog handler would be. He seems to be eager to prove himself. He's very much like a hunting dog waiting to be let loose. The piercing eyes of a German Sheppard watch our every move.

"What's the dog's name?"

"Bullet."

"Seriously?"

"Every year they have a competition to name the new puppies. Bullet was the lucky pick. No matter what his name is, he's the best partner anyone could ask for. He's saved my life four or five times. We're ready whenever you are, Sergeant." Bauer has a military cut under his ball cap, 'Dog Handler' written across the front. A bump on his nose suggest it's been broken more than a few times.

Marilyn says, "Bullet can sniff out bodies?"

"All of our dogs can. On the surface, buried, all levels of decomposition. From his reaction to your dirt piles I guarantee there's a body under each one. Give me five minutes and we'll start searching the rest."

Marilyn nods. As she gives instructions to the other officers I change into my white suit. They will follow behind the dog in a line of blue, using flags to mark any spot the dog signals. As soon as she is finished her instructions, she dons the bunny suit over her clothes and little white booties over her shoes.

As Marilyn and I walk through the grass, I see Dr. Norton already squatting next to Eckhart. Dr. Baron stands beside them watching the tedious job of slowly removing dirt from above the body. Every shovelful of dirt must be saved and sifted to see if there are any particulates or evidence detected. "Eckhart, can we interrupt you for a second?"

He doesn't look up. Over his shoulder he says, "Is there any way I can stop you? What's a name I haven't guessed? Holmes?"

My breath catches. That was close. "What are the chances of this being some old French burial ground?" Marilyn and I stand almost ten feet away giving Eckhart his space. He has already gone over all of the ground around the body, but we can't be too careful.

For a moment the wind coming down from the east stops and I can smell why we are here. The foul smell makes my stomach twist. The smell of decomposing flesh is unmistakable. Much worse than rotting hamburger you forgot in the back of the refrigerator.

"No chance in hell." We all look at Dr. Norton who never looks up from the body. "This body is not old. I would say she was buried not long ago. Possibly just before winter."

Eckhart stops for a moment and adjusts his glasses with the back of his hand.

I take a step to my right and I can see what is there. All around this rectangle of turned-up dirt and spotted tufts of grass is the tall grass that has over grown the island. There is a face in the ground as if it grew out of the red earth, but it's only half a face. It reminds me of fantasy movies where there is a face in a tree or in the ground. It sits there motionless waiting for the

191

adventurer to walk by, then suddenly speaks. I see a nose, cheek bone, and eye socket with loose dirt inside. I want to brush the dirt out of her eye. There is not enough visible to determine age, but I can venture to guess. Dark strands of hair (or are they light strands darkened from the soil) curl and twist out of the ground like pulled roots. An animal has pulled a hand free from the shallow grave and gnawed on the fingertips leaving three as stumps. I would guess raccoon, fox, or the coyote that got the other girl. Those are the biggest wild animals on the island. It's only now that I see the earth is moving over her. A beetle scurries across loose dirt and hides beneath grass. Spiders and bugs of all types crawl around, upset about being disturbed. Now I see the white maggots mixed in with the dirt like spilled grains of rice. Rice that moves and wiggles. This is no fantasy. This is no movie.

"Check this out." Eckhart holds up a large plastic freezer bag. It sags to one corner from the weight of a hand sized rock inside. "This was at the head of the grave sitting above folded grass. I think the face was uncovered recently."

"Recently?" Marilyn.

I take the bag from Eckhart's hand, hold it up in front of my eyes, and twist it around to see all sides. It is just a naturally-formed rock. One side is flatter than the others. Drawn on that flat side is a round circle with two oval circles coming off the top. Is it black magic marker or something else?

"Yes, recently like as in the past few days. This grass here is new growth and this dirt is sitting on it. Someone uncovered her face then covered it back up."

I hand the bag to Marilyn. "It's the same marking as on Kayla Schofield's ankle."

"And the Jane Doe." Marilyn looks to me and back down at the ground. "You're sure you didn't put the dirt there?"

"Hell no." Eckhart sits back on his heels. His hand pushes his glasses up again. Sweat drips down his exposed face sticking red dirt to his skin. "I have pictures before I even got close to the body. I noticed it right away."

"I'll check with the searchers and make sure none of them did it." Marilyn holds up the plastic bag and looks closely at the rock. "What is this? It was by the head of the body?"

"Headstone," I say in less than a whisper. I don't want to look at the face breaking through the ground, but I can't take my eyes from her either.

"A headstone? Why? So he can return to her grave?" I can feel Marilyn's eyes on me.

"He returned to the scene of the crime. It happens. It may not be related." After saying it, I know I don't believe it myself. This is related.

"Why would he mark it?" Dr. Baron asked.

In my head I can hear Dispirito telling us about Ted Bundy revisiting his victims to have sex with their rotting corpses. "A return to what he did. He wanted to relive a past glory." I look up at her and try to form some sort of a smile. "Or maybe he just wanted to make sure he didn't dig up an old body when he brought in a new one." I turn to Marilyn, "This rock relates this to the others. What about the second one?" I nod towards where English stands waiting.

We all look at Eckhart. He pushes his glasses up with the back of his hand again. "I haven't gotten that far yet. We cleared a path though so go ahead."

Dr. Baron moves his hand to gain our attention. "Excuse me, but I thought I read in the paper that the girl's body found the other day was at the beach area. Why would the killer not bury her like this one?"

I shrug my shoulders. Marilyn shakes her head. Eckhart continues his work with the body. We can't answer Dr. Baron's question. I am willing to bet that the *why* will give us the *who*, however we don't know any of it.

As we near where English is standing, she tells us to watch our step. "Something dug up the bones. I don't know if they're all here."

"Everyone stop." Dr. Baron elbows her way around me. "Excuse me Sgt. Moore." She sidesteps around my partner.

"What?" Marilyn looks at the woman who ignores her as she slides past. Both women are slightly taller than I am and standing side by side are intimidating. "What do you think you're doing?"

"There is bone. This is an anthropology situation now."

"Calm down, Cheryl. This is an RCMP situation. I'm in charge. My commanding officer can't even come out here without my permission. You're a guest here. You would do well to remember that." Marilyn does not look too foreboding in a bunny suit with her hair hidden under a hood. But, in both their eyes I could see them battling without a word or move. When two strong personalities clash there are, very well often, sparks that fly.

Dr. Baron raises her hands. "I'm just here to help, Sergeant. In my professional opinion you need a forensic anthropologist to recover the bones and make sure they are all there."

The two women stare at each other waiting for one to twitch or give in. They are two champion fighters sizing each other up. The first one to move loses. Personally, I put my bets on the one with the gun.

Looking around them, I focus on English. Unlike us she is in her full uniform. When the search began, they did not know what they would find. I know that women like men in uniforms, but it goes the other way as well. The day-to-day uniform of the RCMP is not as flattering as the red serge we wear for official events, but some officers (especially English) can pull off the bulletproof body armor and uniform. The sun shines off her cheeks. I can see her gull wing eyebrows over small-lens sunglasses.

Marilyn is the first to give in. She waves her hand for the doctor to take the lead.

I nod at English.

She mouths the word, "hi." Not far from her feet are a couple of long bones dug up from the ground. There is a hole in the ground beside it with claw marks and dirt flung away as if an animal was just there digging. Dr. Baron gets low to the ground. She moves slowly toward the bones, keeping her eyes on the ground. The smell of the sea overtakes any odors remaining from the decomposition of a body.

"Do you have the proper tools for this? Brushes (preferably badger hair) plastic trowels, depth markers, wire mesh?" Dr. Barron looks at each of us in turn. "I'm guessing from your expression that's a no."

"Eckhart should have the trowels, but the rest no."

"Can you mark off a ten-foot square around the remains? I'm going to make some phone calls and get what I need."

Bullet starts barking wildly. All of our heads snap towards the sound. We are hoping for a squirrel or raccoon. I know what this will be though. Police dogs don't go after little rodents when they are on the job. This is going to shake the island completely. One of the officers grabs a flag on a metal post and pushes it in the ground. For a moment none of us move. In our heads we are going over the possibilities. Dr. Baron is thinking about all that she will need and who to call. Marilyn is probably worried about what we may have discovered here. I don't know what to think.

"I have to talk to McIntyre." Marilyn turns and storms back the way we came.

In five minutes I am left standing alone with my wife's best friend over a few assorted bones. Dr. Baron has gone back to the command post to make her phone calls to get the right people here to do the job. Eckhart and Dr. Norton are still back at the first body. I should probably go back to the MCP, but I also want to talk to English and find out what is going on with Hillary. This isn't the place or time, but will there ever be a right moment? I know Hillary and I will talk at dinner. I have always been told never to go into a situation without having some intelligence first.

Deborah and Hillary did not know each other until we moved to PEI. On my first day of work with the Major Crimes Unit, Deb offered to tour my wife around Charlottetown. They started in the morning with breakfast at Maid Marian's and ended up sampling beers at the Gahan House. Now once a week they usually go out for drinks or to the movies. Deb's son, who spends a lot of his time with her ex-husband, is around the same age as Leigh. She is the one of Hillary's friends I really do not mind spending time with because we can talk shop a little. Right now I feel nervous around her. I want to know what she knows.

"How are you?" She is the first to speak.

I want to be out of this damn bunny suit. The sun is making me sweat inside. "I'm good. I don't really know what is going on and all that, but I'm good."

"What do you mean?"

Oh crap, maybe she was just asking how I was in general. She's Hillary's friend so why would she want to talk about it with me? I don't really care. I need to know. "This thing with Hillary leaving, sleeping somewhere else, I don't really know why."

"Oh, she did leave then." Her voicing that statement has my mind reeling. She didn't know Hillary had moved out. So where did she spend the weekend? Leigh said Hillary was at Deb's. She didn't even tell her daughter the truth. "She told me she might. I tried to talk her out of it." She looks over at the officers searching with the dog. They continue to look for any signs of bodies or burial. I keep my eyes on Sgt. Deborah English. When I have a suspect I will often stare at them until they tell me what I want to hear. I don't think it will work this time, but I don't know what else to do. She turns her eyes toward me. "What? I didn't think she was that serious about him."

Him? Who *him*? There's a *him*? I know nothing about a *him*.

Him.

She nods, "I told her not to do anything with him as long as she still want your marriage to work. I'm hoping she just needed time to think things out. She's frustrated, you know." She fidgets from one foot to the other. I can't move myself.

"Yeah me too. Look, I'm going to see what's going on." What the hell is going on? There's a him? My head begins to spin. Who the hell is he? Where the fuck is my wife?

English grabs my arm. "Reid, you're my friend too. If you want to talk, you can call me and we will talk."

I nod until she lets go of my arm.

I have the bunny suit off before I reach the Mobile Command Post. I quickly check my phone. No texts, no missed calls. A quick question lets me know that Marilyn, McIntyre, and Dr. Baron are in the office at the back end of the command post. They are probably arguing over who is going to do what and who has the power to order everyone around.

I check my phone again. I watch a car advancing down the highway. Before it gets close, I recognize LeBlanc behind the wheel. Corporal Longfellow is in the passenger seat. The whole Major Crimes Unit is here.

"Reid, what the hell is going on?" LeBlanc yells at me with his thick French accent. "The reporter leaches are circling the entry gate."

Down the road there is a collection of reporters (which the MCU members had to pass) slowly building in size. Sooner or later, preferably the latter, they will start squeezing their way down the road to get whatever information they can get. They will come at us like a pack of coyotes looking for any scrap they can tear off without caring who they have to plow over. We all know they are doing their jobs, but their jobs directly conflicts with ours. All they want is that little bit of information that gets their story out ahead of all the others. All we want to do is keep all of those tidbits of information to ourselves so that we can use them to trap the killer. It is also a fight between newspaper and video. Certainly the television news gets to more people; however in the day of satellite television, newspapers are needed for that local flavour with your morning cup of coffee. I've had enough run-ins with the press and I want to stay as far away from them as I can.

My wife is fucking around. Maybe. I don't know.

I wait for them to get close before telling them about the bodies.

"So this guy, he kills these poor girls,"

"And he comes here to dump his bodies?" Longfellow runs a finger over his small moustache. "I bet he's *from away*. It could be a trucker or businessman or even a tourist. People come and go from the island all the time. Vehicles don't get searched and the only thing we get are quick video shots of the drivers and licence plates as they cross the bridge, not much of anything if they cross via the ferry. And that's if we ask for the videos."

"Did we ask for them?"

"We have people watching them right now looking for silver minivans. I hear they have a list already as big as my dick."

"So just one van then?"

"Screw you, Reid." Longfellow flashes his smile.

I check my cell phone. "Let's cross reference that list with those at the Bonaventure campground." People are supposed to write their licence plate numbers down when they register.

"An honest killer? What a concept."

LeBlanc checks his own phone and pushes a few buttons to look for anything that might have been missed. Bastard. "You really think our killer is from there?"

Marilyn, McIntyre, Dispirito, and Baron walk out of the back of the MCP. I wouldn't say they are all friendly but none of them look particularly pissed off, nor happy. The doctor is on her phone before she steps from the trailer and starts pacing without heading anywhere near the island grass. Like he is mimicking her movements, McIntyre is also quick to the draw with his cellular phone. I wonder who is on the end of each line. Somebody with little trowels and brushes on one of them, I bet. Maybe the other goes to the Commanding Officer or even the Premier's office. Dispirito and Marilyn walk toward us. Her hips sway. The aroma of her perfume hits me. It's no good. It dissipates immediately and all I can smell is the rotting body over there and the scent of seaweed coming from the water.

I check my phone - nothing. "That was the last place our victim was. Stands to reason someone at the Bonaventure Campground knows something. They probably don't even realize it."

"You want us to head back over there and talk to everyone again?" Longfellow lights a cigarette.

Dispirito puts his hands in his pockets. "A lot of them might have left already. We had no real cause to hold anyone so we have phone numbers and home addresses. Think we should go?"

"No," Marilyn says. Her face looks flushed and tired from the stress of being the primary investigator on a serious case. You hold the sorrows and hopes of the families on your shoulders. Yeah, I know the look on her face because I once had it plastered over mine. I let it drive me to nightmares and the occasional breakdown. "I need you guys here. We're going to have lots of evidence to secure and we'll have to start on getting ID's as soon as possible."

"So again we have to wait?" Dispirito kicks at a rock. His blond hair crests and falls like waves onto his forehead. With a quick flip of his head he throws it back.

Marilyn shrugs her shoulders. She looks at me then turns to face the island. Eckhart is doing his thing. The search group is making its way toward the far end of the island, then will circle back closer to the North side. They have already marked two more spots indicated by the dog. She says, "The one body is at least a few months old. We have no idea where it came from, the definite sex, age, or anything so there's nothing to do right now. The bone lady is calling in some others with the equipment to dig up the other body."

"Bodies." I check my phone.

"Right. When her people show up I want one of us with each one of them to ensure chain of custody. I hope you don't have any plans."

I check my phone.

~ * ~

At this time of year it doesn't get dark until after 10:00 pm. Located at the entrance to Robinson's Island, we are surrounded by trees that block the last of the sun's rays casting eerie shadows. The officers from the Musical Ride left when the search was done. Tomorrow morning they will leave the island to continue their tour of New Brunswick. Even most of the Major Crimes have left. McIntyre left a while ago.

I have been checking my phone all night. No texts, no calls, nothing - not from my wife anyway. Michaels called around 4:30 pm to tell me she was finishing for the day and would get back to work in the morning if I could pick her up at the hotel. When the phone rang I jumped out of my skin. Hillary didn't contact me. I have been too scared to send her a text or call. What would I say? "Hey honey, I can't make dinner for the exact reason you decided to leave." Not the best thing to tell her. I guess I could try, "Will *he* be joining us?"

The grand total is five. Jane Doe #2, the body in the morgue, was the first that Eckhart had carefully unearthed. There were signs that she was strangled and burned into the skin of her rotting ankle was the rabbit symbol. They found what looked like frostbite, so chances are she'd been there all winter. Dr. Baron's people arrived within two hours of her contacting them so no real work could be done until nearly 5:00 pm. She is a smart lady. She allowed only one of her people on the scene beside her at a time so that she could watch what they were doing. Jane Doe #3 had only about two thirds the bones in a human body. Dr. Baron said the pelvic bone showed that she was female. Jane Doe #4 had a full set of bones and they are still working on Jane Doe #5. These last two were found by the dog. Walking back to the entry to the crime scene a member of the search team tripped over a rock. When he looked he saw the rabbit symbol drawn on it in permanent marker – probably Jane Doe #6.

"Do you believe this?" Deborah English holds a cup of steaming coffee just below her bottom lip. The steam rises over her pink lips and around her thin nose.

I check my phone.

The cool air is soaking in through my clothes. The Island air is never overly cold, not even in winter, but the dampness soaks right through. "It's a crazy world out there." I stare across the island peninsula at the large lights set up around the fourth body. They are almost done with that one. Dispirito stands off to the side with his hands in his pockets watching them do their work. Marilyn is beside him, her hands wrapped around a cup of coffee. The spotlights make her hair glow redder than it actually is. "But no, I can't believe this. Not here.," I say.

"This sicko used this island as his own personal dumping ground. Perfect place really. Nobody comes out this way that often so you'd have plenty of time to dig a hole. When I've done patrols down here I think I've only seen one or two cars in the span of a week and those that do come here hike around the outside." She goes silent for a while staring out at the continuing dig. I look at her profile, the blue eyes, the short blond hair. Why did her husband leave her? Or did she leave him? "We have to find out who these girls are."

"You sure they're all girls?" I know the answer.

"Dr. Baron says the first three are."

I check my phone.

"What's with you and your phone? You've been checking it every five minutes."

"I was supposed to meet Hillary for dinner."

Deborah sips her coffee. "Really? Did you call her and tell her what is going on?"

The only person I called was Leigh to tell her to stay at a friend's, unless she heard anything from her mother. She hadn't. I return the phone to my pocket and continue staring at the lights in the field. For a moment, even thinking the words feels pathetic. I tell her, "I never called her."

"That's pathetic."

I can't help smiling. "I know. She told me she left because of the job. I didn't know about some other guy." I look at her.

Deborah turns to me with her face scrunched up. Even that way she is beautiful when she smiles. I can see why they liked to have her in front of the camera for all of the news bites. "Sorry. I shouldn't have said anything. She hasn't talked to me either. I don't really know what's going on with her."

I wonder if the reporters are still out at the entry to the park. A couple of boats have come out of Rustico Harbour and docked within view of the work going on, close enough for photographers to get decent shots. I'm sure tomorrow morning there will be a photo of Robinson's Island with some sensational headline. I don't know how much has leaked out, but something always does.

"So what are you still doing here? Where's your boy?"

"With his father. You're working the music festival right?"

I nod. "I volunteered so I could get the free tickets for Hill and Leigh and now neither of them wants to talk to me."

"Well I'm working it too, so at least you'll have someone to talk to. This must be my relief." She nods at the headlights coming down the road. At least she has relief so that she can go home and get some sleep. "You have my number. If you want to talk feel free to call me, okay?" She runs a hand down my forearm then walks to meet whoever has come to send her home.

I would lie if I said my arm didn't tingle. I watch Deborah's hips sway. Perhaps I should feel guilty for looking. Am I just looking because my wife may or may not be fooling around with some guy? No, I've looked before. Once again, I wonder if I was made for marriage. This job, this life, claims many marriages; but then somehow some of them work. I don't know how. Hillary is not going to be happy with me at all, not only for missing dinner, but I can't walk away from these girls.

I turn and look across the grass to where the trees and the open shore gives way to the ocean. It is going to take a few more hours to unearth Jane Doe #5. I suppose I could go home and sleep in my empty house and let the others take care of everything. I'd rather stand here all night staring off into the blackness.

Chapter 11

It was all there in front of him. He ran his fingers over the front page of "The Guardian," Charlottetown's newspaper. What was it Sherlock Holmes said? "The game is afoot?" It certainly was. Everything was working out the way he wanted it to.

RCMP Recover Remains in PEI National Park.

His wife and kids slowly made their way along the buffet table across the room. They lingered on the scrambled eggs. His daughter loved them; his son didn't, but he would eat whatever Mom put on his plate. They picked over the bacon and sausage, looking for just the right ones and then moved on to the home fries. He knew they would take longer when they got to pastries and fruit.

They found Megan. Did they find anyone else? Megan was a gift to them. When he had Kayla tied up and was satisfied he went out and dug up the other girl.

It took them long enough to find her. He thought the smell of her rotting body would have drawn them to her much sooner. Coyotes or foxes got to Sophia. Such a shame. She was his favorite. Her screaming went on and on like a symphony with encores. She shouldn't have been defiled in that way. Maybe they found her as well. How many did they find? It didn't matter. They found his burial ground just as he wanted them to. It wasn't his only one, but it was enough.

His wife put her plate down on the newspaper, covering the picture of lights and of people digging in the dirt. It looked like the photo was taken from a boat. Without a word she indicated it was his turn to go to the buffet table since his job of watching her purse was finished. He rose slowly and shuffled across the room. He picked up a plate and napkin roll of utensils.

His mind drifted back to Sophia. She wore blue-jean capris, a white belt, a pink T-shirt with a heart on the front in those bedazzled plastic diamonds, and white shoes that reminded him of nurses' shoes when he first saw her. He met her online; he met most of them online. She loved dogs and drawing and singing along with Glee and she loved him. She said she did when they were chatting. Of course she only knew the eleven-year-old him. She knew him as Brad. She told him she loved him after they met in real life too, eventually. He showed her what love was.

He was in a good mood. He scooped a healthy spoonful of eggs onto his plate. He took three strips of bacon and three sausages. He picked out a Danish with cherry jam in the middle.

When he was done with Sophia he buried her naked in the ground. Her clothes ended up in a plastic bag with some of his own kids' old clothes and left in a bin outside a thrift store. He bet some other girl wore them now and proudly showed off the bedazzled heart. If he saw a girl wearing that shirt would he be able to control himself? Would he have to go after her or would he fall on the ground laughing? If the clothes had blood on them, they were burned or ended up in a dumpster far away from where he found the girls or where he left them. He took an item or two from each so that he could remember them, but that was all gone. He never left any evidence on PEI. He was too smart for that. When did he last see Sophia? It was just over a year ago. He still dreamed of her.

"Did you read this?" His wife snatched the newspaper from under her plate. She held it in one hand. The newspaper was crinkled and there was a smear of butter or syrup or something right on the headline. Right on *his* headline.

Without a word, he sipped at the coffee someone had poured him.

"This says they found the remains of more than one body. Nobody made a statement though. This is a crazy world." She shook her head and stuffed her mouth with egg. As she spoke again egg flew out of her mouth at him, "It says it was in Prince Edward Island National Park. We've gone swimming there haven't we? We go there every time we're on the island."

Yes, My Dear. We sit there on the beach, you watching our kids play by the water and me staring down to Robinson's Island wishing I was with my girls. Crazy world indeed.

She didn't know how crazy it was. She didn't know she sat across from the man who found Megan walking down a road outside Montreal, Quebec, over a month ago. She offered to go along with him to give him directions. He said he was looking for such and such road. He didn't force her into the van. Megan was a weak moment. She was so pretty and innocent, and alone. Her brown hair was tied back in a ponytail with a red and white bandana. She didn't know it, but she was dead the moment she sat in the passenger seat and closed the door. He quickly had her unconscious and in the back tied up and covered. He drove from Quebec, through New Brunswick, to Prince Edward Island as if he was just going for a nice little trip. The trick was staying close to the speed limit and giving the police no reason to pull him over. Once on Robinson's Island he had quick fun.

He had her strip naked. Always get them to do most of the work. He didn't understand those savage animals that attacked women and had to struggle to get their clothes off. Megan stood there in the grass looking awkward. One knee was bent, her arms were at her sides, fingers clung together with hands guarding her young womanhood. Tears streaked her face. He licked his lips with the mere thought of tasting her virginal skin. He was thrilled with the idea of caressing her body where no other man had touched, feeling the goose pimples that instantly formed on her skin. She had a mole on her cheek. Another mole on her lower abdomen matched it. He used duct tape to secure her hands above her head and opened her legs. It wasn't nice to do it that way, but they liked it. Mostly he ran his hands over their bodies and tasted them. He pushed himself into them. Megan didn't scream until then. Oh did she scream!

"Are you eating? Are you feeling okay? You're not coming down with something are you?"

It was all her fault. She made him feel worthless and weak. His little playmates he could control; he loved them; he made love to them. Then he burned a rabbit shape into their flesh and jammed a metal rod so far up inside he heard things pop and tear. They weren't going to be like *Her*. He hit them when they wanted to fight, when they thought they were in charge. He was the man. He was in charge. And then he killed them and felt the ultimate release. That was what he craved now.

"I'm fine," he said and smiled across the table. He had killed his wife over and over, in spirit. He couldn't kill the mother of his two children. That would have been wrong.

Sophia was his favorite, Megan was a weak moment, the others fulfilled needs. And Kayla was planned. He had his next one chosen out already. She was going to feel pain the others never felt. She was going to scream until she couldn't scream any more. Then he would wait until she woke again and would make her scream even more. And at some point he would end it, but he knew that wasn't going to be enough.

"What should we do today? Shining Waters or maybe go to the beach?"

Chapter 12

As I drive around to the back of Cassandra Michaels' hotel, I see the Schofields RV parked at the far end of the parking lot. I don't want to look at their vehicle, but I can't stop my eyes from drifting toward it. What else were they supposed to do? Drive back across the country with the empty seat where Kayla should be? Will they even take it back with them? Or are they going to fly back with their daughter in the cargo bay beneath them? And when they get back all they'll see are accusing eyes. Their neighbors will offer their sorrow (*I can't imagine how you must feel*) the whole time thinking about how they are so glad it's not them. "How could parents let their child be taken like that?" At Walmart between the washrooms and above the water-fountain, a dozen children stare out blankly. Photographs of happy times forever frozen, symbolizing the worst time in their parents' lives.

Some pictures include drawings to show age. Fifteen years ago a child vanishes as if the ground opened up and they fell through, never to return except in an *artist's rendering*. Parents continue to hope. They hope someone running to the bathroom (between getting a new pair of socks and looking for the new video game) will look up and recognize their neighbor's child as one of those missing. But they don't. The shoppers run to the washroom with their eyes down on the floor and only look up once they pass the big sign that says the world is a screwed-up place. Someone gets a drink, looks up, a cold shiver runs down their spine, then they quickly catch up to their family as they leave the store. They don't want to look in case just looking would put your kids in danger.

The Schofield's don't know what to do. They came all this way with their baby. Can they go home without her?

The passenger door of my Focus opens. "Good morning," Cassie meets me as she climbs in. She places her work case on her lap and her cap on top of that. The aroma of gingersnaps arrives with her tickling my nose. I suddenly have a craving. I wonder if the aroma is from her shampoo or something she had for breakfast. "I hear you had a busy night." She signals with a rolled up newspaper in front of me.

"Hence the large cups of coffee." I tap the two brown cups in the center drink holders that I picked up at the drive through. "There's sugar on top. If you need cream you'll have to wait for the office. I have to stop by MCU before going to the hospital." I quickly fill her in on some of the details of last night as I proceed down University Avenue.

"Do you think the victims are from the island?"

My head shakes. "A missing kid in PEI makes noise. There aren't many missing girls that age that I know of." Prince Edward Island is like a small city. Somebody screws around on his wife in Tignish on the west end, within a few days somebody in Souris in the east will know about it. Also, it's easy to cut off all escape from the island. If an amber alert for a missing child were to be posted the ferry would be stopped, airplanes grounded, and the bridge to the mainland blocked off.

"Assuming the bodies are the same age as the first victim." She takes her cup of coffee and lifts the lid to breathe in the aroma. The bitter smell of fresh coffee grounds fills the interior, diminishing the gingersnap scent.

"Yeah, assuming." The intact body is definitely about the same age and the rocks with the rabbit symbols, these were victims of the same killer. "Same killer or not, we may need your help in getting identification. Most kids around eleven get reported as missing, but if they're older they might not."

"I think I will have to take the John Doe back to the mainland to my own work space. I had some trouble trying to remove some of the flesh from the skull. I think my equipment back in Halifax would be better."

I nod. My teeth bear down on my bottom lip. I don't want to hear about the removing of flesh from a skull. I know pretty well how it is done. You boil it like you're making soup. I can imagine the smell. Things churn inside my stomach. This is too early in the day to be dealing with this. "We can get you a ride back whenever you want."

As I cross the intersection by Burger King I see a white hatchback parked on the side of the avenue next to HQ's driveway and the minivan on the edge of the loop parking area in front of the red brick building. I know before I see it that the hatchback will probably have The Guardian written on both sides with a picture of a newspaper folded out. The van will be from the *CBC* or *CTV*. More reporters will show up sooner or later. This is bound to be bigger than just local news. As I move around the side of the building I look back and recognize the brown hair exiting the passenger side of the CBC van. A large sheet of "déjà vu" falls over me. The woman who belongs to that hair, who belongs to the heels clicking across the paved parking lot, hounded me before about a different killer. She knows how to get me. Cassie and I move inside as questions are directed at me from the reporter; they are cut off as the door closes.

The air conditioned halls of L Division's Headquarters are comforting to me. At home I sit petting the dog, flipping through channels and feeling like I don't belong. I belong in HQ. I am important. Nobody is going to leave me here. While in this building I get orders, I give orders, I follow orders, I get things done. The grey carpet with blue flecks makes me feel better. The beige walls make me feel warm and safe. I have spent time walking around the halls looking at the framed awards and photographs. My favorite is one of the Musical Ride doing there dome technique. All thirty-two riders on their dark horses dressed in red form a circle facing the inside with their spears all pointed to the center. No wonder I am committed to work, if this is the only place where I feel complete. Even before Hillary left me, there were times where I couldn't breathe until I got inside these halls. Once I'm inside the four walls of Major Crimes I'm home.

I check my cell phone.

"Reid, do you want to look at this?"

No missed texts, no missed calls. Marilyn stands next to one of the white boards. I breathe out a sigh, "Yeah, sure."

To Cassie I say, "The creamer's over there." I do quick introductions with the rest of Major Crimes.

Dispirito jumps up to help Cassie with the coffee creamer, even though it is right out in the open.

Marilyn. "Were you able to avoid Arsenault and the other leaches?"

She puts all of her attention to the whiteboard where she has been posting what little information she has. The photo of Kayla Schofield, showing her state when we found her, is on the left top corner with information written in red dry-erase marker below.

The remainder of the board has photos of the remains found on Robinson's Island with *Jane Doe* and a number written underneath each. Marilyn runs a hand through her hair. "Wylie dropped me off. I was low in the seat so they couldn't see me." She looks at me.

My eyebrow is raised and I can feel the smile on my lips.

"What?"

I give her a big smile, "And what were you doing while you were low in the seat?"

"Shut up." She goes to kick my leg, but I move out of the way.

"This all you have?" There are photos of the marks found on Kayla. Starting on the left and then going across the bottom are photos of the rabbit symbol on her ankle, Jane Doe #1, and then the symbols drawn on the rocks.

"This is it?" McIntyre's voice raises almost squeal. He quickly crosses the room to stand beside us in front of the whiteboard. He's dressed in a perfectly-pressed shirt with black pants and jacket. A grey silk tie finishes his outfit.

"Nice suit. Did you meet Cassie?"

He nods in Sgt. Michaels' direction. "I have the pleasure of meeting with the CO and the Premier's aid and whoever else thinks this is their business. This is all that I have to tell them? Six more bodies and a bunch of rocks?"

"Are you actually going to tell them that?" Marilyn moves her second hand to her hair. Right now she probably wants to pull it all out.

"Hell no. They don't need to know any of it. We're following leads, doing autopsies; we have an anthropologist and a facial reconstructionist here to help with the investigation. I'll baffle them with bullshit. I can't tell them any details, but they are going to want to know what we are doing and how we are proceeding. There will be 60,000 people on the island for the music festival, at least. And that's in three days. They want to make sure we're doing our jobs. They have to put their noses in to make sure the public knows they're involved. What's the plan?"

Today Marilyn wears black slacks and a blue-green plaid shirt with a white tank-top underneath. She is dressed as comfortably as she can be for a day of weaving bunny suits in the morgue. All eyes turn to her. Her face flushes as she takes in a long breath. "I am going to the autopsies of the Jane Does. Dr. Norton, Dr. Baron, and Eckhart will be there. Longfellow will be here reviewing more video tape of the bridge and ferry from Friday and Saturday to look for silver minivans. You're at what - forty-seven already?" There's a nod. She continues, "Dispirito and LeBlanc are going back to Robinson's Island. They'll have regular members and search and rescue personnel walking shoulder-to-shoulder across the whole damn area looking for any more rabbit rocks."

Cassie slowly crosses the room and starts studying the white board. I watch Marilyn. A bit of sweat threatens to drip from her hairline. She holds her head up and her shoulders back.

"What about Reid?" McIntyre's arms are crossed over his chest.

"I thought he wasn't on this case." Marilyn looks at me with big green eyes.

I silently let out a deep breath. Is there really any point in denying that I'm involved? I'm pretty sure that after last night my wife won't want to talk to me, and I'm not sure what to say to her.

McIntyre has the air of a stern man who you never want to cross. "We don't have a choice. The higher ups are on me, so I'm on all of you. Dispirito will go to the autopsy. Reid goes to the search. Let's get some answers."

Dispirito looks white. I can picture him with his head in a sink throwing up within the hour. He's not one for dead bodies. It would be hilarious to watch him trying to hold it together for Cassie though.

"I'll have to go home and change." This morning I dressed in clothes appropriate for being the autopsy room all day. I am not dressed to hike through grass and trees. My day will be swatting mosquitoes and wiping sweat from my face. At least I won't be tempted to spy on my wife. I should call her and apologize or beg or yell at her or something. I don't know if I have the right to be angry. I suppose when it comes down to it you have to get your own emotions figured out first. Whenever I go home I don't know what I hope to see, Hillary there or all of her belongings gone. "Marilyn, can you take Cassie with you to the morgue?"

"Yeah, sure."

"What were they wearing?"

We all stop and look in the direction of the white board. Cassie's back is still to the room. It takes a minute before she turns. Her eyes search the room and lock on me. Her face seems to have lost all colour, turning an ashen gray, and her eyes droop with sadness.

"What were the bodies dressed in?" Her voice strains to get the words. McIntyre has forgotten about his meeting.

"Summer dresses," Marilyn says absently. She looks at me, "Just like Kayla Schofield." Another connection.

"There was nothing else?"

"No. If it's the same guy he takes the clothes. He did with her anyway. We assume he did." She points a trimmed fingernail at the Brackley Beach body photographs. "Why?"

"There have been a couple girls missing in Nova Scotia."

"Seriously? How old were they?"

"One, I remember, disappeared from Halifax. Sophia was her name and, if I remember correctly, she was eleven."

"Same as Kayla."

223

"I don't know all the details. You should call H Division and ask for Sgt. Michael Antcliffe."

"I'll call," McIntyre heads for his office. "Everyone has their jobs to do."

"What about your meeting?"

"Forget my meeting!" McIntyre slams his door behind him.

~ * ~

As I walk from Headquarters building, I throw a hand up to the reporters and that actually stops them for once. As I start the unmarked car I'm assigned, I have full intentions of going home to change. I expect to find Leigh stretched out on the couch eating a bowl of Special K with sliced banana, Frix at her feet, ready for an exhausting day of watching television and YouTube videos in the blasting air conditioning while I'm searching for rocks with the sun on my back. I stop at the avenue and observe the busy morning traffic go by. All I have to do is turn right, then left at the lights and I'd be on my way home. Or I could go straight through those lights and out to Robinson's. Traffic stops beside me. If I went left I'd be heading downtown. Hillary works downtown. I push on the gas pedal and fight the steering wheel to turn left.

I don't really have a plan. As I drive toward the Confederation Court mall I go over in my head what I could say. Do I apologize or do I lash out? Talk to her in private or make a scene? With a suspect I would have no problem. I'd walk into their work place announcing loudly who I am and who I need to talk to and even start listing off private things about their lies until they insist we speak in private. I can't do that with my wife. Our marriage isn't over yet.

Or is it?

Like magic I hit every green light down the hill. University Avenue stops at Providence House, home of the PEI government and birthplace to Canadian Confederacy, only to pick up again on the other side of the building and continue to the waterfront. I don't need to go that far. I turn right onto Grafton Street. A car leaves a parking spot right in front of the bank where my wife works, fifteen minutes still on the meter. This time of day the short journey should take a good ten, fifteen minutes and then another ten more finding a parking space. I'm outside the bank in five. Must be my lucky day.

I check my phone. Nothing.

As I walk in to the bank I see Hillary right away. Usually she's in the back and I have to wait. My luck continues. Goody, goody.

She whispers into a teller's ear and points to something on the computer screen. Her eyes flick up at me and her face instantly changes. The friendly "here to help" demeanour falls away and is replaced by a mixture of anger and tiredness. She whispers again in the woman's ear and looks away from the computer to me. I wonder how many people around here know about our problems. I wonder if the other man works here.

Hillary a smiles at the customer in front of the teller, then quickly escapes to the back. For a moment I wonder if I should ask for her. Maybe she didn't see me. She walks back out, purse slung over her shoulder and walks right past me.

Without a word I follow her down the sidewalk toward the corner. I shove my hands in my pockets. My eyes look at her heels clicking on the concrete. Did she always wear heels to work? My luck has changed. We have to wait at the lights. I think of all the different things I could say; none sound good enough. The light changes. I fall in behind her. As we cross Grafton my eyes travel up her legs. She wears black slacks that hug her ass with no panty lines. Normally I would be walking beside her, my hand rubbing her lower back and occasionally dropping onto her butt. Today I purposely walk slowly while she moves quickly.

Higher to our left and with a wide open space around it is the Confederation Centre of the Arts. Performances take place there year round - plays, concerts, school productions. For two months during the summer Anne of Green Gables, the Musical is performed there. It's been like that for fifty years. Beside that is the Charlottetown Library. Both buildings are connected underground with a little gift shop, a restaurant, and the art gallery that opens up by Providence House. Hillary proceeds up the steps close to the library then heads to the Arts Centre wall. Here we are out in the open, but far enough from others that we won't be heard unless our voices rise. The busy traffic on Queen Street and the clarinet player busking by the Arts Centre entry will also help.

Hillary looks to the side to see if we can be seen from the bank. She crosses her arms, fingers grasping each arm. "Well?"

I let out a breath. "That a new outfit?"

"Seriously, Reid?" her head shakes. "Seriously?"

"What do you want me to say?" I lean in a little, my body shifting so that my back is to her workplace, guarding her.

"What happened last night?"

I'm sure she's heard the news. "Work."

"Dead girls, you mean."

I nod and look at the cars going by. From Grafton down to the waterfront is a residential area, but also on Queen and the streets branching from it are a number of restaurants or pubs, little shops, countless businesses, the Delta Hotel and the Provincial Courthouse so there's much traffic here.

After a long moment Hillary says, "So you're working on the case."

I look at her shoes. Dark red to match the cross chest top and heals of about three inches. Saucy. "McIntyre put me on it this morning. I'm helping out."

"Right." I look up in time to catch her eyes roll. "You could have called me, Reid."

"And have you yell at me over the phone at a crime scene?"

"Oh, God forbid your co-workers know you have a life."

I bite down on my bottom lip. The horse-drawn buggy, that goes around the downtown giving tourists with money a little history lesson, clip-clops down the hill slowing traffic.

Hillary asks, "Do you even want to be married, Reid?"

"Do you?" I turn to her. "I wasn't the one who decided to sleep who knows where."

Her eyes drop. "I've been at Deb's."

I look away and whisper, "Don't say it, Reid," mostly to myself. But if you want to know the truth, I was trying to get her to say it.

"What's that supposed to mean?"

"Nothing." I can't look at her.

"Come on, say it. Say it."

I turn to her and get close to her face. "Deborah doesn't even know where you've been sleeping." Her eyes look away then back at mine. "Is it with the therapist?"

"That's a little cliché, don't you think?" Hillary's brown eyes are moist with tears ready to streak down her face.

I have to swallow hard before saying, "So there is someone."

Hillary's shoulders sag. The tears start to run. She searches her purse quickly for a tissue to wipe them away. "Deb told you?"

I kneel down to get the pen that fell from her purse and skidded across the pavement. "She thought that was why you left." I look at her face. I can't tell if she is sad or relieved. Maybe both.

"Nothing's happened, Reid."

"Yeah, you didn't believe me when I told you that about Marilyn. Did you? I look toward Grafton Street. There are our saviors - my car to get me away and her workplace for her to hide. The stories she'll have to tell her co-workers when she gets back! "So who is he?"

"Reid, stop it. There's nothing going on. We went for coffee a couple times. We talk and text, that's it."

"Do you want something to happen?"

"Are you going to keep working on this case?" She looks up at me and dabs the last tears away. Her light mascara needs a little touch-up.

"I've been assigned to it now, Hill. We get assigned cases. We work 'em. What do you want me to do?"

"I want you to do what you think is right."

My head shakes as I look away and bite my lip. Welcome to the guilt-trip express. Here's your ticket.

The sound of vibration breaks the silence between us. Hillary starts to dig in her purse for her phone, but stops herself.

"That him?"

"I have to get back to work, Reid."

"Must be nice to get texts. You used to text me at least once every hour. Now you don't text me at all. You'd think a major crimes investigator would have caught on to that."

"I'm going back to work." Hillary turns and walks back toward the stairs by the library.

I turn on my heel and head straight across the platform. There are no stairs the way I am heading, only a four-foot drop, but I don't really care.

On my car's windshield is a parking ticket tucked under a wiper blade.

~ * ~

The sun is warm today with a strong breeze coming from the north. By the time I get to Robinson's Island a dozen cars are parked along both sides of the road close to the gatehouse. A square yellow truck is at the entry to the former campground. It's the command post for the volunteer search and rescue team. Most of their training is devoted to searching in the ocean, but they do some training for land searches as well. We need them. Now that the Musical Ride has moved on we don't have enough people to pull in to search the entire area for rocks. I park beside the yellow truck. LeBlanc has talked to the group of volunteers and the members we have working with us. Everyone is basically waiting for me.

It is not the same Robinson's Island that Marilyn and I saw four days ago. The grass has been trampled down, there are stakes stuck in the ground at six different sites all with yellow police tape tied onto them. Flies buzz in and out of the shed where we found Kayla's blood, the brown stain still on the floorboards. I look out at the gulls flying low. Boats are docked close to the peninsula. At one point this must have been a beautiful place to camp. Now it is a graveyard. How long has it been like this? Are there others out there?

I a nod to LeBlanc. "I'm going to take this side." I point to the end of the line of volunteers where Deb English stands. The sun seems to glow off the strands of blond hair sticking out under her blue cap.

"Yes. Everyone knows what to look for and to call out if they find something, but to not touch anything." His French accent is extremely thick. I nod and walk away. The mosquitoes are already around everyone's heads making a constant droning noise.

"Hey, another day of body searching, eh? Rock searching this time, I guess." Deb says as her lips form a smile. She drinks from a water bottle and my eyes take the opportunity to look her over. Dark blue RCMP issue cargo pants mushroom over black boots and she wears a blue tee with the RCMP emblem over the heart. I am used to seeing her in the dress uniform because she is the one going on camera. I like this look. I wish I saw her out of uniform more often.

I move my eyes before she sees me. What is wrong with me? Am I checking out my wife's friend in order to get some sort of revenge? That can't happen. This isn't some episode of Grey's Anatomy.

"You talk to Hillary?" I slap my neck. Mosquito smear covers my palm and disappears into my pants as I wipe it clean. I had my tactical uniform in the trunk of my car so I actually did get to change.

"No."

Deborah leans in close to me. "You could have told me you didn't know about the other guy."

I shrug my shoulders. She is so close I can smell her perfume over the scent of grass and red clay. "I still don't know about him. Hill didn't tell me anything," I say.

"What do you want to know?" Her blue eyes hold mine.

A whistle sounds from down the line. I look over to see LeBlanc taking his fingers from his mouth.

My mouth opens. I stop for a second then bite my bottom lip.

"We should get started," is all I say. I wave my hand to LeBlanc.

There are fifteen of us in total – five members and ten search and rescue volunteers. We start walking in a single line, each of us five feet from the next. We are starting on the southwestern shore with me the farthest inland. We will have to do at least five passes to get the entire island covered with some extra attention to any bends along the shoreline. We all step, pause with eyes going back and forth, then step again. It reminds me of *Lion King 1 1/2* when the meerkats are on hyena watch. Uncle Max said they had to "scurry, sniff, flinch." We quickly realize we have to add *lift the trampled grass* and look underneath to our mantra. Once in a while one of us will stop and reach down to the ground to gently inspect something with a latex-gloved hand. The people on either side lean over to see what they're found. If someone finds something they are to call out and we'll all stop. LeBlanc or I will walk over to check the find and decide whether or not to put a marking flag there.

The spot where Jane Doe #3 was found is along our second sweep as we head back toward the staging area. I look up for a moment and see a photographer snapping pictures with a telephoto lens. We have the road blocked up at the beach but it isn't hard to hike your way in over the dunes or all the way along the beach. At least he is staying behind the yellow tape. I have to give him credit for that.

Doing a search like this is six of one, half a dozen of the other. I find myself getting excited as my eyes search the ground for disturbed earth or a rock with a rabbit symbol then I remember what it would mean to find something. Another body waiting to surface. We are searching for jigsaw pieces we really don't want to find. But if we find more we will have more clues.

Deborah English stops. She bends at the waist and turns over a rock. My blue eyes quickly run from the rock, up her arm, and stop to focus on the blue pants tight around her ass. In my younger days I played a game where I looked at women's behinds and tried to guess panties, thong, or bare. I know I shouldn't be looking.

My eyes flick. She's looking at me. How long has she been watching me watching her? My lips twitch. I face forward again and take a step. I can feel my skin burn. I don't want to lift my eyes.

"Found something," a voice calls out.

The line stops. I walk behind English to the second man down from her. It's nothing. An animal hole. Maybe a raccoon or a fox dug something up, but it wasn't a big enough hole to worry about and there doesn't seem to be any disturbance to the surrounding grass.

As I walk back behind English she asks, "See anything you like?" in a snap whisper.

I bite my lip. My face flushes. This time I look over and she is smiling at me. It's a warm smile showing the dimples in her cheeks. Her eyes are musical. Is this flirting or is it in my head? By this age I should know better.

I check my phone.

In total the whole group spends almost four hours walking back and forth, bending, checking, lifting, stopping, rechecking, and walking again. The mosquitoes cheer us on and the bees announce their annoyance at our passing through their yard as we trample even more grass and wild flowers. As we walk around the sights where bodies have been recovered heads drop, eyes turn away, and we move on quickly. We are tired and sweating as we finish the last sweep. Our clothes are stuck to our bodies or are stained with perspiration.

It is two more hours before LeBlanc and I park our cars behind headquarters. We sent the search and rescue volunteers on their way and searched the shoreline ourselves. English volunteered to stay and help, but I quickly said no. LeBlanc looked at me with a question on his face, then complained about how we could have used the help as we sifted through piles of driftwood as white as cleaned bone. Most of it was in French so I chose to ignore it.

"Sgt. Reid," I hear the voice at the same time I hear the distinct sound of high heels on pavement. I know who it is. I saw her at the front of the building as I pulled in. There will be no avoiding her this time. Catherine Arsenault of the Canadian Broadcasting Corporation blasts me with, "Did you find anything on Robinson's Island? Are there more bodies, Sergeant?" before she even gets to me. Her cameraman plods along behind her. Other reporters try to keep up. How she moves so fast in heels is beyond me.

"No comment."

"Are these bodies connected to something on the mainland?"

I hold up my hand to indicate I'm not answering anything.

"Is it true there's an officer here from H Division?"

"Sgt. Michaels is here helping me with the John Doe cold case - the body that was exhumed Friday." I keep my eyes on the back stairs to the building.

"I mean someone else?"

"No idea."

"The press is calling him the Bogeyman Killer. Any comment?"

I can't control the little snicker that escapes. Bogeyman? Not too creative. But if you look at names of other serial killers they were just quick "also-known-as'" to sell papers.

"What can you tell us about the identities of the victims?"

I don't smile until the door closes behind me. I'm tired of this part. I'm tired of being questioned about everything I do. Even when we do it right we get questioned.

The RCMP has had its issues in the past few years; we can't deny it. From cases mishandled, to allegations of mistreatment of female cadets, to officers being killed because they walk unprepared into situations. Every police force has its problems. The FBI had Wako and the RCMP had the Robert Pickton case. We're only human. The superheroes are in the movies.

At least Arsenault didn't bring up my past and the Playground Killer.

RCMP policy is that we say nothing to the press. We ignore them. We leave the talking for the press liaison people. Deborah English is good with the maggots. Okay, maybe I'm being harsh on them, but they know what our policy is and still they come after us hoping one of us will slip up so that they can have their headline.

As I breathe in the cool recycled air I think of those things I wanted to say to Catherine Arsenault and the others outside.

Bogeyman Killer? Why not The Slayer of Robinson's Island? If they knew about the rabbit symbol they would have called him The Black Rabbit.

I'm covered in sweat and bug bites. Obviously, I was out in the middle of nowhere. How do I know what has been going on?

Bogeyman Killer? Did you miss the class on creativity in journalism school?

Fuck off and leave me alone, bitch.

As LeBlanc opens the door to Major Crimes, I hear voices in lively conversation. Instantly, I recognize Marilyn and Eckhart talking over each other. The moment I step through the doorway everything stops. Eyes turn in my direction. Eckhart adjusts his glasses. Nothing is said.

A phone rings.

Marilyn leans back on a desk and crosses her arms over her chest. "So Reid, do you want to know the good news, bad news, even worse news, or really screwed-up news?"

I shrug my shoulders. "Lady's choice."

She nods and her auburn curls fall in front of her face. With lightning reaction, she takes an elastic off her wrist and is pulling it all back. She says, "Autopsies aren't completely done but we do know all six victims died the same way. They were raped. Probably the natural way, but also with foreign objects. Number 4's bones had two plastic kids' fast-food toys in the pelvic area. They were beaten up and strangled. The force on #5 was so bad the doctors say her spine was crushed. That's the really screwed-up news.

"The good news is that Mike Antcliffe, here from Major Crimes H Division, has helped us identify five of the six Jane Does."

"So you're who the reporters were asking about."

"Yeah, guess so. You look like you've had a rough day." From those two sentences I am not sure if I'm going to like this man. His head is shaved bald and the florescent lights glare off his scalp. Blue eyes penetrate into me and a soft smile forms inside a goatee. There's confidence in those eyes and that smile.

My lips are flat. All I say is, "Yeah."

"Sgt. McIntyre called and told me what you have. He wanted me to send what I had, but I thought it would be best to come myself. Cassie filled me in." He says Cassie's name with a smile. He quickly takes a tube of Chapstick from his pocket and rubs it over his lips.

"Just under two years ago a girl named Patricia Miller disappeared in a small town outside Halifax. She was walking along a road snacking on raspberries and just vanished. It's a busy stretch of road but nobody saw what happened and there was no trace, not even scuff marks in the dirt. I was assigned to the case and, after finding bupkiss, I started looking at missing persons across Nova Scotia. Patricia was eleven at the time she disappeared. She was thin and pretty with long dark brown hair. I looked through the old files and found another girl meeting that description who vanished a year before on Cape Breton and another eighteen months ago in Southern Nova Scotia. Same description. I checked around and found that three months after Patricia, another girl with the same description went missing in New Brunswick. I started watching for missing girls with brown hair between the ages of nine and thirteen. There were some who went missing, runaways and fighting parents mostly, but I found a total of eleven going back over four years that match." He put his hand on a briefcase beside him.

"Dr. Norton matched the dental records Mike had from the missing girls to our Jane Does." Marilyn flicks a hand at the whiteboard. There have been new additions besides the pictures from their recoveries. Almost all have names now. Did they have names to him? The Playground Killer didn't care about their names. To him they were momentary objects, playthings.

"Jane Doe #5 is Patricia Miller," Antcliffe's voice catches in his throat. I look in time to see the Chapstick go across his lips. "As I said, she was last seen eating raspberries and walking on a road she had walked hundreds of times. She was wearing cut-off shorts and a Twilight T-shirt." On the whiteboard her name is written beneath the title Jane Doe #5. On the left is a photograph of her bones covered in dirt and clay. Roots had twisted through her ribs like ivy on a trestle. On the photo to the right she smiles, her face covered in muscle, flesh, and pink skin. Dark brown bangs curl down over her forehead almost touching her long lashes. Her canines are crooked. She'll need braces in a few years.

Oh wait, she's dead.

"Jane Doe #4 was Gabbi Graystone-May. She disappeared twenty-one months ago. She was eleven. She and her mom lived in southern New Brunswick. It was first thought that her father snatched her because he had suddenly moved to Mexico for work. By the time they discovered he didn't take Gabbi, the trail was cold."

"What were the circumstances of her disappearance?" My eyes are stuck on the board. The living picture of this one shows a very happy girl standing up to her knees in the red-tinted surf of the Bay of Fundy, her arms above her head in a V. She wore a one piece bathing suit with purple and black swirls all over. She still had baby fat rolls and her breasts had not sprouted.

I wish Leigh wore suits like that. This year, she has gone for the bikinis. Her early development doesn't make me feel any better about it either. I shouldn't have to give teenage boys and grown men the evil eye for staring at my eleven-year-old daughter.

Antcliffe flips through the file. "She left school to walk two blocks to her home. Her mother didn't get home from work until a half hour later, but, as far as she knows, Gabbi never made it home. No witnesses. Jane Doe #2, Sophia Stinicki, went missing a year ago from northern New Brunswick. She told her mom she was going to see who was at the park. Nobody we talked to who was at the park or lived by the park could recall even seeing her." Compared to the other bodies there was not much left of her. She was the one the animals got to and scattered whatever was left of her. The live picture shows a pretty, happy girl. She was extremely thin like one of the Playground Killer's victims. They had had been at a park when they disappeared.

"I skipped Jane Doe #3 because she actually comes after #2. Ten months ago," Antcliffe continues, "Courtney Brouchard went missing in Shediac, Nova Scotia. She went to the park close to her home and vanished into thin air like a Las Vegas illusion."

She had the same features - long brown hair, dark eyes, thin, innocent, with signs that she would be a lovely-looking woman. But she wouldn't. All she would ever be was a pile of bones and rotted flesh found in a shallow grave. Was she a good kid? Did she ask a million questions like Leigh sometimes does? Did she roll her eyes every time her dad said something?

"Finally, Jane Doe #1 was Megan Morrow. She lived in a suburb outside Montreal. She went for a walk and - poof. A month later she's found here." She is just like the others except that in her recovery photo she is still mostly flesh. Maggots and other bugs hold their place, thanks to the camera. Just looking at the photo I can smell her rotting flesh. The foul odour lingers. Did he uncover her or was it an animal?

I hear Antcliffe smack his lips behind me. "I didn't connect your homicide with these missing girls because she was never reported missing. This is the first time any bodies have been found, not to mention the first time a girl has been taken in PEI."

"How many more do you think there are?" I almost forgot LeBlanc was here.

"Like I said, there is a total of eleven missing girls so there are still five more out there. I don't know how many there are that are not on my list. You sure you did a thorough search, eh, Reid? What is your first name?"

I turn quickly and stare at him. His head is cocked to the side. His tongue slips out to moisten his lips. His eyes stare at mine without faltering. How dare he challenge me in my house. I take a step towards him.

"The bad news," Marilyn begins louder than she needs to, "is that H Division has no concrete suspects."

Antcliffe straightens himself and pushes his shoulders back like a bird showing off his plumage, like a fighter trying to intimidate in the pre-fight interview. There's a smile inside his goatee as he says,

"As long as all of these are connected, and I believe they are, no suspects overlap. We do, however, have reports of a silver, white, grey, or light-blue minivan being seen in the areas of at least three of the five."

I look down at the floor for a moment. What was it a friend said to me with no other way to describe a moron? "Some people's children."

"And ViCLAS didn't come back with anything because we have some information that wasn't known. These are the first victims of this guy, at least first that have been found."

"Bogeyman," I look at Marilyn. Her green eyes show more fear and worry than I have seen in a long time. "The media is calling him the Bogeyman. What's the really bad news?"

"It doesn't look like the bodies are giving us much physical evidence."

"Everything's been degraded by time." Eckhart states.

"You ready for the screwed up news?" Marilyn nods toward Eckhart; the auburn curls bob down over her forehead.

"Mitochondrial DNA," he pushes his glasses up with the back of his hand.

"Eck, I've been out swatting mosquitoes all day," *and flirting with my wife's best friend*, "So you'll have to be more specific."

"Those hairs I found on Kayla Schofield's body …"

I can't stand his pause, so I throw in, "Yeah."

243

He clears his throat. "There weren't any matches on criminal databases so, like always, I had the lab run the DNA profile against the DNA of those on scene. I just like to be thorough." This is the first moment I notice he hasn't been guessing my name. "I got a match, sort of."

"Sort of?"

Eckhart looks from me to the others in the room. He adjusts his glasses with the back of his hand. "Yes, there are variable tandem repeats in the mitochondrial DNA. It's a close match to you Reid, but female. I'm pretty sure the hairs belong to your daughter."

Chapter 13

Leigh had a love/hate relationship with her long
dark hair. She loved her long hair when it co-operated
and she could make it look nice with rollers or braids.
She could wear it up, down, with a hat or bandana.
She had pictures of it flowing out behind her as she
rode Dakota. At the moment she hated it because the
brush pulled hairs out, making her wince in pain. She
often pulled all her hair back and looked at herself out
in the mirror, considering how she might look with
short hair like her mother. Then she'd drop her hair
and decide that cutting it short was something that
would have to wait until she was older. Right now she
liked that she could hide behind it.

In Leigh's eyes she wasn't naturally stunning like
her mother. Men stopped and looked at her mother.
Maybe she had too much of her father in her genes.
Hillary Reid had a thin face with defined cheek bones

and lovely eyes, all of it perfect with her short hair. Leigh Reid had a round face. Her eyebrows were bushy, she wasn't brave enough to tweeze them. Her cheeks were, "chockfull of baby fat," as her grandmother often said. It was usually followed with a rapid, and overly-hard squeeze of her cheeks. She hated having baby fat. When would the word "baby" be removed from it, and she'd just be "fat?"

She didn't want to be seen as a baby or having fat. She was growing up; she'd be a woman soon. She was already able to get pregnant and her boobs were as big, if not bigger, than her mother's. And she was only eleven. She wanted to be seen as sexy.

Lapin thought she was sexy.

He loved the pictures she emailed him. Leigh sent him photos of her wearing everyday clothes, in her bathing suit, and riding her horse. Last week she sent him one of her wearing only a bra and another completely topless with her arm across her chest. He said she was hot and beautiful and sexy. He'd never asked for a picture of her fully naked, but she thought he would want one. What would he say about her belly?

Her Dad joked and asked when her baby was due. Dad was clueless.

For a guy who caught killers he didn't have a clue about his daughter. Leigh bet he didn't even know she shaved her legs. Any time the conversation went to her becoming a woman he always left the room. He joked about how he was going to threaten any boy that came to the door to date her.

She knew Lapin was there for her. He let her talk about her problems and he showered her with kindness and loving words. He understood her.

~ * ~

He looked up as a girl's high-pitched scream squealed across the waterpark. A teenage girl shot out the end of the waterslide and slowed to a stop sending up a wave of water. Hundreds of kids ran around the waterpark in various stages of undress. This was an amusement park as well so there were other rides and places to explore, but it was the huge slides that attracted most people. The parents got to sit around sunning on the deck chairs while the kids ran up the stairs all the way to the top and came sliding down just to do it again.

His wife was asleep in the chair beside him, her head bobbing with her snoring. He probably should have woken her to tell her about her bad sunburn. It'll be up to him to rub her down with aloe vera later.

He sat where nobody else was likely to come around or look over his shoulder at what he was doing. He turned his tablet on and connected to the hotspot from his phone. The beauty of being shy when he was young (back when home computers were first introduced) was that he had plenty of time to find out how to use them. He was certain that if he continued his current use, the Internet would be his eventual downfall. No matter how well you covered your tracks, remotely erased everything, and bounced your signal around the world there was always a trail. Someone just had to dig deeply enough. He was usually careful, but he was getting sloppy. Normally he would never sit out in the open.

Dark sunglasses hid his eyes as he watched a girl exit the waterslide tube and start running toward the stairs. She didn't know enough yet to straighten her suit, leaving one cheek exposed to the wind as she ran.

A bing came through his headphone. There was e-mail waiting.

~ * ~

Leigh, satisfied with her hair, laid the brush beside the computer on the coffee table and logged onto her e-mail. In the inbox were a few e-mails from friends, some spam, an update from the Justin Bieber fan club (something about which she would never admit her participation) and an e-mail from Lapin. All it said was that he had to do something with his parents so he may not be around.

Now what?

She stretched out on the couch, head on the armrest, and absently flipped through channels on the TV. Pop music bounced around the room.

She peaked through the drapes at the empty driveway. A little kid pedaled past, weaving his tricycle on the road, no parent in sight. That was safe! She fixed the drapes so they blocked out the light and went to lock the door. Her Mom was at work. Her Dad was off with dead people or something. Both were too busy with their own lives to care about what she was doing.

Leigh pushed a function button on the computer and plopped down on the couch. Her own image popped up on the screen. She adjusted the laptop monitor until she was centered. She adjusted her body, pulled her shirt down in the front to show a line of cleavage, and tried to get comfortable. She didn't really get why men liked boobs. She asked her dad once but he pretended he didn't hear the question. Leigh held her breath and pushed the image button. The screen went black and made an old camera sound. The image came back showing a still picture of her two seconds ago. Lapin would like more pictures. She promised him more. He asked for sexy ones, but he never said naked. The question was, how far should she go? For the next photo she grabbed her collar and pulled it down while puckering her lips. When she looked at the frozen photo it was a little fuzzy, but she saw a nipple showing beside her fist, pulling down her shirt. She sent that one with the title, "Wish ya were here."

She thought she should strip down and do an all-out Titanic "naked on the couch" pose. Lapin would love that, the horny boy he was. He always said she got him excited. Just the thought of her made him that way. He said he had dreams about her.

She saw in movies what adults did. She had seen pictures. Now she was going to be in the pictures.

~ * ~

He settled back in his chair with one foot on the other knee. His wife was asleep. Both kids came down the waterslide together. This was the first year his son was tall enough to go down the slide by himself. The boy waved. His daughter just turned and walked back to the line for the slide.

His eyes lingered on her swaying hips too long.

He opened the first e-mail. There was HorseRider holding her top down with her lips pouting like a bottom-feeder fish. Why did little girls think that looked good? They had to learn. It took time and gentle coaxing, but over time he could get them to do anything. Send photos, video, locks of their hair, meet him on a road down from their house or in a park. He was running out of time though.

He opened a second e-mail. In this one HorseRider, Leigh Reid was her real name, was stretched on a couch laying on her side. She had no top on and he could tell her jeans were pushed down. Long dark hair cascaded over her shoulders. Her arm crossed her belly.

My, my, what would Daddy say?

Chapter 14

As I pull in behind Hillary's SUV, I think back to our phone conversation a half-hour ago.

She answered her cell phone, I caught the last of a sigh before she said, "Hello." It was better than the attitude I usually got from the receptionist when I called her at the bank. I was hoping she would have been too busy to answer her personal phone.

"I need you to meet me at the house. We have to talk to Leigh." I didn't give a greeting.

Another sigh. "Talk to her about what?"

"I'll tell you when you get there. How is twenty minutes?"

"Okay."

"You can leave work?"

"I'm not at work," and she hung up.

I checked my watch. It was 4:00 pm. Hillary wasn't supposed to be finished work for another hour.

~ * ~

I wait by my car as Eckhart pulls his truck to the curb in front of the house. Marilyn exits the passenger side.

This is my own home and I don't really want to be here. I'm not sure what's going to be inside or what we'll find out. I open the front door and move aside to let Marilyn and Eckhart in, but Marilyn stops in her tracks and motions me to go first. Sure, throw me in the line of fire. I didn't tell Hillary that anyone else was coming. This is not going to be fun.

The inside temperature of the house is about twenty degrees cooler than the outside. Leigh has had the air conditioning cranked up all day. Hillary's heels are discarded on the inside mat. I can hear the television playing and the dishwasher filling. Great, Hill's doing my dirty dishes. I'm sure I'll hear about it later. She probably thinks I can't take care of myself. Does that work in my favor? Frix plods out from the kitchen. She stops in front of me and looks up with sad eyes starting to milk over from cataracts which seem to say, *"please don't fight with Mom."* I rub the top of her head and run my hand down under her chin. She takes it as her sign to sniff the others.

Hillary steps into the archway leading to the kitchen. She wrings her hands in a dishtowel.

And so it begins.

252

"Marilyn, Greg, I didn't know you were coming." Hillary smiles brightly looking at the woman beside me. It disappears instantly the moment her eyes flip to me. They're quite red and her cheeks look puffy.

Marilyn pauses, probably waiting to see if I will say anything, "Sorry, Hillary. We are actually here on RCMP business."

"What's going on?" My wife's eyes dart between us.

I stand up, Frix keeps looking at me. "We need to talk to Leigh."

"You said that on the phone." She's still in her work clothes. There's a little splash of something on her blouse. Her make-up has been fixed. That for me?

I feel a paw scratch my knee and quickly crouch down to scratch the Springer behind her ears. I quietly say, "It's about the case."

Her chin goes up, arms cross over her chest. Hillary's eyes stare at me with fire and hate and worry all in one package.

Without making any sound, Leigh looks at us from the couch. Her laptop is in front of her on the coffee table surrounded by the destruction of several *Kool-Aid Jammers*, a pudding cup, and an empty Swanson's frozen dinner. I can tell that in her mind she's going over everything she has recently done and what anyone could have said or reported.

"We have to talk to you about something. Can you turn off the TV?"

"But I'm watching something."

"Leigh, I'm not asking you."

Her big eyes roll in their sockets as she snatches the remote control, pushes the mute button, and drops it back on the table. She falls back on the couch, arms crossed. A gush of air pushes through her nostrils, her lips purse, and her eyes look off to the base of the potted plant to my left. This is her classic, "*I didn't do whatever you're going to accuse me of*," face. She's prepared to deny and argue over anything ask. After a few silent moments her dark eyes turn to us. Her shoulders go up, "What?"

The tension in the room is like a giant spider web. You can see it strung among us in thick sticky strands. No matter how we move, we're going to get stuck in the threads. The more we struggle, the more we get twisted up and stuck. Then, all we'll have to do is wait for death.

Frix gives up and waddles off to her end of the couch.

Marilyn pushes her hair back. "Maybe we should all sit down."

Eckhart puts his kitbag on the floor and kneels behind, "Maybe I should get my sample so I can get it rushed to Halifax?"

Frix flops off the couch and comes to investigate.

"Leigh, I need a couple of your hairs."

"No way." She lifts her foot, so that her knee protects her, and pushes herself into the back of the couch.

Like he always does, Eckhart pushes his glasses up before dawning latex gloves. "It only hurts for a second."

"What's going on, Reid?" Hillary demands.

My mouth is dry. I know I should say something, but my world right now is surrounded in flame.

"Leigh," Marilyn sidesteps around me, "Did you know a girl named Kayla Schofield?"

"Who's that?" Her face twists with a curled lip and raised eyebrow. My daughter, the pissed-off Elvis impersonator.

"That's the girl who was found at Brackley Beach. You ever hear her name? How about this picture? Do you recognize her?" Marilyn takes a photograph from a folder in her hand and crosses to my daughter. Hillary shimmies onto the couch beside Leigh. Marilyn says, "Look closely. Do you recognize her at all?"

"No. Should I?"

"Why would Leigh know anything about this girl?" Hillary takes the photograph from Marilyn and holds it close to her face. "This was her? She was pretty."

"Our crime scene team found evidence that connects Leigh to Kayla Schofield."

"Evidence?"

"We found a few hairs which the lab discovered are similar to Reid's DNA. The only person with those hairs would be Reid's daughter. Just to make sure, Greg is going to take a hair sample and see if it is indeed a match."

"Wait, her hair was where?" Hillary hands back the photograph.

I finally look up and say, "They were on the body, Hill. They didn't fall off of me so they had to get there somehow."

"I didn't do anything. I never saw that girl before."

I catch Eckhart looking at me. "Leigh, let Greg take the sample."

"No. You never believe anything I say." The tears start flowing down her face.

"Leigh, Corporal Eckhart is going to take a hair sample one way or another. As your father I'm giving him permission." I give him a wave with my hand.

Leigh stares at me the whole time. As the technician pulls out a couple of hairs from the root she lets out a loud, over-the-top, scream with a throat growl behind it. More tears fall. In a mumble she says, "I wish you weren't my father." I hear it clearly.

Eckhart puts the hair in a vial. "I'm going to rush this out. Reid, you'll give Marilyn a ride back?" I nod in reply then he's gone.

The air seems thick, it has a taste to it. Frix climbs back on the couch but keeps her eyes on us, unsure whose side she should be on. The only sounds are Leigh's sobs and the ticking of the grandfather clock.

"What the hell are you two saying?" Mama bear is ready to strike.

I don't know what I'm supposed to be right now. Am I the caring father, angry husband, or cop looking for answers? I'm all of them, I guess. Angry husband can wait. I'm not officially investigating this homicide, I suppose all that is left is to be a father. I say, "Please, Hillary, Leigh, this is important."

Hillary stares at me for what seems like a long time. She's obviously been crying since we talked this morning but I have to wonder whether it's about the break-up of our marriage or something else. She wasn't at work when I called her. Where was she? When did she leave work? Who was she with? She tells Leigh to turn off the television and suggests we sit in the dining room before spinning around.

Leigh follows her first. The silent music video plays on.

Frix re-adjusts on the couch.

By the looks of the kitchen Hillary has been here for a while. Maybe she was here when I called. I look back over my shoulder, but her bags aren't here. When I left this morning, the sink was overflowing; now the dishwasher hums and the stainless steel shines. The mess I'd left on the dining table is now in somewhat organized piles with bills needing to be paid on top. I watch my wife pour water from the water cooler into a kettle and plug it in. She takes down three mugs and busies herself with putting a tea bag in each mug and getting sugar and milk ready. As soon as she is satisfied, she leans back against the kitchen counter; a hand goes back through her short black hair. She has had her nails done. Funny how even when other things in your life are going to hell some people can still find joy in the simple things. When did she have time to do that? Was it already done before we talked?

Leigh flops into a chair on the far side of the table in the open dining room. Her fingers tap the surface, repeating the beat in her head. Her hair has been brushed removing all the tangles that were normally there. Her eyes are dark from mascara and her lips shine. One button on her shirt is in the wrong place.

Marilyn sits in a chair beside her. She takes her notebook out and flips it open to a new page. I don't know where to go. I want to help Hillary, but don't know if she would accept that. At some point I will have to start being a man. I lean against the wall.

The moment the hot water boils Hillary pours it into the mugs and brings them to the table. She says, "So who's going to tell me what's going on?" She mixes the sugar and milk into my tea without my saying a word.

Marilyn stirs sugar into her mug. "Just like we said, on Saturday morning the body of Kayla Schofield was found in the showers at Brackley. Corporal Eckhart found hairs on the body. They were tested and it was found that the DNA is similar to Reid's, but with female attributes. Therefore it's most likely his daughter. Unless Reid has another daughter, the hairs must have come from Leigh." Normally we would never tell anyone this much information, but family is different. Marilyn gazes at my daughter. "We need to know how those hairs got on her body. We need to know if you ran into Kayla somewhere. Did you give away any clothes lately? Because the clothes she was found in were not hers?"

"No. I never met her, okay."

"When was the last time you were in Cavendish?"

Leigh shrugs her shoulder. When she looks at Marilyn and sees that is not going to be a good enough answer she says, "I don't know."

Keeping her eyes on Leigh Marilyn asks, "You don't know when you last went to Cavendish?"

Shrug.

Hillary says, "When did you go with Sarah and her mom?"

"I don't know. Like, two weeks ago. I didn't see that girl." She yells the last sentence.

Marilyn maintains her cool. "What about Brackley?"

"I don't know. Like, a while. I don't know, it's been like a few weeks, like, yeah." She puts her head down. Fingernails dig at a scratch on the tabletop.

I stare at my daughter for a while. She doesn't get it. "Leigh," my voice rises, "this is serious! Right now you're our only suspect in the deaths of seven girls."

"I didn't …"

"We know you didn't do it, but how the hell did your hairs get there? Who has access to your hair?" I put my mug down. The light brown liquid splashes over the rim.

"I don't know. Maybe it was …"

"What?"

"I don't know." She lowers her elbows and pulls her hair down over her face.

"Leigh this is important." I hate repeating myself. "Maybe it was what?"

"Reid watch your tone with her," Hillary says and turns her back to the rest of us.

I stare at the back of her head. I bite down on my tongue threatening to break through the flesh. "Excuse me? Hillary, something's going on here that I need to know about. A girl's been killed. A lot of girls have been killed."

"What a surprise." She throws her arms out to the sides. "Your thoughts go to dead people. Dead girls instead of your own little girl."

"This isn't about me."

She turns around. Her eyes are moist with tears. I don't know how this conversation became about us, but it did.

Leigh pushes her chair away from the table and stands.

"Leigh, sit down."

"No."

My hand hits the table making it shake. "I need to know what you did with your hair."

"I didn't do anything!" Spit flies from her lips. Her hands are clenched in tight fists making her knuckles white. "You two just care about your own lives, so you won't believe anything I say. I don't know how my hair got there. I never saw the girl so just leave me the hell alone."

"Watch your mouth, little girl."

"Don't fucking call me that!"

"Excuse me?" I feel the fire in my eyes and the tension in my jaw. If I had reacted like that when I was eleven in front of my mother, I don't know what my father would have done. I once called him an asshole and he didn't talk to me for three weeks, I think because he didn't know what to do. I don't have a clue either. Hillary's fingers circle my arm. I hear the words, "Choose your battles," whispered in my ear.

Hillary says, "Leigh, go to your room."

The girl thumps off, her feet hitting the floor hard with each step back through the house and up the stairs. Nobody speaks until her door slams.

"Once those lab results are back I'll need to have a more in depth talk with her." Marilyn stands next to the table. "Thank you for the tea, Hillary. Reid, are you going to drive me back to headquarters?" I nod and she adds, "I'll wait outside." Her way of telling me to talk to my wife.

Hillary takes two trips from table to kitchen sink with the leftovers from our tea. I want to put my hand on her back and soothe her, tell her this will all be sorted out soon enough. I think maybe I should just take her in my arms and hold her until we know what is going on. Maybe then things would change. Change how? Change back? Back to us fighting every few days about how all of my time is spent on a case, or that I'm not giving her enough love and attention or to the part where we don't even talk to

261

each other because we can't think of anything to say? Instead, I lean back until my shoulders touch the wall and I watch her bare feet on the floor.

"So," she begins eventually. Enough time has passed that the dishwasher is on the dry cycle. Steam escapes through a vent. "Any thoughts on anything else?"

I look up. Our eyes lock, but not in the love-at-first-sight way. All I say is, "About what?" and hope she says something. I really don't know what more can be said.

"Reid."

I walk halfway to the front door before turning back.

She leans against the archway, but this time she won't look at me. She says, "I'm going to spend the night here so maybe you should sleep somewhere else. Okay?"

I look away. Sleep somewhere else? I've just been told I can't return to my own home. What the hell is that about? I blurt out, "Where the fuck am I supposed to go?" without thinking.

Hillary says, "I don't really care. My daughter needs me tonight and I think right now it would be a whole lot more comfortable if you stayed at a hotel."

"That hasn't bothered you the past few nights has it? Your boyfriend's needs have been more important." Give me a suspect and I can think about what I am saying. I take my time. I cut out what I know will get a bad response. Put me in a room with

262

my wife and I say the stupidest things without a single thought.

She stares at me blankly. "I already told you Mitch and I have just been talking. Nothing's happened. You and Marilyn have done more."

"We kissed, Hill. That was a while ago. It was different."

"It's always going to be the same, Reid. Your work life is always a different world. Well, maybe I need something different. Something or someone different?"

"You're my wife," is all I say.

"I haven't been your wife for a long time, Reid. Your work is your wife."

"That's bullshit."

"No it isn't and you know it. Mitch listens to me and cares about what I say. He answers when I call him. Feelings started to grow, so I had some thinking to do."

Mitch? Mitch who? "Who's Mitch? Who is he?"

Her arms tighten around her. "Mitch English, Deborah's ex-husband. He listens to me. We just sit with a cup of coffee and talk. You never want to talk. He tells me about his day. You can't do that. I can't keep living like that." Tears smear mascara down her cheeks. She looks older now, like us fighting has taken the youth out of her. I'm doing this to her. Before I went into the RCMP I knew I wanted to be in Major Crimes. I can only apologize so much for doing what I've always wanted to do. After a while it isn't enough.

I leave my house.

~ * ~

"Know what you're going to order?" Marilyn takes a sip of her wine. We had gone back to Headquarters so that she could get her car. As far as the case went, she was running out of options. At HQ I had nothing to do but sit at my desk, staring at the framed photos on the corner. My family. As soon as Marilyn was finished she grabbed me by the shoulder and pulled me toward the door. "No matter how serious the case, we have to eat. Let's go to Wylie's restaurant."

I look at the one page menu, but my eyes can't seem to focus. We sit at the bar in her boyfriend's restaurant. As we left HQ, I just went along with her without any protest. What else am I to do?

"Reid, you have to get out of this funk. You know our lives don't always mix well with other people's expectations. We do our job for more than just them." She puts the wine glass to her lips again. She has covered them in a pale pink lipstick. Before we left headquarters she also darkened her lashes and changed her clothes to tight black slacks, a bright blue blouse, and her spike-heeled black boots. Before she sips her wine she says, "Look at what happened to me."

"Marilyn." A thin waitress with a pretty face is suddenly across the bar from us. The servers here wear black pants with white shirts and thin black ties. Classy but not over-the-top, so that the regular person can still feel comfortable. She smiles and says, "Chef Wylie said to tell you that he will make something special for you and your friend and that it's on the house." She gives me a bright smile.

Less than two minutes later small square plates are arranged in front of us with two "bites" on each. One plate contains a few thin slices of Kim Dormaar's Medallion smoked salmon on a house-made cracker with lemon-dill cream cheese, capers, and house-pickled vegetables. Most restaurants in PEI use Kim Dormaar's smoked salmon. The other bite is a halibut ceviche with tomato water and pickled sliced red onion. The ceviche is very fresh and awakens my mouth. The salmon is very classic. Our second course is a salad of micro-greens from local farmers, fresh fruit, spiced candied pecans, and a honey-lime vinaigrette. We are told that the next course will be clams with local forest-forged chanterelle mushrooms, fresh horseradish, and yogurt. Fourth course is going to be whiskey-braised lamb shank with a bunch of local vegetables and PEI potatoes, of course.

We eat quietly. The food is full of flavor, freshness, and excitement. The best restaurants on the island pride themselves on featuring local ingredients. Marilyn samples different wines. I start with a Pepsi then move to rye and cola before the first drink is finished. The salad is bright and vibrant with the fine mix of honey and lime juice. The candied pecans - I would buy bushels of them. The clam dish is interesting, but not my favorite. I bet the mushrooms and clams were delivered to the restaurant this morning though. It was cooked with the skin still on it, so it is crispy. The lamb falls off the bone. With it are the creamiest mashed potatoes. By the time that plate is finished I am satisfied. It has been a while since I ate this well.

While eating in silence I take the time to think about everything happening in my life. The wife - Hillary and I have not really talked for a long time, until today. Even in therapy we didn't really get down to it. She hates that I have a job I can't talk about, one that takes up more time than she receives. She needs someone she can talk to and share with. But her best friend's former husband? Does English know? Their daughter - something is going on there. Does she have something to do with these other girls, with Kayla? Was she there? Did she lie to us? The dead girls - it's not my case so I should step aside. I'm haunted by other girls. The last thing I need is more young faces floating above me at night when my eyes are closed. John Doe - Cassie is doing all the work. I can't do much until she is done, but I should do something.

Marilyn taps my arm and nods to a man walking our way. He's under six feet and looks healthy in a white chef's coat with strong arms and a confident stride. Blond hair is spiked back on his head, his face is smooth, and he smiles with pearly-white teeth. He places a round dish in front of each of us. Both he and Marilyn lean inward and press their lips together.

"You must be Reid. Wylie Renier." He reaches his hand out. His shake is strong, his fingers squeeze my palm.

"Thank you for dinner. Best food I've had in a long time." My body is relaxed and warm from the inside out. I can feel the rye in my system doing its thing. I turn to the woman beside me. Her face is glowing. She is happy and I don't think it has to do with the wine.

Renier's smile builds. "I hope you left room for dessert. I brought you some crème brule." The smell of melted sugar and vanilla is strong in the air.

His eyes turn to Marilyn, "You look great."

I think about jokingly asking how I look, but I know. Everything on my body feels like it is saggy from my skin to my eyes to my clothes. What am I going to do for clothes tomorrow?

"So how are things? Where's your wife tonight?" Renier touches my arm lightly.

I pick up the teaspoon a server has placed in front of me and dance it around in my hand before taking a small scoop of brule and shoving it in my mouth. The caramelized sugar, silky texture, and taste of vanilla bean make me forget everything else for a moment.

Marilyn places a playful hand around her mouth and half whispers, "He just got the boot."

I look at her sharply. She mouths the word, what.

I look back to Renier. "We have some issues to work out."

"That sucks, man." I notice a tattoo down the underside of his left forearm that reads, BE CREATIVE. "We haven't had any issues yet have we, Hon?"

Marilyn swallows a spoonful of crème brule and says, "That's because the only time we see each other is to have sex and sleep." Both smile and stare at each other with loving eyes.

"I picked the wrong time to come out here." Behind Renier stands another man wearing a white coat. This one is a little younger. "Schedules done, Chef."

"No worries. Reid, Zeke. Zeke here is my sous chef for the summer, but he's going off to work with Chef Spencer Alcrest after that."

Zeke gives a half salute then disappears the way he came. Everything seems to move efficiently here. People know their jobs. They do their jobs, collect their paychecks, and go home. There aren't any dead bodies being found, or dug up here. I wonder what types of surprises happen in a restaurant.

Renier circles to the other side of the bar and pours himself a beer from the tap. It's one of the brews from the Gahan House on Sydney. He gives his thanks to a few leaving customers before turning his attention back to us. He folds his arms on the bar and leans in. "So, what's happening with the dead girls?" His blue eyes bounce back and forth from Marilyn to me.

I look at Marilyn and again she says, "What? You know I never follow the rules." Maybe that is also why her new relationship is working. Her last man hit her and drove her down. With this one she is making her own rules.

"I'm sorry," Renier flips his hand. "It's all my fault. I love mysteries. In my spare time, well I haven't had any since March, but I like to read Indie authors like Cheryl Bradshaw, Jill Edmondson, Lorne Oliver. You ever hear of them?" I shake my head. "Well, they're good. So, what have you found out?" He's too excited for me. I slip from my chair and find the men's washroom.

The moment I return I hear Renier say, "What about the Internet? You say there's no connection between these girls so what about websites, or chat rooms? You always hear about pedophiles stalking kids online, right?"

I check my phone.

"I should leave." My head is starting to spin. "I have to find a place to stay."

Marilyn grabs my arm. "Why don't you stay at my place? I'll stay with Wylie." Her big eyes look at the chef.

"Yeah that would be great. I don't have to go to the fish market tomorrow so it'll be perfect. Why don't I call you a cab? It's on me." Is he really this nice or is he sucking up to me like he would to her father? Maybe it's because I carry a gun.

"Here are my house keys. You know where I live." The thought in my head is, "I should know since we almost had sex there." I wonder if Wonder Man Wylie Coyote knows that tidbit of information. How far does Marilyn's new openness go? She kept the abusive boyfriend a secret for a long time.

Marilyn is going to have sex tonight and I get to sleep in a bed that smells like her. I can't remember what it felt like with Marilyn's tongue in my mouth fighting with mine or what her lips tasted like and we have agreed nothing like that would ever happen, but it doesn't mean I'm not going to think about it. Hillary and I don't have sex much anymore. It is probably more my fault than hers. I know it is. She complains about it. Too repetitive, too boring, too short. I compensate with other things, but it isn't enough. It's stupid that I think about the crazy wild kind of sex but when it comes to my wife, I'm bored. I guess that should be - *I WAS bored, it WASN'T enough*, and she complained. She's off having wild sex with Mitch English. I wonder if they have done it yet. Maybe she's lying to me about that too. I wonder if they are doing it now in my bed.

The address I give the taxi driver isn't Marilyn's.

~ * ~

"Reid, what are you doing here?"
I don't know.

"Did you know your husband is screwing my wife?"

The look of confusion on Deborah English's face turns to one of sadness. She opens the door a little wider, one hand still on the door and one on the frame.

I lean forward and then back. I say, "And right now they are having sex in my bed."

I can hear a television inside her house. English lives about thirty minutes outside of Charlottetown in the rolling hills and trees that make up much of PEI. I'm glad Chef Wylie is picking up the taxi bill. When we pulled in, I saw that just one light was on, on the main floor. The blue light of a television made the window glow. Now here in front of her I feel stupid. What am I doing here?

I don't know what I was picturing in my head while coming out here, but it isn't what this is. Deborah's wearing blue jeans, a Charlottetown Rockets hockey jersey and is barefoot. She's not wearing make-up. Her hair is flat, but has the shampoo scent of just being washed - melons I think. Her head cocks to the side. There is a dimple in her cheek. She says, "I don't think they've gotten to that yet, but they are headed that way. And Mitch has our son tonight so I doubt he's in your bed."

My shoulders slouch. My arms and head feel heavy. I want to drop to her wood deck and curl into a ball in front of her door and just let the mosquitoes feast on me.

She rises on her toes to look around me. I stare down at her feet. "Have you been drinking? Come on in and I'll get you some coffee." She smiles and a dimple appears in each cheek. "How did you get here?"

I'm ready to give in. I think on the ride out here I was hoping she would just grab me and screw me right there in her doorway. I don't remember what the plan was. Now every thought feels silly. I follow her through the house watching her feet pad the hardwood floor. I'm a grown-up. At what point do we stop acting like high schoolers?

"A cab. So how long have you known?" I lean against the wall and watch her make a cup of coffee in her Keurig machine. A large tabby cat comes from nowhere and starts weaving in and out of her legs. This is the second time today I've watched a woman make a hot drink. Earlier, it was because Hillary had to do something to keep her mind set.

Deborah waits until she hands me the mug and makes her own. She scrunches her face and says, "Since the beginning. Both Hillary and Mitch told me. I guess he went to the bank to do some business and asked her if she wanted to grab a coffee. It was innocent at first, Reid. Neither one of them wanted anything, but I guess Mitch started finding reasons to see her. Hillary wanted to tell you herself, so I promised not to say anything."

But you gave me hints.

"Is that why you flirted with me today?" I follow her to the living room.

"Who says I was flirting with you? And you flirted with me too."

"I can admit to that. I'm just curious if you flirted with me because of them."

She curls one foot under her as she sits on the end of the couch. Her toes poke out behind her leg. The tips of the nails are white. When I was younger I had a thing for bare feet. She presses mute on the remote. "Maybe some of it. I tell them I'm fine with their, whatever it is, but I don't know if I am. Part of me enjoyed you looking at me." She sips at her coffee. Blue eyes look at me through the steam. One of her gull wing brows goes up at a strong angle.

I sit at the other end of the small couch, but on the edge. I place the coffee cup down on her oval table, keeping my fingertips touching it. "Well I enjoyed looking."

"Are you blushing?" Her fingers pinch my side. "That's so cute. Don't worry though. I'm not putting the moves on a married man."

I sip at my coffee. I don't want to look up at her. I am blushing. My face is burning.

"Look, Mitch and I got divorced because he wanted more of me than I was willing to give to him. Hillary wants more of you than you can give her, or what you both want has just changed. The two of them seem to want the same things. I don't believe marriage is forever. I'm happier now than I was when I was married. I think the main reason we got married was because that's what people were supposed to do."

The thoughts are back in my head. When I was a teenager, any time a relationship didn't go the way I wanted it to, I went looking for something else right away. Many men do that, I guess. They need that warm body to make them feel better. Do they actually feel better? Would I actually feel better? Maybe for a moment. Then tomorrow I will feel ashamed and guilty. But am I even really looking for that? I want to talk, I want to flirt, I want to imagine, but I don't know if I want more. Of course, I don't know if I would stop myself either.

"I should probably go home."

You don't have a car, Reid. Are you going to call another cab? "Why don't you sleep here tonight on the couch. I promise I won't take advantage of you." Her hand grazes my knee. "I'll get you some blankets."

As she walks away, I lean back and watch her curves. I don't think I would mind being taken advantage of by her. I close my eyes and welcome sleep.

Chapter 15

There was screaming.

Screaming from the dark shadows.

A woman screaming from somewhere. Or was it a girl?

Who was screaming? Hillary? Marilyn? Leigh?

I had to stop them. I had to save them. One of them was being tortured. Killed.

Leigh.

"Reid."

My eyes open. *Where am I?* Water drips on my shoulder.

"You okay? You were dreaming." Deborah. She stands over me, water drips from her damp hair. One hand holds a towel to her chest. "You were screaming."

"I was?" I look around the room. This is Deb's living room. I came here last night and I was drinking. There's a Smurf blanket covering me.

"What were you dreaming about?"

Screaming.

"I don't know," I say. My eyes travel up her bare legs to the fluffy towel barely covering her naked body. *Dream? What dream?* Something stirs. "What time is it?"

"Almost 6:30. Did you want to take a shower?"

I can barely recall how I got here. "I'll shower at headquarters. I don't have a car, do I? Can I get a ride?"

She smiles at me and leaves the room. I can't help but watch her (the towel sashays back and forth, ready to drop at any second) until her body disappears around the corner.

~ * ~

"I made good progress yesterday." Cassie says the moment she is in my passenger seat.

Antcliffe climbs in the back. "You didn't get me coffee?"

Two cups of Tim Horton's coffee sit in the holders between the two front seats. "Didn't realize I was picking you up too." After Deb dropped me off I quickly showered in the headquarters gym. I had to put the clothes I was wearing last night back on. They smell a little like booze and sweat.

"No point wasting the tax-payers' money on two hotel rooms, right?" Antcliffe taps my shoulder. In the rear-view mirror I see him gaze at Cassie with a genuine smile across his lips.

"So you made progress?" I pull out onto University Avenue.

"Yes. I would have made more progress if I was in my own workspace and all the autopsies weren't going on. I get distracted easily." She glances over her shoulder.

"Are you two a couple?"

"Engaged," Cassie says without a beat. In the rear-view mirror I see Sgt. Michael Antcliffe with a giant smile on his face. Out comes the Chapstick.

"I have to ask, what's with the lip balm all the time?"

"Two parts nervous habit, one part quit smoking." He gives a toothy smile.

Charlottetown is like any big city first thing in the morning. Everyone has to get in to work at the exact same time, many of them coming from outside the city. University Ave., St. Peter's Rd., Brackley Point Rd., the Hillsborough Bridge and the Perimeter Highway get clogged with people trying to get where they need to go. And of course, where they need to go is much more important than where the person in the next car has to go. I pull in behind a truck pulling a horse-trailer. The animal's tail swishes side-to-side over the back gate. If Leigh we here she would be all excited, hoping to see what kind of horse it was. Everyone snails along. The city is awake.

"Are you two going to stick around for the music festival?" The horse-trailer moves into the turning lane and I push on the gas pedal to take its position.

"Not me. I'll be done what I can do here by tomorrow, maybe even today. The preliminary sculpture should be done and then it's details. I should be able to give you something to work with. I'll have to do more detail work back home with my own equipment." Cassie watches the cars go by. She yawns and continues. "The depth markers are all on the skull. I now have to start with modeling clay." The way she looks at me, and with her short hair, I feel like I'm hearing about a high school student's science project. "Much of the reconstruction from here on is based on artist's perspective. You try to be impartial, but your experiences and prejudices still play a huge part."

"Your perspective's been pretty good so far." Antcliffe announces from the back.

The past reconstructions Cassie has completed have helped greatly in identifying the victims with no names or faces. The last one had been a body found in a fire. The family recognized the face Cassie had built the moment they saw it was printed in the paper asking the public for help to identifying the man. Her *artist's perspective* had been right on. Even the hair style she gave the man, matched photographs of the real person.

The car stereo shuts off. I hold my breath. My Blackberry is synced through Bluetooth to the car so when I'm in there I don't have to use my hands to answer phone calls. The ringing comes through the speakers. The dashboard display says it's Hillary.

My thumb pushes the button on the steering wheel to answer it. "Hey."

Has she talked to Deborah? Did her best friend tell her I got a morning chubby while she stood in front of me in a towel?

"Leigh's staying home," her voice comes through the stereo speakers.

"Okay?"

"I told her to call you if she goes anywhere with her friends. She's pretty upset though. She thinks you were calling her a serial killer."

My eyes flip to the rear-view mirror. "I wasn't saying that."

"I know." There's a long pause. "Where did you go last night?"

I move into the turning lane to the hospital. I bite my tongue for a moment trying to think of what to say. I'm not sure whether to hurt her or be kind. "A friend's," I say. "Look, Hill, I have someone in the car. I have to go." I wait a second before pushing the button to end the call. Instantly the phone starts ringing again as if it were waiting to pounce.

"Hi, Marilyn."

"Is Antcliffe with you?" No greeting whatsoever. I tell her he can hear her. "I want you both in MCU ASAP." She says it, "eh-sap."

"Give us fifteen." I turn the phone off. "I guess you're on your own, Cassie."

~ * ~

As I pull into HQ the reporters are swarming. There are more of them now. This morning I had Deb drop me off across the street in front of the Indigo Bookstore and then I walked across. They didn't expect that.

"Sgt. Reid, are you prepared to answer questions?"

"No. You're trespassing." I can barely get out of the car before Catherine Arsenault is in my face. The other piranhas seem willing to let her get the first taste of blood then they'll be on me.

"Are you any closer to catching *The Bogeyman*?"

"Did you come up with that name?"

"Any suspects?"

Red fingernails holding a microphone appear closer to my face than I would like. Catherine Arsenault steps directly in front of me. She's wearing a red blouse and a matching skirt. A long gold chain forces the eyes down from her neck to between her breasts. In another lifetime and at a younger age I would have watched her on the news and got hard thinking she was a world-class MILF (Mother-I'd-Like-to-Fuck) but this is not that lifetime.

She looks at Antcliffe and takes another step.

I plow through the space between her and my car. My shoulder twitches, hitting the reporter hard in her own shoulder. A noise escapes her throat. Something hits my temple with the heat of fire in the corner of my eyes. I turn fast and, almost in slow motion, watch Catherine Arsenault spin on one of her heels. The other foot slips on loose gravel. The microphone flies into the air. Her cameraman moves forward with one awkward hand to try and catch her while the other hangs onto the expensive camera. She bounces off the pavement on her backside and we are back in real time. Her hair flies around her head. The microphone thumps off the hood of my car and rolls off the far side in front of Antcliffe.

She flips her head and her hair is back in place. Her eyes shoot fire at me. "Nice, Reid."

Part of me wants to help her to her feet. "Stay in the front like you're supposed to," I say as I step over her leg and head to the doors into HQ.

Antcliffe matches me step-for-step. From the corner of my eye I can tell he's trying to keep his laughter inside.

"Shut up."

"I'm not making a sound," he pleads.

"Yeah, right."

"How long till the shit hits the fan?" He moistens his lips.

As I open the door for him I look back towards my car. Catherine Arsenault is on her phone. Her eyes still burn in my direction.

"Did you know you're bleeding?" Susan Daly asks, without stopping her fingers from typing.

My hand goes to my temple and comes away with red stickiness on my fingertips. It isn't enough to run down my face, but enough to sting. "What hit me?" I ask Antcliffe.

Susan hands me some tissues from a lime green box and gets back to typing, never missing a beat.

"I don't know if it was the microphone or her hand."

"She hit me?"

"Not on purpose. You sent her ass-over-teakettle, man."

"Are you guys ready?" Marilyn stands by the whiteboards with her hands on her hips, toe tapping. Today she is dressed in black and white. Very FBI. "What happened to you?"

"Nothing." I shake my head.

All five members of the Major Crimes Unit are here. We can see and hear from our desks, but move in closer and lean against them instead. Longfellow finds a chair. Antcliffe joins us, standing firm with his arms crossed. Coffee cups are forgotten. Susan does her best to answer phone calls so we aren't interrupted.

I hear McIntyre come from his office and stand behind us.

Marilyn clears her throat. "We have to start narrowing things down. Right now this guy's playing us. All of our victims are from off island; one from Quebec, one from BC visiting the island, four from the two Atlantic provinces, and one unknown. New Brunswick and Nova Scotia are checking missing persons, but there isn't much to go on."

"I know every missing girl for the past few years in both provinces." This is the first time I've seen Antcliffe look so stern. Another obsessed police officer? *My people.* He continues, "If the dental records I have don't match, then they won't be there. I'd suggest calling Maine and Quebec, then branch further out."

"Good, you make the calls and talk to an officer, no messages. So, we know this guy can travel. Mike says he's had similar disappearances for years and our bodies are within the last couple of years, so he moves undetected. ViCLAS doesn't have any other victomology like this, no rabbit branding or anything, so the victims are usually well-hidden. He snatched a girl in southern Quebec and buried her here. How? Why? That's a long way to travel with her."

"Perhaps he's home grown, from the island." LeBlanc states what we are all thinking. "He did not take a girl from here before. Maybe this is to keep attention away from *the island*."

"Why dump them here then? Doesn't that move suspicion on the island?"

"He could grab them, never planning to kill them at all; then when he gets home, he's so full of guilt that he has to get rid of them." Longfellow uses his hands to talk.

"Guilt would explain putting them in summer dresses." Antcliffe moistens his lips.

"So guilty he jams fast food toys in 'em and brands 'em." We can all hear the anger in Dispirito's voice.

"Guys," Marilyn raises her voice, "let's not get out of control. "The kids' toys. Does he take the girls to a restaurant? This happened to only one of them, so was it just something he had with him?"

Longfellow snorts. "You'd have to be pretty psycho to have your own kids and do this to other kids."

"BTK killer in the States had kids. He killed ten women over seventeen years." Dispirito says.

"My point exactly." Longfellow got up from the chair.

Marilyn writes the word *kids* on the whiteboard with a question mark after it. "So possibly a family man. We can definitely say he shows anger, but is it toward girls or women? All the girls have long dark hair, brown eyes, and are pretty. This means something to him. We don't really have any answers yet, so I want all of us to find some answers today. Longfellow has a list of vans he saw on the video tapes so he's going to review that. Find out who owns the vehicles and have an officer in the area talk to them. Call the FBI too; see if they can enlighten us.

Antcliffe, you're going to call the other places about missing persons. Then I want you to call the investigators of all the missing girls. See if there's some connection. Ask about Internet usage, did anyone see strangers around the time of the disappearances, any strange phone calls."

"I know a couple of the girls went to the same chat room, Chatter's, I think that was the name of it." Antcliffe makes a quick notation on his notepad.

"Reid, I want you to talk to the Schofields. I think we can safely say they're not suspects; but maybe now that things have settled, they might remember something. Eckhart says we should have the results on the hair samples this afternoon. If they come back positive, I want you to bring your daughter in and wait for me. Dispirito and I are going out to Bonaventure Campgrounds to re-canvas everyone. Let's get some answers before we get more bodies."

Go team, go. Everyone scatters in their own direction to get to work.

I down the last of my cold coffee.

"Reid, my office." McIntyre spins and walks into his office. He holds the door waiting for me. As I enter he says, "Sit," and slams the door shut behind me.

"Wayne, I ..."

"Don't talk Reid."

Slowly I slip into the chair in front of his desk. My shoulders slouch forward. I keep my eyes on the floor. I'm suddenly back in Principal Bailey's office after being caught throwing mud with Matthew Gertz. I'm guessing Catherine Arsenault's pretty red fingers did some walking.

McIntyre walks to his side of the big desk and pushes his chair out of the way. "What the hell did you think you were doing?" Spittle flies from his mouth. He pulls his chair back and sits. "You want to tell me what happened to your head?"

"Cut myself shaving," I say this as if I'm some cocky smartass TV cop. At least I know where Leigh gets her mouth.

"Bullshit!" I can feel the force of his voice from across the desk. I'm pretty sure a window rattled. "Do you want to tell me why the CO's getting calls from lawyers threatening to press charges against the whole division? Why he's threatening me?"

Her fingers did do some walking. I'm guessing the phone chain went from Arsenault to her boss, her boss to the lawyers, a hundred dollar phone call from the lawyer to the Commanding Officer, then to McIntyre leading us to this very moment. I really do hope I bruised her ass. Now there's a whole line of people looking for some sort of satisfaction and I'm probably the one to get screwed.

"They shouldn't have been around the back."

"You knocked her on her ass. Catherine Arsenault. You know she's high profile. You made her high profile. Don't you think the RCMP has enough bad press? We don't need members looking for it."

"I wasn't looking for anything. She got in my space. It was an accident."

McIntyre takes a deep breath. His office is the only closed office in Major Crimes and it's the cleanest area in the unit. His desk has a perfectly-organized "in and out" system with his laptop on one side and pictures of his kids beside that. Hanging on the wall is a photo of him and his wife on their wedding day. The tops of his filing cabinets have piles of papers and books that also look organized. I don't know if McIntyre or Susan should get the credit, but I do know I could learn a thing or two. My desk is a mess. Even the smell in the boss's office is good.

I can't handle the quiet. "I'm the one who almost lost an eye," I say.

He remains silent and continues to stare at me. I don't know if this is over, but I don't want to risk getting up to leave and have him blow up again. "You have to make a public apology," McIntyre says after a couple of minutes.

"What?" It's been a long time since my voice has gone that high.

"You have to make a public apology to Ms. Arsenault."

"No fucking way."

"CO's orders. Or you'll be suspended."

"They had me boxed in. I had to get inside. I'm not even on the frigging case."

"Reid, you don't have a choice. Do you know how lucky you are that she wasn't doing a live report?

287

Don't be stupid. Go out there on your way to interview the family and, in front of her reporter buddies, tell her you're sorry, then stay away from her."

I'm in the wrong profession to be upset when I'm being told what to do. Some people in this job hate being given orders. They have huge egos and want to be the bully at the top of the pile. We need A-type personalities willing to put themselves in harm's way, but at the same time we're the ones who get in trouble. Unfortunately in the world of law and crime, we are near the bottom of the pile.

Out in the main area of the Major Crimes Unit, those who agreed to make phone calls are sitting at desks; Antcliffe has taken over my desk. He scribbles quickly with a pen. He looks up at me with the phone cradled in the crook of his neck. He starts to get up, but I stop him with a hand.

The reporters aren't in the back when I go out and I actually get to a car without incident. They must have chased Marilyn when she left. As I drive around their heads turn and follow me. I should pull over, get out of the car, and apologize to her. At least I slow down. Arsenault's eyes follow me as I drive past.

~ * ~

The Royalty was the first hotel owned by the Rodd family which eventually became the Rodd Hotels and Resorts. They own hotels and golf resorts throughout the Atlantic provinces, but primarily on the island. I walk into the lobby and up the main stairs to the second floor.

Emily Schofield answers my knock. She looks tired. The lines on her face seem to sag, her clothes hang from her body. She shows no sign of recognition in her eyes and no sign that she cares.

"Hi, Mrs. Schofield. I'm Sgt. Reid. We met the other day." *You know, on the worst day of your life.*

For a moment she stands there staring at me as if I'm not even there, or she's seeing something else far away. Then something clicks and her eyes begin of glow. "Yes, come on in. You'll have to excuse me; I'm packing our things. We're taking Kayla home tomorrow."

The hotel room looks as though two ghosts have been staying in it. The blankets on the bed are barely wrinkled. There is a stack of belongings beside the closet near the door. Even though it is a no-smoking room I can smell the bitter scent of cigarettes in the air. A chair sits against the window. I'm sure that if I looked outside there would be a pile of butts in the grass. There are empty liquor bottles falling out of the garbage can. Plates with barely touched food sit on a tray from the restaurant downstairs. Empty suitcases are open on one side of the bed. On the other side are carefully folded piles of clothes. I'm guessing they are Kayla's clothes. There are bright-coloured shirts beside a stack of pants and shorts. Emily Schofield takes one of the shirts from the pile, unfolds it, folds it again, hesitates a moment, then starts a new pile.

"Where's Mr. Schofield?"

"Wayne is showing someone the RV."

"You're selling it?"

She grabs another shirt to unfold and refold. This time she holds it close to her nose for a moment to breathe in whatever is left of Kayla. "We can't take her home in it. We have to fly." She folds another shirt. The next one she holds to her chest, then turns and sits on the bed. The pile leans in toward her. "We just bought this shirt at a store in Cavendish," she says. "It changes colour in the sunlight. Do you have children, Sergeant?"

"A daughter. She's the same age as Kayla."

She takes a shuddering breath. I can tell tears are ready to fall. How much has this woman cried in the past few days?

"Do you know how people say they felt it when their children got hurt or killed? A mother knows, right?" She smiles slightly but that is gone as quickly as it came. "I didn't know. I didn't have a feeling. I did when I couldn't find her, but not before that. What kind of mother doesn't feel when her child is in danger?" She looks up at me as tears stream down her face.

I want to tell her that predators like this know when to strike. They know when people are at their most relaxed and when they can slip in unnoticed. All I manage is, "I'm sorry." I wait for her to calm down before continuing. "I know this is hard, but I was wondering if you've been able to recall anything. Do you remember seeing anyone paying attention to Kayla or anyone walking by your campsite often? It would probably be someone you recognize. Someone you see around Bonaventure."

She shakes her head. "No, no we're all family out there."

Well maybe Uncle Joe got a little too friendly, I think. "Are you sure?" I ask.

"I've gone over it. I don't remember anyone doing anything."

"Okay, that's okay." I can't help but wonder what Hillary would be like if something happened to Leigh. It would probably be the end of us altogether. These people have to go through it twice. They have to pack her things here, then when they get back home they have to walk into a quiet house and unpack it all.

"Mrs. Schofield, did Kayla have or use a computer?"

"She had her own laptop."

"May I see it?"

She looks worn out. Her skin is almost grey. She has aged in just five days. Without a word she gets up and walks to the pile of their belongings brought in from the RV. She digs out a computer, runs her hand over it, and passes it to me.

There are stickers over the top. I won't let Leigh put stickers on hers. Several of the stickers are of horses and unicorns inside sparkly outlines. Kayla and my daughter could have been friends. "May I borrow this? I'll get it back to you before you leave."

Emily Schofield stares right at me. "We didn't monitor her Internet. She said she was old enough and responsible. She was responsible too, more than I was at her age. Did he get her through this? You always hear about it." She stumbles back.

I catch her with one arm and lower her to the corner of the bed. A stack of clothes tumbles off the edge scattering across the carpet.

She stares down at it, tears dripping from her lashes. Her entire body shakes as she pulls in a long breath. "Sergeant, can you do me a favor?"

"Of course." I'm a little startled at how calm she has suddenly become.

"When you find whoever took my daughter can you imagine he took yours," her eyes come up to meet mine, "just for a moment? And then do to him what you would do if it was your daughter?"

I tell her, "That won't solve anything," because that is what I am trained to say. I said that once before and didn't listen.

~ * ~

The reporters avoid me when I return to the office, so I am quickly in the Major Crimes Unit booting up Kayla's computer. Antcliffe is still at my desk. I take a table close to the wall near the whiteboards. Every time I look up, those faces are smiling back at me.

292

The computer is what you would expect from an eleven-year-old girl. The main background is a picture of a unicorn on a hill rearing up on its hind legs. There seem to be more games on it than anything else. The music file is loaded with teen pop songs, especially from the TV show Glee, and a couple of oldies. On Leigh's computer there are probably more older songs than newer ones. I swore I would not do to her what my dad did to me (he forced me to listen to his country twang and fifties and sixties rock) but I did anyway.

I click on the Internet and find the browser memory empty. According to this she either didn't ever go online or she erased what sites she used. Or someone else did. If Kayla did it then she had something to hide. The recycle bin file is empty. I doubt I will get much more from her parents. My only real hope is to find it on the computer.

I click on the Pictures folder - 367 files. Again they are what you would expect, but when I was younger I would never have kept things out in the open for parents to stumble upon. Amongst the horses, unicorns, movie stills, and family pictures are pictures and quotes I bet she copied from Facebook.

I get up and head to my desk. Antcliffe is on the phone talking in a soft calming voice. Gabbi Graystone-May's file is open in front of him. I lean around him and log onto my own computer. We have blocks on our system so that people can't get onto our computers and we can't use certain websites. You can get onto them, but you have to be able to justify it because a red flag will go up and you will be questioned about it later. Yes, I have a Facebook account. I only use it to talk to family and old school friends; I barely use it. That's why I have eight messages waiting for me. I ignore those and type Kayla Schofield into the search line. I have to scroll through until I find one with a profile picture that matches. I'm always amazed at how many people in the world have the same name. Her profile pops up on the screen. It has the word Unicorn in brackets after her name. Usually that means she also goes by that. There's no security here. I can get onto her photos and timeline. Nothing spectacular. Her last status update was the day she went missing saying she was having fun at the pool.

Antcliffe puts his hand over the phone. "No luck?"

"Not yet. You?"

He shakes his head.

On Kayla's computer I click on the Documents folder. It pops up and there are almost as many files as pictures. There are also more folders inside the folders. I'm not going to have much choice but to start reading all of them.

It's in the file Funtimes that I sit up and pay attention. There in the file is another file folder labeled Chatters. After reading through some of her homework and a few poems she had written, I think I have a sense of how she writes. Another file is labeled Lapin 1, but it doesn't sound like Kayla's writing. It is a poem about dreaming of meeting someone and uses different words than the other works, more advanced words. This sounds, I don't know, older, more flattering than the other things I have read. After several files with the word Lapin and a number is a file with only a date labelled. The date is from seven months ago.

This is a conversation between someone named Lapin and someone named Unicorn. I'm guessing Kayla Schofield is also known as Unicorn in the Internet chat world. It's just conversation, many lines with *lol, jk,* or *rofl* which mean laugh-out-loud, just kidding, and rolling-on-the-floor-laughing. At first it seemed like two kids talking and getting to know each other. Then half-way through the first conversation after Lapin said, "I bet you're really cute," Unicorn asked if the other wanted to exchange photographs. Lapin said he was thirteen and lived in Moncton, New Brunswick. He liked sports, especially soccer, horses, and girls - especially brunettes.

The next line in their conversation is what grabs my attention. It is Kayla's e-mail address.

How does a girl with no Internet activity on her computer have a Facebook and e-mail account?

For the next half hour I read through conversations between Unicorn and Lapin. A lot of them are nonsense. They talk about how they hate school or how their `rents are nagging at them. Lapin sprinkles his messages with compliments to the girl and occasionally asks for more pictures, trinkets, and a lock of hair.

Leigh.

I close the file I am reading and open one named Chat Friends. It is a small Word document. There are usernames along the left, then on some the name of a city and a number that I assume is their age. Lapin – Moncton – 13 is the seventh one down. As I look over them I see there are three from PEI; Shadow123 – Summerside -12, HorseRider – Charlottetown – 11, and Widget – Charlottetown – 11.

HorseRider.

My heart is suddenly in my throat. I rush back to my desk, push Antcliffe out of my way and log onto my computer. I know I've seen that before. I don't want to be right.

"What's your problem?"

"Shut up."

"Excuse me!" Antcliffe replies.

I get online and log onto Facebook.

Antcliffe throws his arms up. "Are you serious? What, did you forget to tell everyone what you had for lunch?"

I type in my daughter's name and press enter. It takes just a moment and then there it is, *Leigh Reid (HorseRider)*

"Everyone stop what you're doing," McIntyre bellows as he comes from his office to the main room. I take a quick look and see him attaching his holster. "We have a situation and everyone's going."

We snap into action. Desk drawers are unlocked and our Smith & Wesson's come out.

"Where are we going?"

"Bonaventure Campground."

Marilyn.

Chapter 16

Everything had changed. That was the one truth about which he was positive.

Even sitting at the campground pool, he felt that things had changed. Even deep inside his own body, his own psyche, everything was changing, evolving. Through dark sunglasses he still watched the young girls swim and play and run around laughing right in front of him. He still held the magazine he pretended to read holding it low in case his bulky shirt wasn't enough to hide his excitement. But what he pictured in his mind's eye was different. He imagined these girls begging for their lives. He imagined their blood warming his hands. And he heard their screams. Things in the world certainly were different.

"Is anyone sitting here?"

He dropped the magazine to his lap. The children's playful screams drowned out the thumping of his heart in his chest. *Had he ever been so excited?*

The woman in front of him looked from his face to the empty deck chair beside him. *Could she see the change in his face?* He said, "No go ahead," and folded his hands over the magazine. He felt what was hiding underneath.

"It's so hot today, eh?" She was a talker. "I'm so glad our RV has air conditioning."

She was dressed in a one piece bathing suit that did nothing to hide the roll in her mid-section. She kicked off sandals and wiggled her pedicured toes. At least three fingers on each hand showed her wealth. The ring finger on her left hand had about six rings itself. With that hand, she pulled her dark hair up and let it fall over the back of the chair. She wore four gold chains of different lengths and thicknesses around her neck.

Her neck. He stared at it for a long moment as he listened to the tale of her vacation so far. The only thing remarkable about her neck was how long and untouched it was. There were no birthmarks, no blemishes, no scars. It was just pure clean flesh. As he stared he saw her throat move when she swallowed. He looked so hard he was sure he saw the pumping of each pulse of blood.

Then he pictured his hands. He imagined them circling her throat, his thumbs pushing on her trachea. He could hear her screams change to gurgles as his fingers squeezed every last breath out of her. He pictured his fingers entwined with the gold chains, using them for grip. He even saw the life leaving her eyes.

Oh things were going to be so different.

"I mean, if the cops can't find this psycho, then we all have to be careful. Am I right?"

"What?"

She stared at him through oversized rose-coloured glasses. "The RCMP are here again asking questions. Otherwise I wouldn't be out in this heat. If the cops can't find the," she leaned in close to him and lowered her voice, "killer of those girls, then why should we expect the lifeguard to watch them? Am I right?"

He checked his watch. In just over two hours he was going to go for a drive. And in that drive he was going to stop at the Haunted Mansion in Kensington. HorseRider was being dropped off there. She was going to meet thirteen-year-old Lapin and his family for a little fun, then they would drive her home. Only that wasn't exactly what was supposed to happen. She wasn't going home. She was going to play his end game.

Why did it have to end?

"I have to – excuse me." He got to his feet and walked away from the pool holding the magazine at waist level in front of him. He heard his daughter call out for him, but ignored it.

The game didn't have to end. It could change. It could evolve.

He felt a strong warmth in his chest. He knew he enjoyed the innocence. He enjoyed being their first, but that wasn't what he craved any more. That wasn't what he dreamed about. The thing most in his thoughts was their fighting, their begging, their screaming, and being the first to see the light go out. Not just the first – the only. *Yes.*

As he crossed the main road leading from the office through the campground his eyes fell to the left. Two RCMP officers were there at the guard shack. They were dressed in casual clothes, but he knew it had to be them. He saw the dark-haired woman who was always in the morning paper and on the news. *Only two?*

They still didn't have a clue. There was still time for him to change his life.

He walked quickly around his gold-coloured van and took the stairs into the camper in one step. The kitchen was a mess. All the dirty dishes still sat waiting for him to clean them. On the kitchen counter, plates were caked in drying egg yolk. His fork and the steak knife he had used were right there where he left them.

"Hello?" His wife was in bed. She had too much fun yesterday at the waterpark. Her skin was such a bright red she almost glowed.

She was awake. He had woken her. She was probably going to yell at him.

Change your life.

"It's me," he called out.

"Come here."

Five steps lead to the upper level where the bathroom and master bedroom were located. The kids' bedroom was in the back.

He walked slowly up the stairs and past the bathroom. The bedroom was like a grey cave where he was always belittled and torn down. How was that going to change?

"What are you doing here?" His wife lay on the bed stark-naked, patches of white showing where her clothes had been. The skin of her face was beginning to look like red leather. "Where are the kids?"

"At the pool."

"Then why the hell are you back here?" She let out a yelp as she pushed herself to a sitting position. Her dark hair cascaded down to the pillow. "Go back and watch them. Come back when *they* are done."

"No." It came out with his breath.

The skin of her face tightened even more than what the sun had already accomplished. She said, "Excuse me," and glared at him. "I told you to go watch the kids. You do what I tell you to do …"

It was a new day.

"… not the other way around. Now you go out there …"

He didn't want it to end.

"Fuck you!" He didn't know where the voice came from. It was his, but it was different. Was that confidence?

He also didn't know where the knife came from, but there it was suddenly rammed into her skull from under her chin, his fingers wrapped tightly around the handle. Hot blood ran down over his hand and forearm like a bright crimson glove. It was just like the daydream. His wife's eyes were wide with pure shock. He grabbed onto her hair with his free hand. Every time he pulled the knife out and stabbed there was the wet sound of blood, then grey matter.

Finally he stopped. He let the body fall back onto the bed. It bounced. A molten lava fountain of blood spurted into the air from the hole between neck and head. It was quiet. She couldn't say a word. The only sound was the air conditioning coming through the ceiling vent.

He felt satisfied. Her blood warmed his hand. There was wet heat in his underwear from his internal excitement erupting. This was more than a new day. It was a new life.

"Daddy?"

His head whipped around. His daughter stared at him. Her eyes fell on his red hand. She looked so much like her mother. As if hearing his thoughts she let her gaze fall on the bed.

"Mommy? What did you do?" She turned.

He lunged forward. His fingers snatched her hair and tugged her head back. The fine strands slipped through the bloody palm.

She reached for the door. Her head turned to see where her father was.

His hand clasped around her throat. He liked this new life. Both hands squeezed. He twisted her around and slammed her back against an inside wall. That took some of the fight out of her. Her fingers slipped on his bloody hands. She was a product of her mother. She was going to be just like her. He saw her eyes almost pop.

In seconds it was done. Both of them were quiet. Everything was different.

He moved his daughter into the bedroom with her mother, quickly washed himself and changed his clothes from top to bottom. Everything was forever changed.

The moment he had a few things packed there was a knock at the door.

Chapter 17

"Do you want to put two hands on the steering wheel?" One of Antcliffe's has one hands was squeezing the life out of the armrest and the other pushing against the dashboard.

As if that would even help him, driving at this speed.

It would have been better for him had I taken my own car, but I opted for the department issue car instead. With my car I could have verbally asked it to dial Marilyn's phone instead of having to do it myself. The unmarked cars' engine is stronger and it has flashing lights in the grill. Sometimes I wish we had those flashing lights they had on old cop shows - the ones they reach out their window and put it on the roof of the car.

"Marilyn's not answering her phone." I say and put my phone on my lap. Both hands grip the steering wheel.

"She's probably busy with whatever's going on. You drive as crazy as Cassie."

Without touching the brakes, I turn the car at the Bonaventure sign. The back end fishtails and leaves a skid mark.

There are more people here compared to when I was last here. The cabins all have cars in front of them, or at least signs of life, and there is a small gathering of tents in the large field. The music festival starts in two days. People have to stake their spots. The main parking lot at the top of the hill has been taken over by the RCMP.

I park my car beside a white one with its roof lights still flashing.

Crime scenes start off as controlled chaos. The first on scene, in this case I'm assuming it's Marilyn and Dispirito, secure the area and call in reinforcements. They check victims for vital signs and, if need be, administer first aid. If possible, they take the perpetrator into custody.

They have the entry and exit blocked off again. The main action is inside the gated RV camp. The owner, Greg Montgomery, and a man who I assume is his partner are also at the gate trying to ease the growing crowd.

All members of Major Crimes get out of their cars and start walking toward the gate. Antcliffe stays close to me.

McIntyre takes the lead. "Do we have anyone at the back of the campground?" he barks. "I want members on every outer edge of the campground all within eyesight of each other. When Tactical is mobilized they'll start searching every damn camper and hiding spot in here."

"Is that really necessary?" Montgomery gets in McIntyre's way.

"Are you serious? You know what's going on here, right?"

More cars arrive. Some of these are from the Charlottetown police, some personal vehicles. Tactical (the team that would deal with things like hostage situations) in Prince Edward Island is like a volunteer fire-fighting team. It is comprised of members from both police forces on the island - RCMP and city police. They receive special training like any SWAT team would and when their beepers go off, they have to respond.

I'm starting to think we haven't been told everything.

We're pointed in the right direction and start walking down a side road, LeBlanc and Longfellow on one side, Antcliffe and me on the other. The closer we get, we see that the area around a motorhome has been taped off. A couple of uniformed officers are telling people to go back to their campers. Their eyes barely look at us.

The RV looks like the rest of them from the outside. It's huge - the popouts on either side are open making more room inside. This thing costs a good penny.

"Reid, over here." Deborah is around the front of the RV, outside the crime scene tape.

As we get closer to the front, I can see the strain on her face. Her cheeks are puffy and red. Her eyes glisten with moisture. There are streaks of something dark on her thighs as though she ran her hands down them to clean them.

"So what's going on?" I ask.

Her eyes drop. Dispirito sits there in a lawn chair. He's slouched forward, his elbows on his knees, his hands holding both sides of his head. Between his feet and splashed onto his shoes is a puddle of vomit. His strawberry blond hair is a mess.

Strawberry blond? No, there's something red mixed into his hair. It's there on the side of his face by his hands. It's blood. There's blood on his hands.

"Where's Marilyn?" My eyes move from the sitting officer to the standing one. My heart clenches in my chest. I hear the others around me breathe in as they put it all together. I don't want to.

Deborah's hand touches my arm. "Reid." but the rest is lost.

I look at her hand. Is that blood around her fingernails? "Al, where's Marilyn?"

Disprito doesn't move. I can't even tell if he's breathing. If it wasn't for his entire body shaking he could be a statue. A corpse.

"Reid," Deborah squeezes my arm. "She's in the camper." She fights to keep composure. "She's dead."

I lunge for the camper. More hands than Deborah's are suddenly on me, holding me back.

"You can't, Reid." Longfellow is in front of me.

"I have to. Did anyone check on her?"

"I did." Deborah raises her voice.

"She might just be hurt. We have to check on her."

Deborah's fingers grab my chin. She pulls my face so that I'm looking right in her blue eyes that start to overflow with tears. "I checked her. She's gone, Reid."

~ * ~

I'm sitting in the grass far away from the camper when Eckhart arrives and begins to process the scene. Longfellow is in charge now. LeBlanc and Antcliffe are off conducting interviews of everyone in the campsite. Members from other units have arrived to offer their assistance and are interviewing as well. Dispirito has been looked over by Ident and Emergency Services. The world still spins.

My phone rings. It's in my hand. I'm not sure how long I've been holding it.

"Hello?"

"Reid," Hillary's voice comes across to me. "Are you okay? The news on the radio's been saying a member was hurt."

I look up. Dispirito has been moved to the back of a car. Deborah stands by it, but her eyes are on me. I say, "I'm fine. It wasn't me." I breathe out. "It was Marilyn."

"Oh my God. Is she okay? The radio isn't saying …"

"She's dead, Hill. Marilyn's dead."

Silence. She says something to someone else, but can't find the words to speak to me.

"I have to go, Hill."

"Wait, what happened?"

"I don't know yet." I stare blankly at the RV. Do I really want to go in there?

"Did you catch who did it?" I can hear emotion in her voice. She's upset and concerned. Or is she thinking about what our marriage is going to be like without the thought of Marilyn and me?

"No," is all I can say. "I have to go, Hillary."

"Just wait. Have you talked to Leigh today?"

"No," I watch Eckhart, decked in his bunny suit, enter the camper.

"She called me and said Sasha's mom was dropping her off at the Haunted Mansion in Kensington and that you were picking her up."

"I haven't talked to her. I have to go." I push the end button on the phone.

Nobody says anything as I step up beside Longfellow and start pulling one of the white bunny suits over my clothes at the back of the Mobile Command Post. I'm not sure when the MCP got here, sometime during my daze I suppose. I don't even know how much time has passed since we got the call. Almost two hours, I think.

The search of the campground has been completed. Officers with guns already have already searched all the places that someone might hide. The RCMP and Charlottetown sniffer dogs have gone over everything trying to flush out a perp. Parents are keeping their children close. Some people are complaining. For a little while they will have to put up with the chaos. Officers circle the area and check everyone coming in and out. Reporters have collected by the restaurant. This is the place to be today.

I don't want to be here.

"Reid," McIntyre is behind me. "You're an observer on this. Let Longfellow do the work."

I pull the hood over my head. "No problem."

As soon as Eckhart gives the word Longfellow pulls the yellow police tape up and ducks underneath.

I do the same. My heart races. The blood pulsing through my temples makes my head spin. We've been told roughly what is in there, but seeing it for the first time with my own eyes is not something I am sure I can handle. I have to though; she would have.

As Longfellow goes up the steps and moves inside the camper, I hear a muffled, "Shit."

I take a deep breath and let it out slowly.

You can smell death the moment you get to the top of the stairs. As you duck your head and cross the threshold it becomes overwhelming. It's there like a thick cloud sitting above everything. There's a very metallic odour.

This is a newer motorhome. It has a flat-screen TV, comfortable-looking seats around a table, large kitchen area, bedroom in the back with its own TV, upper floor, blood splatter on the wall – your typical camper. There are dirty dishes in the sink. A fly buzzes ignoring our intrusion. On the table are two cups, one standing across from another on its side as though two people had been sitting there having a conversation. Marilyn's notebook is there beside the tipped cup. There's no pen. *Where's the pen?* There are red splashes on the table and across the curtains covering the window. On the seat behind the standing cup is a cast-iron pan.

My eyes fall to the kitchen floor and the body that Eckhart crouches over. It is Marilyn, but it's not. Her skin is whiter than I'd ever seen it before. Her eyes staring at the ceiling, have milked over. Her red-wine hair has spilled out behind her head. The right side of her face is coloured deep crimson. Her skull seems to be broken above the temple. There's a pool of blood beneath her head, mixing with her hair. Her pen sits in the pool. Her blouse has been torn open and her bra pushed up to her neck, exposing her breasts to the world. There are holes in her body, fine slits where a sharp object has gone in and out. My eyes move down. Marilyn's slacks and panties have been pushed to mid-thigh.

I look away before I can see anything else that has been done to her.

"There are two more bodies up in the front room," Eckhart says.

"Start with Marilyn," I say and quickly have to clear my throat.

"Alright," he goes back on his heels. The back of his hand adjusts his glasses. "From the blood splatter she was sitting at the table when she took a blow to the head. Dr. Norton will tell you for sure, but I'll bet that first blow killed her. There's bruising to her throat, so he probably tried choking her afterward. These stab wounds," he points to her torso with a gloved hand, "look to be post-mortem. Very little blood flow."

"What else?" Longfellow points lower.

I bite down on my tongue.

"It doesn't look like she was raped. Maybe he realized she was dead, or that he had to get out of here."

We all go quiet. If this was done to someone else, we would probably be all business and it wouldn't phase us. She is our sister. She's going to wear the red serge one more time.

"Can we cover her up?" My voice barely makes it past a whisper.

"I will." Eckhart replies. "I have to finish first and then I'll cover her."

"There are other bodies?" Longfellow asks.

Eckhart nods toward the stairs leading to an upper level. "I haven't processed them yet, but you can take a look. The woman was stabbed in the throat and bled out. The girl was strangled, I think."

Longfellow goes to the top of the stairs and takes a look. As he turns back, his face is pale. "Do we know who they are?"

"That's your job." Eckhart gives him a brief smile, then as if he remembers who's on the floor in front of him, it's gone. "There's a picture on the wall of two adults and two kids. They look like the mom and daughter to me. Oh and Marilyn's gun's gone. And Reid …"

I stare at Eckhart trying my best to control myself.

"The hairs found on Kayla Schofield matched with the sample I took from your daughter." He returns back to his work.

What does this mean?

As I follow Longfellow out into the warm afternoon air, we both take deep breaths filling our lungs with freshness. It's a different world. People go on. People are living their lives. Even here in this campground, people have their kids at the pool as though nothing was wrong. I don't see how that's right.

I strip off the bunny suit and place it in a bag.

"You satisfied?" McIntyre asks.

Far from it. "Al talk yet?"

McIntyre puts his hands on his hips. Maybe he's trying to decide whether to tell me anything. He strokes his goatee. "They split up. He went down one road and she the next. When she didn't meet him at the end, he started back on her road. The camper door was open. He went in, found her. There was nobody else around."

~ * ~

"We can't recover from this," Greg Montgomery paces back and forth nibbling on a fingernail. "The girl was one thing, but this?" He's talking more to his partner who is standing with us, not moving. "People don't lock their doors here. Now we're going to be known as the RV camp where campers got slaughtered. Oh my God, we're an eighties slasher flick."

Under normal circumstances, Dispirito would have piped up and told us the whole history of the slasher movie franchise. But right now he is busy smoking every cigarette he can get his hands on.

"So, whose camper is this?" I ask.

"The French officer already asked me all these questions."

"And now I want you to tell everyone else," LeBlanc says as he and McIntyre walk down the MCP ramp.

It's too hot to be outside, but also too hot to be inside the converted pull-behind camper.

Montgomery rolls his eyes. "It's owned by Julie Coniglio. For years they've been coming here every summer."

"Coniglio," Longfellow taps his notepad. "She own a silver minivan?"

Big sigh. "Do you know how many people come through here every season? I can't keep track."

"Greg, they're just doing their jobs." Trevor Attansia is obviously the calmer one in the relationship. He continues, "I'm pretty sure they drive a minivan, Caravan I think, but it's more golden-beige than silver."

"I put an all-points-bulletin out on it the moment he told me," LeBlanc states. "They had the licence plate number on file."

Longfellow leans toward me. "Julie Coniglio owns one of the vans we saw on the videos from the bridge and ferry." To the campground owners he asks, "Were they here last weekend?"

"They got here Monday." Montgomery starts tapping his foot.

"Not Friday?"

Montgomery's eyes go to the blue sky as he breathes in. The tip of his tongue peaks out between thin lips. "They came on Monday."

"They don't have to sign in at the security gate do they?" Longfellow doesn't look impressed.

"No."

"So you can't say for certain if they were here Friday."

"I guess not, but security knows what camp sites are being used. They would have noticed. They weren't here."

"But if somebody were to just come on site for a few minutes you wouldn't know, would you?" I spit out, controlling myself as much as I can.

Montgomery looks at me as if I had just sworn in church. "The people here wouldn't do that."

I bite my tongue and try my best not to say a word about all the dead bodies around the campsite. Personally, I want to grab this man by the face and scream at him until he quits screwing around, but I'm just observing. I watch Dispirito stomp out his cigarette and start walking toward us.

"What can you tell us about the family?" Longfellow is a lot calmer than I feel.

"I don't know. Husband, wife, two kids. I think Julie was a teacher. That's why she and the kids spent a lot of the summer here while her husband was back and forth with work. He works with computers I think." As Montgomery talks his hands fly wildly. "They were a pretty quiet family."

"You said two kids?"

He nods. "A boy and girl. She's was around eleven and he's younger." All the campground owners have been told is that dead bodies have been found in the camper. "Are they not all dead? I thought you said - wait was it …" His skin changes to an off shade of green.

"What can you tell us about Mr. Coniglio?"

"He's a mouse." Attansia grunts.

"Coniglio?" Dispirito.

"He did whatever his wife told him to do." Montgomery says.

Dispirito touches my arm. "Why did he say, Coniglio?"

"It's the name of the RV owners."

"Coniglio is Italian for rabbit."

The two of us lock eyes. The symbols burned into the ankles of the seven girls. The permanent marker ink on the grave markers. Both crude versions of the Playboy bunny. Rabbits marking death. Things click. *Rabbit.*

"He didn't put sunscreen on the kids once and she let him have it in front of everyone." Montgomery is telling stories about the mouse of a man. The bunny of a man. *The rabbit.*

"LeBlanc," everyone looks at me. Dispirito and I look back at them. "How do you say rabbit in French?" I know the common words, enough to get me by at least.

"Lah-pehn," he says.

Things are moving in my brain. Gears have shifted. "How do you spell that?"

He looks at McIntyre then back to me. "L-A-P-I-N."

"Shit. He's a computer guy. That's why there was nothing on their computers. That's why Kayla Schofield's browser was empty." I look around at the confused faces. I quickly go over everything I learned while searching through the girl's computer. I tell them about her chat room conversations with this Lapin boy and that he got her to send him things. I wish I had looked at the newest conversations. "He talks to these girls, pretending to be a boy their age, then lures them into meeting him near their homes. That way, they'll feel safe. He flatters them. He gets them to send pictures and things."

Lock of hair.

"As soon as you're alone he has you," Antcliffe states.

HorseRider.

Chapter 18

Three female voices sang along with the song blasting from the car stereo.

"I've been living in a blue room
I've been crying tears at night
I've been living in this sad, sad world
Baby, I'm too tired to fight."

Leigh studied the CD she had bought from the woman at the Farmers' Market. Maeve Campbell was her name. She looked pretty. She had long blond hair that fell down her back. Leigh pulled some of her hair forward to look at it. What would she look like as a blond? Her mom said her hair was too dark to dye blond, but movie stars and pop singers did it all the time. Katy Perry changed her hair colour every week.

"Are you sure it's okay to just drop you off?"

Leigh looked up at Sasha's mother's big eyes, watching her through the rear-view mirror and said, "Yeah."

She had come up with the plan herself. Okay, Lapin helped a little. The hardest part was getting a ride, but things clicked into place when Sasha said she and her mom were going to Summerside for a street fair. Kensington was on the way.

To Leigh, the Haunted Mansion in Kensington was the best attraction on the island after Shining Waters. It was a large Tudor-style house decked out inside like one of those haunted houses in traveling exhibitions. You walked through dark passageways looking at scary scenes and having things jump out at you. In the basement was a replica of a Victorian London street. At the very end you walked out into a beautiful garden with its own waterfall and things to play with and see. Over the last few years they had added carnival rides out front. At Halloween they went all out and made the house even more frightening with actors dressed up and hiding in the dark hallways.

~ * ~

He flicked the turn signal with his pinky, slowly moving the minivan to the side of the highway, and held his breath. His eyes locked on the white police cars beading straight toward him. Their wailing sirens could be heard over the radio and the cold air blasting from the vents. The lights on the tops of the cars and in the grillwork flashed red and blue. They got closer and closer. He thought of the pistol on the passenger seat under his rapidly packed bag of clothes.

His eyes followed the cars as they sped past. His foot found the gas pedal and he eased back onto the road. The police were on their way to Bonaventure. They'd found the bodies.

The female Mountie wanted to ask him he heard anything or knew anything about a missing girl.

"Would you like some lemonade?"

"I would love some. Mind if I come in? Mind if I grab a seat?"

Mind if I pretend to wash dishes, spin, and flatten your face with my favorite cast iron pan?

He smiled when he thought of the sound her skull made as the black pan made contact. He remembered waiting for the school bus as a kid, stomping all the end of winter ice with the heel of his boot. That's what her head sounded like.

He stared at her for what seemed like minutes, but was probably just seconds and then he was on her. His hands grabbed her throat. He knew it was pointless. She wasn't moving. Even the blood seeping from her skull wasn't making a noise.

How was he going to know if he could kill a grown woman with his hands if she was already dead? He tore her blouse open and pushed her bra to her neck exposing her firm breasts. There were no breaths. She was nowhere as pretty and innocent as his girls. She was a woman. She was like his wife. His wife was the cause of all this. She took away his manhood. She stomped his soul into the ground to the point that he had to fight. He had to fight to feel alive. He had to kill. A knife was in his hand again and he stabbed and stabbed. There was no satisfaction there.

"Dad?"

The speedometer creeped over 110 kilometers per hour, so he lifted his foot. The maximum speed limit in PEI is 100. He didn't want to be pulled over for something stupid. He wasn't going to be caught.

He thought about when he struggled to pull down the woman's pants to see what was there. He hoped she was clean and looked like one of his girls. She wasn't like them. There was a line of hairs, a landing strip, which was nothing like the others. She wasn't innocent. She was dirty.

"Dad?"

There was just one thing he had to grab before leaving the campground.

"Where are we going Dad? Where's Mom?" His son asked from behind him.

And then there was one thing he had to pick up in Kensington.

~ * ~

"You're sure? We can wait with you."

"I'm sure." Leigh smiled and looked around the parking lot. She couldn't see him anywhere, but Lapin said he would meet her in the garden. She looked at

Sasha's Mom. "My dad will be here any minute. He's always running late." She focused on the car until it backed down the driveway through the open wrought iron gate and was back on the road.

She had never seen the parking lot so full. Kids were screaming from the carnival rides as they spun round and round. Leigh checked her pocket. She had enough money to pay admission and a little extra for treats. She had never gone through the Haunted Mansion by herself before. Usually she held her mom's hand and stuck to her side as things jumped out at them. Dad never wanted to go in there. He didn't like the dark.

~ * ~

There she was.

Leigh got out of the car, smiled brightly at whoever was stupid enough to drop her off and waved as they backed down the driveway and left.

"Dad."

She was prettier in person. Her hair was tied back in a ponytail. Her big eyes looked around full of excitement and curious energy. She was looking for him. She wanted to be with him. She proved that by sending him pictures and a lock of her hair.

The plan was to make her his final conquest. He left her hairs with Kayla so that the police might find her. They were going to be too late. He was going to love her and then kill her. And then he was going to wait for the police.

He thought about what lay under her t-shirt and shorts. All he had to do was take her. Her screams would mix with everyone else's as they walked through the mansion. Nobody would know.

"Daddy, when are we going in?"

He thought about the gun under his bag of clothes. It wasn't his style, but desperate times. You can't refuse a gun.

Trevor started kicking the seat in front of him. "Daddy."

He had killed the police woman. He didn't get the satisfaction he wanted, but he had done it. He killed his wife, he killed her daughter. He did all that. He was showing them all. He could do anything.

"Wait here. I have to get something," he said as he put the gun in the small backpack and stepped out of the van, slinging the backpack over his shoulder.

Chapter 19

I pull into the Haunted mansion through the open wrought iron gate. A gargoyle overhead seems to be watching. I drive to the black-and-white three-story house and get out of the van. Antcliffe exits the passenger side. An automated mannequin opens an upper window and looks out. Kids scream on the carnival rides. My eyes circle around. There are kids everywhere. There are men all over. It's like looking for a needle in a yard of moving needles.

Leigh's not out front.

A patrol car speeds into the parking lot and pulls in beside me. Deborah and her partner, Joe Hart, get out. She automatically starts looking around.

"Joe, you stay here. You know what my daughter looks like?"

He nods. I had shown him the picture from my wallet and he had seen her at functions. His eyes start roaming every face.

"Don't let anyone leave." I look at the others. "You two go to the gardens and look for her. I'm going inside. Look for her and anyone watching her."

"Are you sure this guy would even come here, or that he's after Leigh?"

My breath is caught in my throat. I know he could already have her. I know what he has done. "I don't know," I say, finally.

All we have to go on with respect to Coniglio is the family photo on the wall of the camper. We know he's skinny with dark hair and eyes. He also has a police-issue handgun in his possession.

I walk in the front doors to the mansion, around some people waiting to pay who all look at me as if I'm the rudest person they've ever run into, and step to the front counter. I flash my identification and Leigh's picture to the older lady behind it. "Have you seen this girl today?"

She takes the photo and holds it close to her glasses. She reminds me of the Crypt Keeper. For a second, I wonder if she's just one of the automated displays. "I don't know," the lady says. "We're really busy today." She just wants me to go away.

"She probably would have come in alone. A man might have come in with her or right behind her." What if he already has her? He could be gone with my daughter in the back of his van. I try to shake the thoughts from my mind. I can feel my heart trying to pound its way out of my chest. I can't seem to catch my breath.

The woman takes a closer look at the photo. She hands it back and says, "I think she might have gone in there. Yes, I thought she was a bit young to go alone, but kids are always trying to show off."

"Okay, I need you to hold off letting anyone else in for a while."

"What?"

People waiting to pay admission start complaining.

"You're about to have all of the RCMP in here," I cut her off. "I don't want to have to arrest you, but I will." I walk down the hallway past a sign reading, "*abandon hope all ye who enter here.*" There are more complaints behind me.

After getting your admission ticket, the first room you enter is a study. There's a fireplace, a portrait on the wall, candles, a suit of armour with a white skull looking through the helmet, and a bookcase in the far corner. It is through the bookcase that you enter the dark hallways. The sign here says, "*turn back now.*"

I can't.

My hand goes to the Smith & Wesson on my hip. When I was a kid I was scared of the dark. The older I get the more I have to deal with bad guys and the evil things they do and the more terrified of the blackness I am. Most of the Haunted Mansion is in the dark. Some hallways are so dark all you can do is feel along the walls and take one step at a time knowing that what you are stepping on is not solid floor. Your whole body tenses as you wait for something to grab you.

I can't pull the gun out of its holster. Things jump out at you in here. Things make noise. People in front of you scream as something frightens them. The last thing I want to do is start shooting randomly.

I push open the moving bookcase. A blast of air shoots down from above. My hand squeezes tightly around the handle of my gun.

"Jesus Christ!" *This is what it's going to be like, eh.*

As I near a corner there is a loud hissing noise. The moment I turn a large snake head, the size of a basketball, bounces above me. I suddenly remember I'm holding my breath. I exhale but have to fight to take in more air. Along the sides of the path are lighted boxes with giant spiders and bugs in them. Everything is fake, but even a coat hanging from a hook can look like someone watching you in the night.

I left my Maglite in the trunk of the car. I have another small flashlight in the glove box, but I forgot that too.

Around another corner a small room is lit. A desk is covered in books and papers. There are cobwebs on everything. A mannequin that looks like a skeleton sits in a chair in front of an old-school typewriter.

"I said I didn't want to be disturbed." The voice comes from nowhere. I think I know some writers who will end up like that.

"Let me out," a man grabs at a cage beside me. The metal rattles.

My hand half pulls out my gun. I take a step back.

"Before she cooks me, let me out." It's just a dummy. Behind it is a female mannequin standing at a stove.

At every pulse point of my body, I feel my heart race. These things are fake.

There's a scream. Was it real? Yes, it had to be.

Was it Leigh? Was it someone else? Was it me? Maybe he has her already. He has her in one of these cubbyholes among the animatronics doing what he wants in plain view of his audience. *"It's so lifelike."* He is already killed three people today.

"Leigh," I call out before even realizing I'm doing it.

I turn another corner and run into a family. For a second I think they're just another display.

"What's going on?" The man questions. Is he Coniglio?

I quickly look him over. He's rounder than the man in the picture. The woman beside him has her hand on his shoulder and there are two girls with them. They look older than my daughter.

"Sorry. RCMP. We're looking for someone." I have to swallow hard. "Just stay together and keep moving forward." I quickly walk around them.

Two more corners and I call out my daughter's name again.

"Dad?"

Around the next corner she stands at the base of a staircase. My eyes take in everything. There's no one with her. There is no one up the stairs. She has this look on her face that says, *"what the hell are you doing here."*

"You're alone?" My breaths come quickly. My hand is still on my gun.

"Ah," her big eyes do a quick circle, "yeah."

"Let's go." My hand goes to her back and I push her up the stairs.

"What are you doing?"

"We have to go."

At the top of the stairs, the darkness ends. I keep my eye on the turning handle of a giant Jack-in-the-box inside a child's bedroom. I know there's a demonic jester inside, ready to jump out. As we turn to leave it pops up with a cackling laugh that makes my spine hurt. The main part of the top floor is supposed to be a typical 80's middle-class house, I guess, but with a twist. The body parts in the oven and skull in the microwave are a little Jeffery Dahmer. The brown water running from the kitchen tap reminds me of camp when I was a kid. I think it's supposed to be blood. Out the window I see the parking lot has been taken over by RCMP vehicles. A chair starts to rock by itself. The next area is a dining room where a female rotting corpses sits, having supper with a mummy. Its wrappings are coming undone. A picture on the wall behind them slides down, revealing a waiter who complains about having more guests. This one's not a very good dummy. A body hangs inside a brick fireplace. In front of the far wall is an old electric organ playing without anyone at the keys. It looks exactly like the one under the stairs in my parents' home. A large dummy next to it mechanically stands then sits again.

"What's going on, Dad?" Leigh thumps her feet down a little harder than usual as she walks in front of me.

How much do I tell her? "Where are you meeting Lapin?"

Her feet seem to stutter. "Who?" She asks over her shoulder.

"Don't lie to me, Leigh."

She stops and turns to me. "How do you know about him?"

"Keep moving." I push her along. "Are you meeting him here?"

We pass some more people who back away when they see my hand on my gun.

Leigh doesn't say anything until we step through a door into the streets of London. Inside windows of old shops are artifacts that could have been found in old London, maybe even in White Chapel where Jack the Ripper did his thing.

"I'm supposed to meet him in the garden. He's here with his family. How do you know about him?"

"Do you know anything about him?" I don't like this part of the house. There are more people here looking at the displays. It's a dark city street where the killer could be anyone.

"Of course I do. We've been talking for a long time. He's thirteen, he likes sports."

"Do you send him things?" My eyes lock on the glowing red exit sign. "Eh? Pictures? Poems?"

Leigh shrugs her shoulders and drops her eyes.

"What about in the mail? You ever send him some of your hair?"

It's as if a light suddenly goes on and she gets it.

That's my confirmation. Until now I have been hypothesizing, but now I know. She sent him her hair. He left it at the first crime scene. And here we are.

As we go through the exit door, the light of day momentarily blinds us. We are transported into a beautiful garden. An archway over the door is covered in green vines. There are bushes of colourful flowers on either side bringing us to an area fenced in by growing walls. Huge trees stand guard throughout, their leaves making a canopy to filter the sun. Wonderful smells touch our noses as the happy voices of children touch our ears. A replica of the Eiffel Tower, but a lot smaller, stands vigil. It is like walking from night into day or evil into good. It reminds me of movies where the characters are in a horrible place, then walk through a painting on the wall a door or armoire and are instantly transported to a place of beauty. We are Alice and this is Wonderland, but the movies it always turns out to be just a fantasy.

336

I expect to see Marilyn waiting to bring me up-to-date.

Deborah walks over to us. "Anything?"

"I didn't see him."

Leigh looks between us with a face showing confusion and anger.

"Get them to turn up the lights in there. We'll have Tactical do a sweep." I keep moving forward into the garden pushing my daughter along. My eyes move over every face. "If he's here we'll find him."

"Reid," Antcliffe jogs over to us. "This lady says her car is missing and Coniglio's van is here. His son's in there."

I take Leigh's hand and follow him back to the parking lot. The rides have stopped. Everyone is corralled to one side.

Along one lane of parked cars is a golden mini-van. Here in Atlantic Canada you only have to have your license plate on the rear of the vehicle. He backed it into a spot so we couldn't see the plate on the first pass. As I walk to it, I don't know what to expect. He stabbed his wife and strangled his daughter, so what would he do to his own son?

As we get closer I see the boy's head and shoulders over the dashboard. He is alive.

~ * ~

I lift my chin as Deborah slides her fingers between my coat and neck. She gives it a little tug to straighten the collar.

"Are Hillary and Leigh coming?"

I check myself in the mirror. The red serge uniform is an amazing thing. It can change any man or woman into a symbol. "They're marching with Marilyn's family."

The scarlet uniform brings out Deborah's blue eyes. Except in photos I don't think I have seen her wearing the red serge before. She looks better in it than I do.

Today the symbol of Canada will be a red wave flowing down University Avenue from headquarters to Providence House. The Premier of the province will talk about how much the people of Prince Edward Island owe to the memory of Sergeant Marilyn Moore and the sacrifice of the RCMP. Someone will talk about who she was. The Musical Ride has come back and will lead the sombre parade to the downtown followed by off duty officers from PEI, the other Atlantic provinces and others who have come from all over the country because they knew Marilyn as far back as when she first joined. The Charlottetown City Police are marching as are members from other police forces. Some have even come from the United States. Even though the RCMP wear red we all wear blue, police blue.

Marilyn would have hated all this. She probably would have rather had a party and a lobster bake.

Dressed in her red serge, she lies in a coffin in the back of a hearse. After the ceremony, she will be taken to her home town of Souris on the Eastern tip of the island where her family will have their own quiet moment before she is buried in the family plot.

"Any word?" Deborah doesn't have to specify. I know what she means.

It's been three days. "This morning a guy reported his boat missing." I look into her eyes instead of looking at myself in the mirror. "He can't say when it went missing. He last used it on Tuesday. They found the stolen car a half kilometre away so it looks like Coniglio left the island."

"That's why nobody's spotted him at the bridge or ferry." Since Wednesday every vehicle trying to leave the island has been searched. "He's gone," Deborah adds.

My phone rings. I think about not answering it, but I've had enough of that. I've had enough of hiding from everything. I put the phone to my ear. "Reid."

"It's Cassie. Sorry I couldn't be there today. I had to get back to work."

"It's okay. Duty calls."

"Yes it does." I can hear her smiling through the telephone. "I wanted to tell you about the progress we've made. We might have a name on the John Doe."

"What?" A smile erupts on my face for the first time in a long time.

"Gordon Ledoux. His aunt is one of our secretaries. She was walking past my office, glanced in and stopped in her tracks when she saw the reconstruction on my desk. She swears it's her nephew. When he was twenty-four he bought a boat and decided to sail south to the Caribbean to run charters. Nobody's heard from him since. His mother is coming in so we can take DNA, but it looks good. She's not sure how they would have missed it all those years ago. Mike wants to talk to you."

There's silence as the phone is handed over.

"Hey," Antcliffe starts. "We've been looking into Peter Coniglio. Not his real name by the way. He wiped down the van but your boy Eckhart found his dirty fingerprints on the knife he used on Marilyn." He pauses for a moment. "His real name is Peter Hamilton from Manitoba. When he was twenty-two, he was arrested there for groping a young girl. He was a youth pastor at a church. The girl convinced her parents it was mutual or something and the charges were dropped. He went to college to study computers and, from what I can tell, he came out as Coniglio. I think he's a lot better at this computer stuff than we know."

I fill him in on what we found out about the car and boat.

"With his computer skills he could go anywhere."

"Looks like we won't get our man this time," I voice, not to the man across the phone, but to the ghosts around me. "Are you working on the why?"

There's a snicker on the other end. "Everyone we've talked to says the wife dominated ol' Peter. She treated him like crap. It sounds like he was pissed off at his wife so maybe to show he was the man he wanted to dominate little girls."

We say our goodbyes and talk-to-you-soons. Deborah and I join everyone outside ready to march through the city. Today is a sad day. I hold in the tears as long as I can. They can wait for the march. This is one day I don't want to be in my red serge.

Chapter 20

"This is not the sword you should carry." He tossed the metal replica of a broad sword down the aisle between the pews. It bounced on the carpet with a metallic thunk and came to rest. His eyes searched the eyes of the few people sitting in the first few pews right in front of him. Most were children from eight to sixteen.

Gina let out a squeal.

"Don't worry. That sword is just a replica. It's very dull." He gave her a bright smile.

Gina was eleven. She had long dark hair and a pretty, innocent face. She was just his type. Too bad she lived in his new town.

"The Israelite army ran. They were extremely outnumbered, so they hid in the hills. Some even joined the other side. Our Lord God. Jonathan knew that they did not need an army. This is the only sword they would need." He lifted his left hand where, squeezed between his fingers and thumb, was an old leather bound bible. When he was a child, he studied the bible. He had been a youth pastor before, but that had been in a different lifetime. Falling back into it was easy. All it took was the right paperwork.

He was a computer guy. Changing identities was easy. He had a new name. He had a new symbol to mark his playmates. The difficult thing about his new life was controlling his urges. He had access to all of his flock, but he couldn't let himself be consumed by his needs. He drove long distances to fulfill those.

He looked up as someone began walking down the aisle toward him. The person was dressed in dark grey with a hood covering his head and dark glasses over his eyes.

"This is the only sword you need in your lives. With this sword you can fight any battle. Jonathan and his armour-bearer went out to meet the entire Philistine army with only two swords and their belief. Our Lord God. The two of them went by themselves to attack the Philistines, knowing that God would be on their side. They killed twenty men before panic struck. An earthquake shook the ground and the Philistines began fighting each other."

Many of the kids had their smartphones in their hands ready to read an upcoming passage. Gina's youth bible sat on her lap. Just two nights earlier he treated himself to someone just like her. She wanted to fight him. He didn't go after only girls any more, sometimes he found women to satisfy his needs, but girls were still his favorite. He liked their taste.

"This sword is sharp."

The person dressed in grey picked up the broad sword and looked at it as if didn't know what it was. He held the replica at arms-length looking straight down his arm and along the blade.

"You don't want that sword. That is an unsharpened tool. That is a weapon of those without faith. This," he slapped the bible, "is a sharp sword. This," he slapped the bible again, "can be your shield as well. With this you can fight any battle. Shortly after Jonathan and his armour-bearer began to battle the Philistine army, the land shook with an earthquake. Which sword do you want, sir?"

There was a flash. His mouth opened wide as the dull sword was thrust through his stomach and out his back. The skin made a ripping noise.

For a moment there was nothing. Nobody in the pews said a word or made a noise.

Then blood spurted from his body.

Girls and women screamed. Everyone moved away from the front and the middle aisle. They climbed over pews to escape.

The pastor fell back onto the floor. Bright crimson shot from him like the fountain in the gardens behind the Haunted Mansion in Kensington, PEI. The sounds that came out of his throat made it seem like he was under water. His eyes saw nothing. He had always been terrified that the ghosts of the girls he played with would be there as dark shadows standing around him, but in his last moment, there was nothing. Everything was cold.

The stranger bent over and pushed a piece of paper into the pastor's hand. Without a word the stranger turned and walked back the way he had come. Beneath the sunglasses was a faint smile. He thought about the look on the pastor's face and the words written on the piece of paper that the man was never going to read.

Red Rover, Red Rover, send Sgt. Reid over.

From the Author

So, what did you think? I'd love to hear your comments and thoughts and even your complaints. You can email me at redislandnovel@gmail.com

If you enjoyed this book please tell your family, tell your friends, update your Facebook status, Tweet about it, put up a notice on your work bulletin board, write about it in the snow (guys know what I'm talking about), if possible smoke writing from a plane would be really cool.

If you haven't read **Red Island** (the first in The Sgt. Reid Series) you really should. It's the first time relatives began telling me I'm sick and twisted.

Check out **The Cistern** (first in The Alcrest Mysteries)

I have some great things coming up in the future…

…The Menu – second book in The Alcrest Mysteries…

…Just by Accident, a romance novel I wrote about 15 years ago is being worked on…

…and Red Rover, the next Reid novel is being written. A lot of answers will come out in that one, including Reid's first name. Don't tell Eckhart.

Find me at
Lorneoliver.blogspot.ca
Facebook.com/oliverauthor
And @LorneOliver on Twitter